BLACK SUN

BLACK SUN

BLACK SUN

PAUL COX

FIVE STAR
A part of Gale, a Cengage Company

LIBRARY OF CONGRESS CATALOGING-IN-PUBLICATION DATA

Names: Cox, Paul, 1950– author.
Title: Black sun / Paul Cox.
Description: First edition. | [Waterville] : Five Star, 2021.
Identifiers: LCCN 2020008547 | ISBN 9781432876418 (hardcover)
Classification: LCC PS3603.O9246 B57 2020 | DDC 813/.6—dc23
LC record available at https://lccn.loc.gov/2020008547

First Edition. First Printing: May 2021
Find us on Facebook—https://www.facebook.com/FiveStarCengage
Visit our website—http://www.gale.cengage.com/fivestar
Contact Five Star Publishing at FiveStar@cengage.com

Printed in Mexico
Print Number: 01   Print Year: 2021

CHAPTER ONE

It was just past sundown in Columbus, New Mexico, when I crossed the weather-beaten platform and boarded the eastbound El Paso and Southwestern train. Even though the car I entered was nearly vacant and all the windows down, the temperature inside was well over one hundred degrees. I had no desire to converse with any of the passengers so I took a seat in the back and slid over to a window.

As the train jerked and then sluggishly rumbled out of Columbus, I peered through the twilight at the sprawling military camp on the south side of town. Watching rows of canvas tents light up with the amber glow of kerosene lanterns, I could hardly believe that only a few hours earlier I had been sweating nervously in a court-martial hearing, a neophyte news reporter facing a charge of treason and possibly a firing squad. But thanks to the stunning testimony of some key witnesses and a bizarre twist of fate, General "Black Jack" Pershing had abruptly dismissed the charges. Even more difficult for me to absorb, however, was the fact that some of the uncanny discoveries made during the trial had proved instrumental in averting an all-out war with Mexico.

The circumstances surrounding the entire affair were as complicated as they were mystifying, and I was exhausted from trying to make sense of it all. As the hours passed and the air streaming through the windows began to cool, I started to relax and slowly unwind. My thoughts drifted pleasantly for several

7

minutes but then abruptly snagged on a troublesome domestic issue that awaited me in New York City, a dilemma that was, in some respects, as grave as Pershing's court-martial had been.

To fully appreciate my situation, I must first explain that I am a Weston. That is to say, I am the son of a Carnegie Hill Weston. For centuries, our seafaring family has been in shipping, international shipping to be precise. And as a result, it would not be an exaggeration to confess that we are world-renowned shipping magnates and proverbial masters of the seas.

Be that as it may, a few days after graduating from Harvard I chose to ignore decades of cast-iron tradition and adamantly refused to take my place in the family business. With aspirations of following in the footsteps of William Randolph Hearst, I boldly proclaimed to Father and Mother that my intention was to someday own my own newspaper. Days later and much to the chagrin of my parents, I took an entrance level job as a lowly news reporter for the *Chicago Tribune*. There, without question, I naively accepted my first assignment, which was to assist a veteran reporter and cover something called the Punitive Expedition. Later, I came to find out that expedition was not an exotic adventure into Egypt, China, or even Africa, but rather a military operation deployed to capture a Mexican I had never heard of, a revolutionary named Pancho Villa.

After Pancho Villa's murderous attack on Columbus, New Mexico, President Wilson had called on the army to cross into Mexico. Their mission was to apprehend the so-called general and bring him to justice. However, over the coming weeks, even though thousands of our soldiers marched hundreds of miles into Mexico, supported by scores of civilian drivers and a dozen newsmen, the glorified bandit was never even seen, much less caught and punished.

During the military campaign, I had not been able to get word to Father and Mother for various reasons. And during my arrest and court-martial, contacting them was out of the question. By the time of the trial, several weeks had passed since they had heard from me. I knew they would be dreadfully worried, but until the legal proceedings ended there had been no way to communicate with them.

Naturally, I was anxious to get word to my parents but that was the least of my worries. What kept my mind churning that night on the train was how to break the news that my homecoming was only to be a short visit, and that I was determined to return to the Southwest as soon as possible.

As the train rhythmically clacked over the rails that night, I began piecing together bits of information I had gathered while listening to various soldiers and officers throughout the campaign. Eventually I was able to formulate what I felt was a plausible excuse for my return to the border, a story honest enough for Father and Mother to accept. In actuality, however, I could not have truthfully explained my decision to anyone, for I didn't fully understand it myself.

One thing I did know. As William Cabott Weston III, I had been raised as a pampered lapdog, but as Billy Cabott in Mexico, I had broken my leash and run with timber wolves. And since then, I have imagined many times, if not actually felt, the hot pirate blood of my grandfather's grandfathers pulsing through my veins. How, I wondered, could I explain *that* to Father and Mother without them thinking I had lost my mind?

Such unsettling thoughts kept me awake long past midnight and it seemed as though I had just fallen asleep when a sudden jolt disturbed me. I opened my eyes and discovered it was close to daybreak and the train was already pulling into the El Paso station.

While passengers loaded and unloaded, I exited the train and used the telephone in the depot to call home. The sun was just rising over New York City when Mother picked up the receiver.

When she heard my voice on the other end of the wire she was frantic. After calling for Father they eagerly shared the earpiece and, heads together, listened as I quickly assured them all was well. I then apologized profusely and sincerely for my prolonged lack of communication.

After my apology, though, I was forced to curb my sincerity. With lighthearted jests and short cavalier answers, I deflected their many questions regarding the exact nature of my long silence. As loathsome as that may seem, it was the only way I could think of to juggle an armload of fragile half-truths while attempting to avoid outright lies.

To begin with, I explained rather loosely that my silence was in part the result of a news blackout ordered by General Pershing. Being that news reporters had been allowed to accompany the expedition, a good portion of that particular excuse was true enough. I left out the tidbit about me eventually being arrested and then charged with treason against the United States. And I failed to mention anything regarding my trial and how General Pershing hoped to sentence Monte Segundo and me to death by firing squad. I did admit that Monte Segundo was indeed a newfound friend and that we had met in Columbus. And yet, it was only in passing that I mentioned Rosa, Rosa del Carmen Fernandez Bustamonte. I thought it best to say nothing of her exquisite beauty or of the bloody battles she had participated in while fighting as a soldier in the Mexican Revolution.

As for Monte Segundo, I did eventually elaborate, at least to a degree. I told Father and Mother that Monte was in the Idaho National Guard and that he was a bull-of-the woods lumberjack that stood just under six feet and weighed two hundred pounds. I also revealed to them how Monte had once lived with the Kootenai Indians and could track as well as any Indian. Everything else I left out, including the Mexicans I had seen him kill and how his legendary feats had spread throughout Mexico, a phenomenon strategically employed by Pershing to prevent the invasion of the United States by Mexico.

It must be kept in mind that telling Father and Mother everything would have been pointless if not cruel. Father would have reacted one way and Mother another but the reality of what I had seen and done, both the barbaric and the wonderful, would have been far more than they could have absorbed.

When the telephone conversation ended I was greatly relieved. The ice had been broken and my plan to reveal my imminent, and possibly permanent, departure from New York City was on course.

The following afternoon our chauffeur, driving a spotless Packard limousine, picked me up in front of the Grand Central Terminal and drove me to my home on Carnegie Hill. There, to my surprise, I was met with an impromptu homecoming party that was attended by many of the finest families on the hill. A few eligible and attractive young women were also present but as I conversed with them I could not resist comparing them to Rosa Bustamonte. When I did so, though I covered it well, my interest in them waned considerably.

Had Father and Mother known that I had hardly slept a wink on the train they would never have invited guests for me to entertain. However, though I was tired, I soon discovered that the long days and hard rides endured in Mexico had toughened me more than I had imagined. It was nothing for me to be charming throughout the entire evening. I joked about my sun-darkened skin and calloused hands. I then amused everyone with tales of dusty wagon trains, airplanes in the skies, motor trucks stuck in the sand, and cavalry marches over the mountains. And for a finale, I thrilled them with a whitewashed version of the heroic battle of Ojos Azules, where not a single American soldier lost his life.

Afterwards, as the men gathered in the smoking room to light up their cigars and the women moved into the parlor to gossip, my stories grew more serious. Recounting what I had learned from the officers during my time in camp Colonia Dublán, I confidently declared that despite what was being reported in the newspapers, there would be no war with Mexico. On the contrary, the powers that be had all but decided that the United States would enter the European war, likely before the year was out. It was at that point, standing next to Father, I remarked that the inevitable conflict in Europe was going to require vast amounts of copper. Then, glancing at Father through a haze of tobacco smoke, I added that the rush on copper would result in enormous profits for Phelps Dodge.

At the mention of copper, Father flushed red. Phelps Dodge was a New York–based import-export firm. The company, as I well knew, was a major competitor of ours but had recently expanded into copper mining in Arizona. Seeing the color in Father's cheeks gave me the courage to continue with my report and my plan.

I offered that in light of the upcoming war, I thought it best that I resign from the *Chicago Tribune* and use my recent experiences in Arizona and New Mexico to locate a number of rich zinc deposits. When an elderly man standing next to me asked "Why zinc?" I nonchalantly explained that Phelps Dodge controlled most of the copper in the southwest but not the zinc. And that it required copper *and* zinc to make brass, brass that would be needed for millions of cartridge cases.

In unison, the men erupted with a blend of surprise and hearty approval. Several slapped Father on the back, congratulating him on raising such an astute son. Then "chip off the old block" reverberated through the entire room as Father, still a bit ruffled, nodded and grinned.

Very shortly, Father totally agreed with my proposal. I

breathed a sigh of relief and yet felt a wave of guilt for zinc mining was, at best, very low on my priorities list.

From that moment, however, and for the remainder of the week, when Father and I conversed, the subject was always the same; zinc mines, brass casings, and the upcoming war. And after Father explained to Mother that in the event of a world war, those involved in the production of ammunition would likely be exempt from military service, she was ready to pack my bags.

After Father went to work in the mornings, I spent much of the day in the library researching zinc mining. I brought home several books that I often read late into the night. Most of the books I shared with Father and even some with Mother. However, the books that most intrigued me, the ones I did not share, were about Mexico.

While riding through that country I had been exposed to more poverty, corruption, and cruelty than I could have ever imagined. Since then, I had often wondered how a sister republic, a country blessed with as many natural resources as the United States, had gone so terribly wrong. I was keenly aware that Mexico possessed enormous potential and yet most of the people I encountered there were poverty-stricken peons, thousands of them fighting and dying in a barbaric civil war that few of them even remotely understood.

It was obvious to me that somewhere in the country's past, the nation had tragically veered off course. And eerily, Mexico was a nation with striking similarities to our own. For, just as we had won our independence from England, Mexico had won theirs from Spain. Then we had written a stellar constitution and a few years later Mexico had done the same. And now Mexico was involved in a civil war just as we had been not many years in our past.

In fact, General Pershing had been a small boy during our

Civil War and when he graduated West Point, General William Tecumseh Sherman had handed him his diploma. And Major Dodd, who recently attacked Pancho Villa at Guerro, was a teenager at the war's end.

But our Civil War, for the most part, was fought with a sense of decency by both North and South. The Confederates, even in their darkest hour, never abandoned their code of honor. But what I witnessed in Mexico's conflict was nothing more than roaming hordes of undisciplined barbarians that murdered at will as they raped and ravaged across the countryside.

Deeply disturbed by all that I had witnessed in Mexico, and hoping to find answers to at least some of my questions, I read a dozen books on the history of Mexico. I started with Spain's conquest of the Aztec Empire and finished with a recent publication dedicated to the genius of Porfirio Díaz, president of Mexico for the last thirty years. And finally, I spent a few hours reading the latest newspaper articles on the revolution. But when I finished reading, instead of answers, I had more questions than when I started. All I had done was unearth grotesque pieces of a puzzle that plainly did not fit together. And too, I came to the chilling realization that the only thing separating the lawlessness of Mexico from the United States was a razor-thin line that had been scratched in the sand.

Having experienced the anarchy of Mexico and the dangers of the borderland, I managed to secretly procure a thirty-eight caliber Smith and Wesson, a small-framed pistol. I also purchased a snug shoulder-holster in which to conceal it. After smuggling those items up to my room, and only when I was certain Father and Mother were fast asleep, I practiced drawing my weapon for an hour each night.

The thirty-eight was not as powerful as Monte's forty-five but it was an excellent fit for my hand. And after a week's worth practice, I felt confident and prepared for anything.

When it came time for me to leave, Mother did indeed pack my suitcase, but, unlike before when I left to become a news reporter, this time she tearfully gave me her blessing and wished me well. And at the front door, on the top of our marble steps, Father heartily shook my hand.

As our chauffeur loaded my suitcase into the trunk of the waiting Packard, Father implored, "Pease, keep in touch this time."

"I will do my best, Father," I said, and then kissed Mother on the cheek.

At the bottom of the steps I turned for one last look. I felt excited and sick in the same instant. "I will write as I am able," I said boldly. "There are very few telephones where I'm going."

With that, I slipped past the open door of the limousine and into the back seat. I waved as we drove away. I had not intended to look back but when I did I saw Mother weeping on Father's shoulder. Tears formed in my eyes but to keep them from falling I forced myself to think of something else. The first thing that came to mind was the powerful and stoic figure of Monte Segundo.

Where was Monte? I wondered. Had he found the graves of his father and mother? Did Rosa let him search for them alone or had she gone with him? Had they become more intimate or were they still quarreling, each attempting to understand the feelings of the other?

Such questions kept me occupied until I reached the busy Grand Central Terminal where I was to board the train that would take me out of New York City. It was late afternoon and Father had insisted on sending me off in proper style, so when I arrived at the station I was directed to a Pullman Palace Car and informed that I would have the entire sleeper to myself.

I glanced around at the ornate interior and chuckled to myself. Knowing it would be my last taste of luxury for quite some time, I decided to thoroughly enjoy everything at hand. As the train began to roll I rang for the porter and ordered an early supper, a combination of seafood, steak, and prime rib. I also ordered an excellent bottle of red wine.

Easing back into the plush comfort of my window seat, I gazed out through the glass, hardly noticing the dingy bulk of concrete skyscrapers that impaled the New York skyline. Instead, I was envisioning the limitless reaches of the western horizon and hearing the desert wind as it rushed over the barren sand, through the mesquite, and then hissed past the outstretched arms of the ancient saguaro.

Eventually, however, my thoughts drifted back to the train platform in Columbus. Had it only been a week since I stood there watching Monte and Rosa board the westbound train? Neither of them had voiced their feelings for the other but I had seen the attraction between them from the very beginning. Each had tried to deny it and at times to resist it but both had failed. Yet standing on that platform that afternoon, with the train ready to leave, I was deathly afraid they were about to go their separate ways.

Monte was not one to wear his feelings on his shirtsleeve, and that day when I saw him look at Rosa it was easy to see that he was struggling. I had never played the part of Cupid but the situation at that juncture was dire. I was about to intervene when Monte finally found the right words and asked Rosa to join him. To my relief, she agreed and then, ahead of Monte, had boarded the train. He had a few more things to say to Lieutenant Patton who had defended us in the court-martial. Then, Monte also stepped inside the passenger car and took a window seat. He gave me a quick nod and then the train took them away.

The porter knocked on my door, interrupting my thoughts. He brought in the wine I had ordered. I sampled it and then nodded my approval. He poured a bit more into my long-stemmed glass and then placed the bottle on my dining table.

After the porter had gone, I raised the glass and smiled, thinking of the toast I would someday make at Monte and Rosa's wedding. Oh yes, I had no doubts they were a perfect match. All they needed was time to smooth out a few dents and wrinkles. And after spending the last week together, I was certain that, by now, they would be strolling down the primrose path that led to marital bliss.

But I should have known better. Since the day the Apaches murdered his mother and father and left him to die, nothing in Monte Dell Segundo's life had come easily.

I later found out that when Monte first stepped into the passenger car he had paused, looking over the heads of two dozen passengers, trying to find Rosa. Then, before the train had even left the station, he spotted her sitting by a window toward the rear of the car but deep in conversation with another man.

The man was sitting next to Rosa and leaning toward her as he spoke. He was well-dressed, likely in his early thirties, and wore a grin that reminded Monte of a snake oil salesman. He was speaking excitedly and gesticulating with both hands.

Rosa glanced up from the conversation. Seeing Monte staring at her, she quickly averted her eyes.

Monte felt something deep within begin to boil. It was a rising fury, the likes of which he had never experienced. With his gut twisting and his face flushing with heat, he worked his way down the narrow aisle. He took an empty seat opposite Rosa and glared out the window.

Monte had no idea what was happening to him. He wanted to grab something and rip it apart or better yet to take the interloper and pulverize him with his fists. But, intuitively, Monte knew there was absolutely nothing he could do, and for the first time in his life he felt weak, even helpless.

As the train pulled out, he could not help but hear what was being said across from him.

"But you never wrote," Rosa said. "Not once."

"No?" questioned the man. "It must have been the revolution. I wrote you many times."

"What was I to think?" snipped Rosa. "It has been three years!"

"But Rosa, I was told you were killed at Agua Prieta. My heart was broken. And, of course, I wrote no more after that."

That was enough for Monte. He took a deep breath, and as he had done so completely as a child, attempted to smother his emotions, to shove them down into the same black hole that had, for so many years, imprisoned his most painful memories. With grim determination to feel absolutely nothing, he turned his head and deliberately locked his eyes on Rosa. In seconds, their eyes met again but this time they held. Rosa expected Monte to show a bit of curiosity or perhaps a twinge of jealousy, but the emptiness she saw in his expression stunned her into silence.

The man next to her noticed Rosa's stare and twisted his neck to investigate. For the first time he saw Monte Segundo. However, all he noticed was a powerfully built man wearing a general issue military uniform.

"Sir," said the man, with only the faintest edge to his voice, "this is a *private* conversation."

Monte's dark eyes shifted to the speaker. He was slight in build. His hair was black and slicked down. And, he was handsome, almost too handsome. He reminded Monte of a painting of Jesus he had once seen. All except for the eyes. Those were black and reflected the sinister glint of a cat watching a mousehole.

"That is Monte Segundo," offered Rosa. She desperately

wanted to say more but the words would not come. "He is . . . he is . . ."

"National Guard," Monte said flatly.

The man looked uncertainly from Monte to Rosa. "Do you two know each other?"

Rosa hesitated but did not take her eyes off Monte.

"I got discharged from the army," said Monte. "She's a revolutionary who got arrested. They took both of us to the train and kicked us out of Columbus."

Monte paused. He gazed at Rosa, holding on to one last hope that she would in some small way reach out to him. But Rosa said nothing.

Rosa, on the other hand, had just met a former lover, a man she mistakenly thought had abandoned her years before. She could not deny her past feelings for him and yet Monte Segundo was unquestionably the man she loved. But there Monte sat, not the least bit jealous and offering no explanation of how he had invited her to join him on the train. No admission that they were supposed to be together. And to make matters worse, Monte was not showing the slightest interest in her. Nothing!

Monte clenched his jaws and turned his attention to the sinister-eyed intruder. "We know each other but that's about all there is to it."

Rosa's eyes flared with indignation but Monte had already looked away. Had he seen the anger in her eyes, things might have been different. But such is fate.

"Yes," Rosa huffed. "That is all there is to it."

"It seems like," Monte said to the man, "the two of you go way back."

The man seemed uncertain. "Way back?"

"I mean the two of you have known each other a long time."

"Oh, yes," the man said. "And now after so many years here we are together again!"

Monte could feel the muscles in his neck starting to knot. "I can see that."

The man sighed and glanced starry-eyed at Rosa. "A few minutes ago, when she first walked in, seeing her was . . . was like a miracle. I thought she was dead but here she is sitting next to me."

"It looks to me," Monte said dryly, "her getting on this train today turned out a lot better than she thought it would."

Rosa blinked. Rolling Monte's words over in her mind, she attempted to grasp the meaning of what he had said but she was too distressed to concentrate.

Satisfied that Monte was no threat, the man began to grin again. He leaned toward Monte and stretched out his hand. "I am Anthony Ortega. Tony to many on this side of the border and Antonio to many more south of it."

Taking an immediate dislike to Anthony Ortega, Monte shook his hand.

"Where are you bound for, Mr. Segundo?"

Monte pointed straight ahead. "West."

Anthony Ortega glanced at the Colt single action and large hunting knife Monte was wearing. "I'm bound for Tucson, myself. There is lots of opportunity in and around Tucson. If you're looking for work, come to Tucson and ask for Anthony Ortega. Among other business interests, I own a mercantile on Congress Street. I'm always looking for good men."

"I might just do that," Monte said, suddenly coming to his feet. "It's too crowded in here for me. I'm going to get some air."

With that, Monte took a few steps down the aisle and then ducked out the back door of the passenger car to stand on the deck. For Monte, anywhere was better than sitting across from Rosa Bustamonte and her long-lost lover, Anthony Ortega.

Ortega watched Monte go and for the first time noticed that

he wore moccasins instead of army boots. Turning back to Rosa, Ortega thought for a moment and then asked, "So, why did they run him out of the army?"

Rosa was angry but with Monte's sudden departure she was also confused. "He tried to kill an Apache. One of the army scouts."

Ortega smirked. "That would do it. I read about the Apache scouts while I was in New York City. They are called 'Pershing's Pets,' are they not?"

Frowning, Rosa glared at Ortega. "You were in New York City? What was Antonio Ortega doing in New York? Is that where you got that ridiculous gringo suit you are wearing? And why are we speaking English? Where is your mustache and what happened to your hair?"

Rosa paused to take a breath. She glared at Ortega, taking in everything from his slicked-down hair to his shiny leather shoes. "What has happened to you, Antonio?"

Patting Rosa's hand, Ortega chuckled, "Questions, questions, so many questions. Where do I start?"

Rosa pulled her hand away. "Start with where you got the money to buy such an ugly suit."

Ortega laughed. "You have not changed, Rosa," he said lightly but then grew more serious. "But I have."

"The suit!" demanded Rosa. "Did you steal it?"

Ortega soberly shook his head. "I am making money, Rosa. More than I ever dreamed possible. Soon I may even own my own hacienda with thousands of acres."

"And how," Rosa asked suspiciously, "do you make all this money you claim to have? Are you now a bandit?"

Leaning close to Rosa, Ortega lowered his voice. "It is the revolution, Rosa. There is money, much money, to be made if you know how to operate."

"Operate?" questioned Rosa. "You do not fight in the revolution?"

"I did," said Ortega. "In the beginning. You know I did. But then I was wounded. By the time I recovered I was all alone. I had to survive on my own. So I began to work, work hard.

"That was about the time I heard you had been killed. Oh Rosa, how sad I was. So, I worked even harder to heal my broken heart. I saved my money. When I had enough, I went to Tucson. And then I began to make real money . . . selling arms and ammunition to Villa and his men, to the revolution.

"So you see, I still fight but it is on this side of the border and in my own way. The supplies have to be smuggled very carefully across the border. I often risk my life doing it."

Rosa thought for a moment and then frowned. "But you make money. Fighters make no money. In Mexico we can barely find enough to eat."

Ortega shook his head. "You do not understand, Rosa. I must make enough to pay for the rifles and bullets. The dealer in New York City is a German agent but he looks like an American. To avoid suspicion it is necessary that I look like a successful businessman from Tucson, a man that goes there to buy farm equipment. The United States government is watching everything closely but the Germans always outsmart them. It is the Germans that I deal with and appearances are very important to their operation.

"They sell me the guns and ammunition for very little. Yes, it is true that I make a small profit but I must make something. How else can I run my mercantile?

"When we win the revolution I will make everything right. I have planned for that as well. You will see."

Folding her arms, Rosa said stiffly, "You had plans to come back to me, too, but you never came back. What good are your plans?"

Rosa paused and thought of Monte. "I have my own plans now."

Ortega smiled and leaned back in the seat. "Do your plans include living in a grand hacienda? Do they include fine horses and automobiles? Does your plan include more land than you ever dreamed of and servants to cook and do the laundry?"

"I never dream like that," Rosa said. "What I want . . . what I wanted was *Villisimo*, all the things Villa promised."

"Come with me to Tucson," Ortega said, changing the subject. "You can do more for General Villa there than you ever could fighting in Mexico."

"Come with you?" huffed Rosa. "After so many years you appear out of nowhere and ask such a thing? You remember a little girl. That little girl is the one who died in the revolution!"

Rosa craned her neck trying to get a glimpse of Monte. Only minutes before he too had asked her to come with him, but where was he now? Did he not care that another man was trying to take her from him? Would he give up so easily and walk away? Was such a ferocious fighter as Monte Segundo not willing to fight for her?

Ortega continued to talk but Rosa was only half-listening. When the train stopped in the small hamlet of Hermanas to pick up passengers, she thought Monte would surely return to his seat. When the train pulled out of the station and Monte was still nowhere in sight, Rosa grew agitated.

"I need to use the toilet," said Rosa.

Ortega slid out of the seat, allowing Rosa to stand. He pointed to the rear of the car. "The ladies' facility is back there."

Rosa walked down the aisle but continued out the rear door. She crossed to the next car and looked it over. A porter noticed her and stepped forward to meet her.

"May I help you, señorita?"

Flustered, Rosa said, "I am looking for a man wearing an

army uniform. A big man."

"Was he wearing moccasins?"

"Yes."

"He got off at the last stop. That was Hermanas. Not much there for an army man. Only about a hundred people. Farmers and ranchers mostly."

Rosa felt her heart sink. But then she grew angry.

"Did he say anything before he got off?"

The porter shrugged unconvincingly. "Not to me. He seemed to be having a private conversation with himself."

Rosa glared at the porter with fire in her eyes. Through clenched teeth she demanded, "What did he say?"

Scratching the back of his neck, the porter replied reluctantly, "He said, 'To hell with her.' "

CHAPTER TWO

Monte stood by the tracks and watched the train until it was out of sight. He had experienced the bitterness of betrayal before but never the smoldering rage of jealousy. On the train he had desperately tried to bury his emotions but soon realized that doing so was far more difficult than he had imagined. Sitting there, merely listening to Rosa and Anthony Ortega was more than he could stand. His only recourse, the only way he could think of to curb his anger and salvage his pride was to walk away from Rosa and never look back.

"From the start, you were nothing but trouble," Monte muttered.

A voice to his left broke into Monte's thoughts. "Are we expecting trouble, soldier?"

Monte turned to see an old man leaning on a cane. He had gray whiskers and wore a battered suit and hat.

"What do you mean?" Monte asked.

The old man pointed at Monte. "I heard you mention 'trouble.' Is the army coming here? I thought the military was only taking over Columbus."

Looking to the east, Monte could clearly see the mountains that stood just outside of Columbus. At best they were ten miles away. Then for the first time, he glanced around Hermanas, seeing a few shacks, a corral, and what passed for a train station and post office.

"Nobody's coming. Just me."

The old man studied Monte for a moment. "Not much here for a soldier. Not many folks either."

"How far is it to the Arizona state line?" Monte asked.

The old man licked his lips to wet them. "It's ninety miles, give or take. You thinking of walking the tracks?"

"How far apart are the train stops?"

"About every ten or twelve miles. The ones closest to the state line are Rodeo and Apache. Rodeo's in New Mexico and Apache's in Arizona."

Monte swore softly and then nodded. He left Columbus to find the graves of his father and mother and that was what he intended to do. With that in mind, he started walking alongside the train tracks.

"You best watch out for bandits, soldier," called out the old man. "The damn Mexicans and Yaquis are crawling all over this side of the border. Nobody's safe, especially a man alone and afoot."

Attempting to block Rosa from his thoughts, Monte repeatedly told himself that he was actually quite fortunate, in that, only a few hours earlier he had been in a military courtroom being tried for treason. Now, instead of facing a firing squad, he was miles from General Pershing and, once again, free to do whatever he wanted. Everything, he assured himself, was back to normal.

But less than a mile down the tracks, Monte grudgingly admitted that things were anything but normal.

Just three months before, he had been a bull-of-the-woods lumberjack in North Idaho. His life was simple. He worked hard, played hard, and cared for nothing and absolutely no one. But that was before he left Idaho to join Pershing's army and before his suppressed childhood memories began to haunt him. And, too, it was before he met Rosa Bustamonte.

As Monte walked alongside the rails, he wrestled with the

nagging sensation that because of what he experienced in Mexico and what he had learned during his court-martial trial, his life would never be the same. Eventually, he began to curse the day he left Idaho and wished he had never heard of General Pershing and his Apache scouts. Now, instead of living the good life in the mountains of Idaho, he was traipsing across a blazing desert plagued with a passel of loathsome thoughts he could not get out of his mind.

Too many times, he vividly recalled the horrible death of his father, and he remembered all too well the agonizing pain he had endured after the Apaches threw him into a cactus patch and left him to die. He also could not stop thinking of the lonely graves of his mother and father. But, worst of all, each time he thought of his parents and the graves, he inevitably envisioned the train station at Columbus and then, infuriatingly, Rosa sitting with Anthony Ortega.

Over the next few hours, Monte's jealously festered. Eventually crowding out the other sentiments, it grew so tumultuous that heat no longer affected him. Thirst and hunger did not register nor did time or distance. Fatigue, too, was erased by an unquenchable fire that burned inside him, a savage emotion completely foreign to Monte Segundo.

Engrossed as he was, it seemed to Monte that only an hour or so had passed since leaving Hermanas, but when he approached the train stop of Continental, he noticed the sun was already setting.

He drank his fill of water from a horse trough and only then did he realize how long he had walked without water. Searching around, he found a discarded whiskey bottle that still had a cork. After rinsing it, he filled the bottle with water and stuck it in his back pocket. At a small dry goods store, he spent half of the money he had left on a sleeping blanket, but the air had not yet begun to cool so he kept walking. A short distance past the next train stop of Hachita, he welcomed the realization that he was too tired to think any longer and decided to stop for the night.

He bedded down near the train tracks and had slept for only two hours when the rumbling of the eastbound El Paso and Southwestern jarred him awake. Unable to fall back asleep, Monte rolled out of his blanket and tramped farther west under the starlight.

Existing on nothing but jackrabbits and an occasional cottontail, Monte made it to Animas by late afternoon the following day. Finally completely worn out, he shuffled into the small Burns Hotel and paid one dollar for a room. He slept soundly through the entire night and the following morning used his last fifty-cent piece to buy a hotel breakfast and as much black coffee as he could drink.

Late that afternoon, he walked into the dusty train stop of Rodeo.

Still unable to keep his mind off of Rosa, and with only twenty-five cents to his name, Monte went to the only saloon in town.

Going through an open door, he glanced around the spacious room. Hot and sweaty, he made his way to the bar. A half-dozen tables with chairs were crowded together near the front window. A billiard table was set up in the rear and two electric fans spun lazily overhead. An elderly man stood behind the bar. Other than that, the saloon was empty.

"How much is a beer?" Monte asked.

The bartender's eyes swept over Monte, taking in his army uniform as well as the width of his shoulders. "Two bits."

Monte slapped two dimes and five pennies down on the polished wood. "That's all I got. Any work to be had around here? For a day, maybe?"

"You done with the army?"

"Let's just say they're done with me. And I'm National Guard, not army."

"May be some work down at the livery," said the bartender as he grabbed a glass mug and began filling it. "There's cowboys that'll come in directly. They'll leave their horses there till they get back on Sunday night. The hostler might could use a hand taking care of their stock."

Monte scratched the stubble on his jaw. "What day is today?"

Setting the cold beer down in front of Monte, the bartender's eyes narrowed as he took a closer look at Monte's disheveled appearance. "Today's Saturday, friend. Mind if I ask where you come from? I didn't see no horse out front and from the looks of you, you shore didn't come in on no train."

"I started out in Hermanas," said Monte and then emptied half the mug of beer in one swallow. "I walked from there."

"Long ways," commented the bartender. "Where you headed?"

Monte wiped his lips with the back of his sleeve. Ordinarily he would have ignored such questions but he needed information and the bartender seemed talkative. "Right here is where I was headed. To start with anyway. I'm looking for somebody that's been around this part of the country for a long time, all the way back to the Apache wars."

The bartender put out his hand. "I'm Red. I've only been here since the century rolled over but Deek Coleman is the man you want. He'll be in along with the cowboys. He rides fence for the Bar S outfit."

Shaking hands, Monte said, "Segundo. Monte Segundo."

Red let go of Monte's hand. "Quite a grip you got there stranger. You a miner?"

"Idaho lumberjack."

"Figured you was something of the sort," Red said.

A faint rumbling sound funneled through the front door. As

the sound grew louder, hoots and yells of men blended with the rumbling. In seconds a cluster of horses and boisterous riders thundered past the saloon, leaving behind a rolling cloud of dust.

"That's the cowboys," grinned Red. "They'll be in here to get liquored up good before they get on the train."

Unimpressed, Monte sipped his beer.

"There's no whores here in town, you see," offered Red. "So them cowboys take the train in to Globe. When they get to town they go all night long and then, on the way back here, they sober up before they go back to work. They got their timing figured out pretty good."

"Does Deek Coleman go with them?"

"Not to drink. He used to bend an elbow but not too far back, it got to where the whiskey like to have killed him. He give up drinking the hard stuff about a year ago. Didn't give up chasing women, though. Just drinking whiskey. He'll take a beer or two but that's it for Deek."

Pounding leather heels and the jingling of spurs reverberated off the plank entrance as the blustering cowboys pushed and shoved each other through the door of the saloon.

Monte turned his head. Taking the cowboys in with a single glance, he saw that all of them were young. Each had a pistol belted around his waist as well as large noisy spurs strapped around the back of his high-heeled boots.

Monte went back to his beer. As far as he knew, he had never seen real cowboys but for some reason the fact that they wore their spurs into the bar irritated him. But Monte was tired, his stomach was empty, and he had been fuming for days.

Sipping the last of his beer, Monte found himself yearning for the cool serenity of the deep timber and the life he once lived. In the mountains of North Idaho, he simply enjoyed the good things life had to offer, destroyed the bad things, and ignored everything in between. There was no worry, no anxiety, and no regret.

But that was before Rosa del Carmen Fernandez Bustamonte started haunting every hour of his day.

Monte was at the end of the bar closest to the front door. The jostling cowboys lined up to his left. Almost immediately he was carelessly bumped with a sharp elbow. Making room, Monte slid a step toward the door but when the caterwauling of the cowboys intensified he left the bar and took a seat at one of the tables.

A short wiry cowboy with a light growth of chin whiskers noticed Monte's move. "Aren't we good enough for you?" said the cowboy, his tone jovial.

Monte smiled and the cowboy turned back to his friends. A moment later another man darkened the front entrance but, instead of walking in, he paused in the doorframe and peered inside. He was average height but stooped at the shoulders and very thin. His hair and beard were gray and the bridge of his nose was flat, no doubt the result of having been broken years before.

A different cowboy leaned back from the bar but this one was thickset and well over six feet tall. He eyed the newcomer and smirked. "Come on in, Deek," bellowed the cowboy. "I'll buy you a whiskey!"

"To hell with you, Turk," Deek grumbled, but the noise of the cowboys almost drowned out his words.

Red filled a beer mug and then went to the empty space on the bar where Monte had been standing. Deek went to meet him. As the bartender handed Deek the beer, words were exchanged between the two men. Deek then turned and looked curiously at Monte.

Taking a moment to study Monte, Deek Coleman took a thoughtful sip of his beer. The old man's eyes narrowed with curiosity and then he started for the table where Monte was sitting.

Turk took notice of Deek and then glanced at Monte. "Hey Deek, are you going to tell some of your whoppers to that soldier boy? Tell him a good one and he might buy you a whiskey or two just like the good old days."

The old man ignored the heckling. Standing across the table from Monte, he asked, "Are you looking for me?"

"I am if you're Deek Coleman and you know about some renegade Apaches and what they did to a man and woman that lived near here about thirty years ago."

Sizing Monte up for a moment, Deek hesitated. When he was satisfied, he pulled out a chair and sat down. "I was here back in them days, alright. And I fought the Apache many a time. What are you looking for exactly?"

"Graves. Two of them. My ma and my pa, both murdered by Apaches in eighty-six. I'm told it happened down near the state line and the Mexican border."

Nodding slowly, Deek raised his beer to his lips. He took a long, slow drink from his mug but did not take his eyes off Monte. When he was finished drinking, he drug his palm down over his mustache and beard. "Are you the kid? The one they found in the cactus?"

Monte stared at Deek for several seconds. "Yeah. I'm him."

"I'll be damned," Deek said gravely. "I thought you died. Lord only knows you came close to doin' just that. And what they done to your pa, I won't forget as long as I live."

"So, do you remember where it happened, remember good enough to show me?"

Deek thought for a moment. "I can draw you a good map. They's landmarks down that way you can't miss. You won't get lost. I'd show you myself but I'm on my way to Globe."

"Good enough," said Monte. "I got no money to pay you to

guide me, anyway."

"Hell, boy!" Deek said, shaking his head. "What you went through! I wouldn't take your money even if I was to ride down with you and show you the way. But like I said, I'm bound for Globe. I ain't had a woman in a month."

The tall cowboy was starting to feel the effects of his whiskey. He turned around and leaned back against the bar. Holding a half-empty shot glass in one hand, he pointed at Deek with the other. "Hey Deek, tell him about the time you captured old Geronimo. Or better yet, tell him how you single-handed saved Teddy Roosevelt in that Spanish American war.

"Damn it, Deek, come on and tell us one of your tales. We haven't heard a good lie since you climbed on the wagon."

The other cowboys began turning toward Monte and Deek.

The small cowboy laughed. "Hey soldier, if you offer to buy old Deek a whiskey he'll spin a yarn like you never heard. Why, to hear him tell it, he's a bigger hero than Daniel Boone and Wyatt Earp combined."

Monte stared appraisingly at Deek. The old man clearly had a reputation as a liar. Yet he had mentioned a boy thrown into cactus and Monte knew there was no way he could be lying about that.

Ignoring the cowboys, Monte asked, "How far is it to the graves . . . I mean to where the Apaches attacked?"

"You believe me, then?"

"I do."

Deek sat up a bit straighter. "It's a good thirty miles. You got a horse?"

"No."

Now finished with his whiskey, Turk sauntered over to the table. Standing between Monte and Deek, he leaned forward and rested both palms on the top of the table. "Deek, you old son of a bitch, what lies are you telling this fella?"

Monte had had enough, enough of walking, enough of Antonio Ortega, and enough of loudmouthed cowboys. "That's none of your damned business."

Turk blinked and then blinked again. He wasn't looking for trouble but he had never backed away from any either. He raised up to his full height, filled his lungs, and defiantly expanded his chest. "It's my business if I say it's my business. Who the hell do you think you are?"

Startled by Turk's sudden outburst, the saloon suddenly fell silent. All eyes darted back and forth from Monte to Turk. The cowboys were frowning but, behind the bar, Red wore a knowing smile.

Monte took off his hat and laid it on the table.

"I'd never seen a cowboy until today. Now that I have, I can't for the life of me figure out why some folks think a *cow-boy* is something special. It seems to me that all you really do is hoist your skinny ass onto the back of a horse. You sit there while the dumb brute does all the work and then you go and claim the credit."

Turk was dumbfounded and, for the moment, stunned into immobility. In that instant, Monte stood up and smoothly stepped clear of the table.

With eyes full of reckless fury, Turk took a step forward and swung a right cross, intending it to land on the side of Monte's jaw. Anticipating the move, Monte slapped Turk's blow away with his left forearm. Cupping the back of the cowboy's head with the palm of his right hand, Monte slammed Turk's face down onto the table. Then, lifting Turk by the hair of his head, Monte spun him around to face the bar.

The whole maneuver was accomplished in seconds. Blood began to drip from Turk's nose. His eyes rolled as he struggled to keep his balance.

Monte jerked Turk's pistol from its holster and then took two steps back. "Guns on the bar, boys. Look at me sideways and I'll put a bullet in your chest."

None of the cowboys moved. Monte extended his arm, leveling the barrel of the pistol at the back of Turk's head. "Now!"

Almost in unison the pistols thudded on polished wood.

"Red," Monte said, calmly, "stow those guns down under the bar."

As the bartender gathered up the pistols the short cowboy grew belligerent. "You sucker punched him!"

Monte snickered. "If I'd have done that, he wouldn't be standing."

"Big talk," said the short cowboy, "with you holding a loaded pistol."

Turk came to his senses and then sluggishly wiped the blood from his nose. He turned to see the barrel of a pistol inches from his face. "That was a dirty trick, damn you!"

Monte was mad at the world and he was ready to get even. His eyes darkened as he eased the hammer of the pistol down. "You think that was dirty, do you?"

Seeing the change in Monte's eyes, Turk balked. "I got nothing against you, mister."

"Shorty," demanded Monte, "you come over here with your friend. You both want a clean fight. So to make it fair, I'm going to let you pitch in and help him out."

Shorty took a step but then hesitated. "You still got Turk's gun in your hand."

Monte was feeling good now, his blood coming to a boil. "I'll give it to Deek, here. But on second thought, Shorty, you pick out another cowboy to come along with you. I want to see how tough you are when you have to stand on your own two feet."

Red spoke up, a dire warning in his tone. "Boys, you're looking at an honest-to-goodness bull-of-the-woods lumberjack. And you best only take a good long look or you're gonna get busted up real bad."

"He's more than that," added Deek. "He survived what the Apaches done to 'im as a kid. He's tougher'n any of you will ever be. If you want to stay clear of the hospital or maybe even out of the graveyard, I'd advise you all to eat a little crow and just walk away."

Handing Turk's pistol over to Deek, Monte took out his own pistol and laid it on the table. His eyes locked on Turk. "Make your move, you son of a bitch or I will."

Turk glanced at the bar, his face pale. "Come on, boys. Let's get to the train station. To hell with this."

"What about our hardware?" protested Shorty.

"I'll keep it safe 'til you boys get back," offered Red.

Spinning on his boot heels, Turk stomped out of the saloon. After a moment of hesitation, Shorty and the rest of the crew filed out behind him. Still spoiling for a fight, Monte watched them go, but then went to the door and stood there until they were out of sight.

"Never thought I'd see the day," Deek said.

"Me neither," agreed Red. "Prettiest damn thing I ever saw."

Monte went back to the table. He took a deep breath, let it out slowly, and then picked up his pistol and holstered it.

"We serve steak and beans here, too," said Red. "If you want a plate full, it's on me. That was worth a hell of a lot more than the six bits I charge."

"I'll take you up on it," Monte said and then took a seat facing the door. "I'm tired of jackrabbit."

"Serve me up a plate, too," Deek said, "and two more beers."

Monte nodded. "I could use another. And you don't need to draw me a map. Just tell me about the trail. I can remember what you say."

Deek shoved Turk's pistol behind his belt. As he began giving Monte detailed directions, he used his bony finger and began tracing an imaginary map on the tabletop. By the time the steaks were brought out, Monte Segundo finally knew where his parents had been buried.

With a full stomach and a good three hours remaining before sundown, Monte headed south, crossing over the desert at a fast walk. At dusk, he spotted a stand of willow trees in a shallow wash and then found the nearby spring just where Deek said it would be.

In the fading light, Monte knelt by the water and listened for a full minute before cupping his hand and drinking his fill. A few feet away, in a smooth patch of sand, he built a small fire. He had nothing to cook or any coffee to boil but to a man alone, the flames of a fire are often his only comfort. And for the first time in a long, long while, Monte's realized he was experiencing loneliness.

He was close now, only a few miles from where he used to live, and yet none of the landmarks looked familiar. He had hoped that seeing a distant mountain or perhaps a rocky outcropping would resurrect a forgotten memory, but so far his mind remained a blank. All he knew for sure was that in a few hours he would be standing over the graves of those that had brought him into the world.

For most of his life, Monte assumed it was normal to have forgotten one's early years. Until recently, he had no idea that he had, in fact, blocked out all memory of his childhood. Now, however, gazing into the fire, he wondered about his father and mother, two people that he had somehow erased from his memory. Over and over, he asked himself, who they were and where they had come from. But no matter how hard he tried, he could not remember anything whatsoever about his mother and what little he could recall of his father, he wished he did not remember.

As the night wore on, Monte became increasingly frustrated with his faulty memory but then a memory he desperately wanted to forget wormed its way back into his thoughts. Once again, he could see Rosa together with Anthony Ortega. In the blackness beyond the fire he even imagined he heard Rosa laughing along with him.

Monte swore, cursing his inability to purge the pestilent visions of Rosa from his mind, or to at least prevent their constant intrusion. For the last two days he had tried but again and again he had failed. What he wanted to remember stubbornly remained a mystery and what he wanted to forget continued to plague him.

Watching the dancing flames, Monte swore under his breath and then said out loud, "Damn snake eyes. That's what he has. How could she be such a fool? A blind man could see he was lying."

Unrolling his blanket, Monte paused and then muttered regretfully, "No. It's me that's the fool . . . Damn you, Rosa . . . To hell with both of you."

Wrapping his blanket around his shoulders, Monte stared into the flames. But all he saw until he fell asleep was Rosa, Rosa and Anthony Ortega.

The predawn chill woke Monte and in minutes he had rolled his blanket and was again heading south. Deek's meticulous description of the terrain and landmarks allowed Monte to travel swiftly as he threaded his way around low-lying patches of cactus and then crossed a rolling plain dotted with thorny mesquite and smooth-barked palo verde. Shortly after sunup, when he started angling to the southwest, he knew he was getting close.

A few hours later, he abruptly stopped in the shade of a gnarled mesquite. His heart began to pound. The open ground in front of him fell away for miles in a gentle slope. Here and there a patch of prickly pear added a swath of green to an otherwise parched landscape. A few scattered cholla cactus, rigid and threatening, anchored themselves above scant tufts of brown grass. A half mile in the distance, however, he could make out a sagging frame of charred timber.

Monte gritted his teeth and shook his head to clear his mind. He started for the burned-out building but found himself growing more and more anxious with every step. Having long ago learned to trust his instincts, Monte slowed his pace and began scanning the horizon in every direction.

Was his uneasiness, he wondered, simply due to an over-worked imagination? Was it perhaps whispers of forgotten memories that were now beginning to stir? Was it the thought of standing over the final resting place of his father and mother . . . or was it something entirely unrelated?

Halting for a moment, Monte listened. There was no wind, no sound but his own breathing. After several uneasy minutes, Monte started again. Feeling the hairs on the back of his neck stand on end, he eased his Colt in and out of the scabbard, making certain it was loose enough to draw quickly if the need arose.

When he was within one hundred paces of the burnt cabin he paused once more and studied everything in sight. He saw nothing unusual. Walking softly and slowly in his moccasins, he continued on to the side of the cabin and then stopped.

He stared at a dense thicket of cholla cactus a short distance to his left, and knew instantly it was where he had been thrown by the Apaches and left to die. That much he did remember. But he also remembered a corral where his father had been tied and tortured to death. That had been somewhere near the house but when he looked for it he could see nothing, not a single pole. However, there was a large palo verde shading a bare patch of sand off to his right. On a hunch, he headed toward it to investigate. When he rounded the twisted trunk of a dead mesquite, he jerked to a stop. Stacked a few feet in front of him, in the middle of the patch of sand, were two piles of brick-shaped stones.

The stones on the right were arranged in the shape of a grave but lay somewhat unevenly as one might expect they would after thirty years. But the grave next to it looked entirely different. In fact, it appeared to have been recently tended. The stones on it were neatly arranged over fresh dirt as if the grave were new.

Monte inched his way forward and then paused to study the tended grave more closely. Then he saw something that jolted him. A human finger, covered in flesh, was sticking out from under a stone.

Completely bewildered, he was staring at the finger when he caught a flicker of movement from the corner of his eye. Glancing far to the south, he could make out five mounted horsemen riding at an easy gallop. The land in that stretch of the desert was wide open and the riders were at least five miles away, but Monte had a feeling they were headed straight for him.

He watched the riders veer to the west for a while and then to the east, but he quickly surmised that his hunch was right. The men were clearly following a trail or track of some sort that would soon bring them to the homestead and very likely to where he stood.

It appeared that the riders were trailing someone, but Monte assumed whoever that might have been was already dead. And that person had recently been buried using the gravestones from his parents' graves.

Monte walked to within one step of the newly occupied grave to take a closer look. Then, to his amazement, he saw the finger move. Bending down at the head of the grave and peering into the shadows cast by the flat gravestones, Monte was astonished to see an eyeball staring out at him. And then it blinked.

Suddenly, Monte understood that someone was trying to hide from the riders and, in an act of pure desperation, had taken refuge under the gravestones. As the small posse grew nearer, Monte circled the grave looking for tracks. He spotted them easily enough but Monte Segundo had lived for years with the Kootenai Indians. Most men, unless they were expert trackers, would have missed the subtle marks left in the sand. Whoever was hiding under the dirt and stones was very good at covering tracks, as good as any Indian.

Circling the fresh grave as well as the old one, Monte deliberately obliterated every print the fugitive had left behind. Satisfied with his work, he stood close to the new grave and waited in the shade.

"I won't turn you in," he said softly as he watched the riders close the distance between them. Then noticing the men wore sombreros, Monte said, *"Soy amigo. No tengas miedo."*

Two hundred yards out, the Mexicans slowed their horses to a walk. A moment later, they scattered. After meandering in several different directions they regrouped and then galloped straight for Monte. When they were a few feet away they slid their mounts to a stop, blasting sand and gravel against Monte's moccasins.

Unimpressed with the horsemanship, Monte casually eyed the Mexicans. Even though they were covered in trail dust he could see that each wore the same type of jacket and sombrero. These were rurales.

The Mexicans, in turn, studied Monte, no doubt noticing his military uniform and the moccasins on his feet. Next, their eyes roamed suspiciously over the two graves.

"Buenos días," Monte said.

One of the Mexicans, a lean, hard-eyed man who appeared

to be in his forties, replied, "So, you speak our language," he said with no attempt to hide his arrogance. "I also speak yours."

Monte could size men up quickly and he took an immediate disliking to the Mexican.

"That's good," returned Monte. "Since you're north of the border, how about we stick to American?"

The Mexican sneered. "I am Sergeant Garcia. We are searching for an escaped murderer, a Yaqui Indian. We are in hot pursuit. If you know where he is, your country's neutrality law demands that you surrender him to us immediately."

Monte had never heard of the neutrality law but he had heard of rurales. They were dangerous men and used to getting what they wanted regardless of the law. He also knew that rurales had no aversion to murdering those they had apprehended. Monte was pondering his next move when a thought seemingly came out of nowhere.

"I suppose the law says that," Monte said. "But we've seen no Yaquis around here . . . guilty or innocent. All we've seen is the five of you on the wrong side of our border."

Garcia flinched, his eyes darting to his left and right. "Who is 'we'? You are alone and with no horse. Why is a soldier out here with no horse?"

"Alone?" Monte snickered. He looked back over his shoulder and then again faced Garcia. "Sure, that's what it looks like, doesn't it? We train our horses to lie down in the brush and then we find us a place to shoot from. You know. Sharpshooters with telescope sights. General Pershing's idea. He's deploying units all along the border. We're National Guard from up north, Idaho to be exact. Up there, we shoot elk at five hundred yards like you do rabbits at fifty. That's why Pershing recruited us from so far away.

"And since Mexico claims they're going to invade us any day now, we've got orders to shoot anything that looks like an army, anything at all we see coming north. Carrancista or Villista doesn't make any difference to the general.

"So, right this minute, there's thirty-caliber Springfield rifles with crosshairs on all of your chests. If I give the word, all you'll hear is a thud of the rifle slug blowing your heart out through your backbone. But you'll be dead before the sound gets here."

Garcia was no fool but he was wary. "Idaho National Guard?" sneered Garcia. "Next you will tell me that you are the great El Muerte!"

Monte smiled but his eyes held a threat. "We both know El Muerte is just make-believe. But I'm standing right here in front of you, real as the fires of hell."

Spreading his arms out slightly, Monte's black eyes bored into Garcia. "You want to find out if I'm bluffing? You damned greasers are trespassing. My men have itchy trigger fingers and every last one of them is chomping at the bit, wanting to bag their first Mexican."

Garcia was a tough man but he knew a killer when he saw one. He gathered the reins of his horse. "There is a reward for the Indian. One thousand pesos. You will know him by the marks on the back of his hands. Black suns."

Easing his horse around, Garcia ordered, *"Vámonos,"* and then led off in an easy walk. The rest of the rurales followed in single file, all heading back the way they had come.

When the Mexicans were mere specks in the distance Monte knelt beside the unmolested grave and started straightening the stones. Only then did he begin to realize that he was kneeling above his father and mother. Yet, with the distraction of the rurales and a fugitive concealed under the stones of the grave next to him, Monte was unable to apprehend what certainly would have been a bittersweet if not heartbreaking reunion. Once again, fate had robbed Monte Segundo of one of life's most precious moments.

"You can come out now," muttered Monte as he continued rearranging stones. "You should get away from here in case those rurales decide to come back."

There was no movement. Monte leaned over and looked under the rock where he had seen the eyeball. Now, the eye was nearly closed, almost lifeless.

Monte carefully lifted the stone that covered the fugitive's head. Brushing away a thin layer of sand, he discovered a strip of cloth that had been used to cover the fugitive's mouth and nose. Pulling the cloth away, Monte glared briefly at the gaunt face of a young man and then bent low and listened. The man was not dead but he was barely breathing.

"Oh, hell," growled Monte and then hurriedly jerked the rest of the stones off the man's body. Lifting him from the grave, Monte laid him down in the sand, making certain he was still shaded by the palo verde.

Looking the man over, Monte guessed him to be, perhaps, twenty years old. He was barefooted, grimy from head to toe, and dressed in filthy cotton rags. His hair was long and black. He was average height and Monte surmised that if he tipped the scales at one hundred pounds he would be lucky.

Believing the poor wretch was merely overheated from being under the rocks, Monte left the fugitive to recuperate and went back to tending the graves. When he was finished rearranging the stones, he noticed the man was still unconscious. A few seconds later his labored breathing turned into short raspy gasps.

Monte pulled the whiskey bottle from his back pocket. Seeing there was only a swallow left, he looked back toward the burned cabin. "There has to be some water somewhere," he said to himself. "We had to have water. There's got to be water somewhere."

Monte knelt and slowly trickled the last of his water past the man's cracked lips. As he corked the bottle, a faint memory of a large tree flashed through his mind.

He stood and immediately noticed the trunk of a charred cottonwood protruding from a ravine fifty yards east of the burned cabin. Going toward the ravine, he saw where a thicket of stubby willows had taken root. Sliding down the sandy bank of the ravine, Monte felt around the base of the willows. In a rocky depression, he discovered a scant pool of water no larger than a frying pan, all that was left of their spring.

With no way to fill the whiskey bottle, Monte brought the man to the ravine and laid him alongside the willows. Tearing off the bottom of the Indian's shirttail, Monte sopped up the water and then wrung drops between the man's lips. His tongue, however, was black and swollen and he did not swallow.

Again and again Monte slowly dripped water into the fugitive's mouth. A half hour went by before he was able to swallow. Just past dusk, his eyes finally opened.

"It's about time," Monte sneered, as he squeezed a few more drops of water into his whiskey bottle.

The man rolled his eyes toward Monte but could not speak. In fact, he was too weak to move.

"I suppose I've got to feed you now," Monte said, corking the whiskey bottle and coming to his feet. "But we can't stay here. I got a feeling those rurales will come back tonight. We'll have to move out a few miles and find a good place to camp."

The man managed to shake his head. The movement was barely perceptible but Monte caught it. "Don't worry," said Monte, picking up his hapless charge and then hoisting him onto his back in a fireman's carry. "I've packed many a deer like this. Most of them were twice your size."

Trudging up the soft bank of the ravine, Monte started off in a brisk walk angling northeast. "The railroad is out there somewhere. We'll come to it tomorrow sometime, but we'll need to stop in a while. We both need to eat and get some sleep."

Monte walked for an hour before he found a deep ravine with a smooth sandy bottom and a good bit of brush along the edges. Sliding down a crusty bank into the bed of the arroyo, he then rolled the man off his back and onto the sand. After giving him a few swallows of water, Monte went hunting for something to eat. With a half-moon overhead, and his uncanny ability to see in low light, he had no trouble finding and shooting a cottontail rabbit.

When he returned to the bottom of the ravine, Monte was pleased to see the young man sitting up in the darkness. "Maybe you'll live after all," Monte said, but then the man wavered and fell backwards. "And then again, maybe you won't."

Tossing the rabbit on the sand, Monte gathered some nearby sticks that had been piled up by the last flash flood. In minutes, he was squatting by a fire with the rabbit skewered on a stick, broiling over a plume of dancing flames. As he rotated the rabbit, Monte starred curiously at the stranger that he had been packing for so many miles.

A few minutes passed and then Monte jammed his cook-stick deep into the sand and went over to the unconscious man. Lifting one of his hands, he twisted it toward the firelight, but the back of the hand was too dirty to see anything. Unsatisfied, Monte spit on the hand and then rubbed. He saw nothing so he spit again and rubbed some more. Then he saw the tattoo, a sun the size of a silver dollar with flames extending out from the rim. The flames were yellow but the sun itself was solid black.

"Well, you're sure enough the Yaqui Indian they were after," Monte said, easing the hand down. "Now what the hell do I do with a murdering Indian?"

Monte went back and sat by the fire and turned the rabbit

for the better part of an hour. Occasionally, he climbed out of the ravine to listen to the sounds of the night and scan the starlit desert. But most of the time he spent staring at the flames and the Yaqui.

The Indian, lying motionless in the sand, reminded Monte of a corpse, and he could not help but think of the two graves he had left behind. At times, macabre thoughts of what lay beneath the gravestones crossed his mind but those demons were quickly shoved aside. Instead, he concentrated on the fact that he had finally connected with a tangible remnant of his past. Now, at least, he had a sense of belonging and a place he could call home.

The Indian suddenly stirred, breaking into Monte's thoughts. Leaning forward, Monte realized it was time to check the rabbit. As he peeled off a strip of steaming backstrap, he could not help but recall the *pitoreal* Rosa had once cooked under similar circumstances. He swore under his breath and tried to block that memory, but the face of Rosa Bustamonte highlighted by the soft glow of firelight was a vision impossible for him to suppress.

Monte took a bite of the rabbit. "Damn you, Rosa. I wish I'd never met you."

The Indian struggled up into a sitting position. His eyes strained to open. *"Gracias, señor,"* he managed in a weak, raspy voice. "Thank you . . . for saving my life."

Tearing off a back leg, Monte handed a piece of rabbit to the Indian. "Don't thank me yet. I don't know if I did you any favors or not. We'll see."

The Indian accepted the meat and took a small bite. "I am called Ahayaca."

"Ahayaca?" repeated Monte, pulling the other hind leg off the rabbit. "Sounds like a Yaqui name. Is that what you are, a Yaqui Indian?"

47

Ahayaca swallowed the dry meat with some difficulty. "I am not Yaqui. But it is to their village I must go."

Monte held the whiskey bottle out to Ahayaca but the Indian hesitated.

"It's water. And by the way, you can call me Monte."

Ahayaca nodded and then gratefully accepted the bottle.

"So where is this village?" Monte asked.

Knowing too much water would make him sick, Ahayaca took only a small sip of water. "It is near Tucson, Arizona. A few miles southwest of that town."

Ripping off a chunk of meat with his teeth, Monte chewed as he eyed Ahayaca. "Those rurales back there said you murdered somebody. Did you?"

Ahayaca studied Monte from across the fire. "No. But if I could, I would have. But I did not get the chance."

For several minutes no words were spoken as Monte and Ahayaca eyed each other and hungrily gnawed on the rabbit legs.

After stripping the meat off the bones, Ahayaca pointed at the rabbit. "Is there more?"

Pulling the rabbit off the stick, Monte twisted off a front leg and then handed the rest to Ahayaca. "Well, you don't look like a killer. A starved man like yourself isn't very good at killing or anything of the sort. It must have taken all you had just to get yourself under those rocks."

After chewing on the back of the rabbit for several minutes, Ahayaca paused to take another sip from the whiskey bottle. He took a deep breath and let it out slowly. "I saw you look down at me. And then I felt the horse's hooves pounding the earth. After that there was nothing but darkness . . . until I opened my eyes here by the fire."

Ahayaca squinted at Monte as if trying to see into his soul.

"What happened at the graves? Why did you not tell the rurales where I was?"

Monte shrugged. "That one Mexican, Garcia, tried to order me around. I don't take orders very well, especially not from Mexican rurales. And besides, I didn't like the looks of that bunch."

"Where are the rest of you?" Ahayaca asked. "Where are the other Americans and your horses?"

For a moment Monte was stumped. Then he realized Ahayaca was referring to his uniform. "There's only me. No horses either. I was there by myself."

Blinking several times, Ahayaca tried to focus his bloodshot eyes. He peered at Monte across the fire. "You *carried* me here?"

"Yeah."

"Where are we?"

"A few miles north of the graves where I found you."

Ahayaca studied Monte for several seconds before asking another question. "The graves . . . are those of your ancestors?"

Monte thought for a moment, realizing that for the first time in thirty years the words he was about to speak now had meaning.

"My ma and pa."

Ahayaca bent forward, placed his left palm flat on the sand, and bowed his head. "Your father and mother," he said solemnly. He paused in that position and then brushed the sand from his palm and began eating again.

Monte glanced curiously at Ahayaca. Briefly, he wondered about the odd gesture the Indian had made but then dismissed it as some sort of tradition peculiar to his tribe.

"The rurales told me there was a big reward out on you," Monte said. "What makes you so special?"

Ahayaca ignored the question. Instead he said, "They will not give up. This I have to tell you. They will come for me."

Looking up into the star-filled sky, Monte said, "The moon

has gone down. If they come, it'll be first thing in the morning. They'll circle around where they lost your trail and then they'll cut my tracks. If they're any good at all at reading sign, they'll know I was carrying something heavy. I figure, they'll find us an hour or so after sunrise."

Still holding onto the rabbit with one hand, Ahayaca set the whiskey bottle in the sand and then attempted to get to his feet. He made it to his knees but could go no farther. "Then I must go. They will kill you for what you have done."

Monte finished nibbling the meat from his rabbit leg and then tossed the bones into the fire. When Ahayaca finished eating Monte came to his feet. Stepping around the dwindling flames, Monte pocketed the whiskey bottle and then knelt with his back to Ahayaca. "Climb on. Our only chance is to make it to the railroad and then follow the tracks to a station before they catch up."

"It is no use. You must leave me here."

"Fat chance," Monte said. "I started this and I'm going to finish it. Now get on. You've had some food and water. You'll feel better in a few hours. If you do, then you can walk some."

Ahayaca grabbed Monte's shoulders and held on as Monte stood and locked his arms around Ahayaca's legs.

"Anyhow," added Monte, "we're almost out of water and it'll be cooler walking at night. I doubt it's more than ten or fifteen miles and we can make that by sunup."

"You cannot carry me fifteen miles," protested Ahayaca as Monte trudged out of the ravine heading north. "And, anyway, the rurales will come to the train station looking for me. There are five of them."

Monte changed his direction slightly, angling a bit to the west. "I just spent some time down in Mexico and I came to notice a big difference between them and us. Americans might break the law from time to time but down in Mexico, the law is just plain ignored.

"Those rurales are used to their own lawless ways but up here they'll find out soon enough that things are different. They can't just cross the border and take you away without some sort of proper paperwork."

"But," protested Ahayaca, "what if there is no law at the railroad, no sheriff?"

"Doesn't matter," Monte said. "The whole border is a powder keg right now. There's talk of a Mexican invasion and the Americans are sending thousands of soldiers down this way to stand guard all along the border. Those rurales will be on mighty thin ice just being in this country. They won't start any trouble, sheriff or no sheriff. Not if they're smart, anyway."

Monte had gone over a mile before he eased Ahayaca off his back. Ahayaca, however, could barely stand, much less walk, so after a few minutes rest they continued on as before. Working their way across the sprawling desert, they stopped at intervals to rest but as the night wore on, the rests became more and more frequent. Even so, by first light Monte was able to make out a straight line in the distance, a black thread that stretched across the entire horizon.

"There it is," Monte said, allowing Ahayaca to slide off his back. "There's the railroad."

Holding onto Monte's shirt, Ahayaca steadied his legs. "I do not see anything."

"It's there, alright. Closer than I thought. It veered southwest somewhere and now it's headed for Globe."

Ahayaca let go of Monte's shirt. He rubbed the grit from his eyes and then looked back in the direction they had come. Straining his eyes, Ahayaca pointed. "What is that?"

Monte turned and saw a fuzzy gray speck, a speck that seemed to be moving. He could make out a rider. He was on their trail and closing fast.

"Looks like we're not going to make it," Monte said, and then tossed Ahayaca over his shoulder and trotted to a shallow arroyo. Dropping down behind a knee-high bank, Monte drew his pistol. "Stay low," he ordered.

"I am sorry," Ahayaca said. "I brought this on you."

The rider was closing rapidly. Monte could now see the *rurale* was leading a second horse, but a horse with no rider. Monte drew his pistol. He searched left and right and then behind him looking for the other rurales who would be trying to surround him. Monte was confident he could hit a man-size target at one hundred yards with his pistol but against five rifles, he knew he had little chance to survive.

"You watch my back," Monte said. "Let me know if you see anything, anything at all."

"It is an honor to die with you," Ahayaca said. "You are like the *jaguar.*"

"I only see . . ." Monte began and then stopped. "One rider. He's leading a second horse. No one's on it so the other rurales may already be circling behind us on foot."

In moments, Monte could see the rider more clearly. He stared in disbelief but there was no doubt. Whoever was barreling toward them wore a hat but it was not a sombrero. And the second horse had no saddle.

"What the hell?" muttered Monte.

The rider was in range but Monte did not take aim. In seconds, the horseman rode past the arroyo where they were hiding. But then, after taking a few more strides, both horses abruptly slid to a stop.

"Monte Segundo," the rider called out. "It's Deek Coleman! Rurales are hot on my tail. We got to move and move quick!"

"I'll be damned!" Monte said, as he stood in the growing light. "Over here, Deek."

Deek trotted his horses over. He glanced at Monte and then settled his attention on Ahayaca. "So that's it. I wondered what you was totin'."

"He can't walk," Monte said.

Deek nodded. "Put him up behind me. You hop on my mare. We gotta hightail it, pronto."

Lifting Ahayaca, Monte placed him behind Deek Coleman. Taking the lead rope from Deek, Monte grabbed a handful of mane and then swung up onto the bareback mare.

"I can see 'em," Deek said, pointing. "Five of 'em. We'll head for Bernadino."

Spurring his mount into a full run and with Monte following close behind, Deek rode directly west. Dodging mesquite and bounding over cactus they raced across the desert, angling toward the railroad. Soon a small cluster of buildings could be seen alongside the tracks.

Deek's horses were fresh and they crossed the desert with ground-eating strides. Just before sunup and well out in front of the rurales, Deek and Monte reined in their lathered horses on the outskirts of Bernadino.

The rurales were less than a quarter mile away when they began to slow and then finally come to a stop. One of them could be seen looking through a pair of binoculars.

"What do you think they're up to?" Deek asked.

Monte took a good look at Deek. His scraggly hair had been cut short. All that was left of his beard was a well-trimmed mustache but, unlike two days before, Deek now wore a pistol.

"Most likely figuring out their next move," Monte said.

"What're they after, anyhow?" Deek asked.

"Me," offered Ahayaca. "They won't stop until they have me."

Deek nodded toward the rurales. "One's comin'. Reckon he wants to parley."

A door was heard slamming somewhere in the town.

"Not many folks in Bernadino," Deek said, looking back over his shoulder. "But they're startin' to stir."

The *rurale* approached at a walk. With his reins in one hand, he held the other hand high in the air. It was Garcia.

The Mexican halted a few feet away. His eyes rested appraisingly on Monte. "You have much *machismo, señor.* It would be such a pity to have to kill you."

"What do you want?" Monte asked.

Garcia's eyes swept over Deek, taking in the pistol around his waist. "I will give you one thousand pesos for the Indian. Paid in Mexican silver."

"A thousand pesos!" exclaimed Deek. "You'd pay that much for a skinny peon?"

"Sure," smiled Garcia. "Why fight each other when we can all be friends?"

Monte frowned. His eyes were locked on Garcia, watching for him to make the slightest wrong move. "I don't need any friends."

"You got any papers?" asked Deek. "For a thousand dollars he must be one bad *hombre.*"

Garcia slowly reached inside his jacket. "From the state of Sonora," he said.

Taking out a folded piece of battered paper, Garcia leaned forward and then handed it to Deek. "You are a sheriff?"

Deek unfolded the paper. "Used to be an Arizona Ranger. I was a Ranger a couple of times but not no more. But I know the law."

"The law," scoffed Garcia. "What good is the law along the border? If you were a Ranger you have heard of Kosterlitzky. He knew how to handle criminals without the law getting in the way."

Studying the paper in his hand, Deek answered, "Sure, I

knew the colonel. But I heard he quit the rurales a couple of years ago. Retired on this side of the border . . . for his health you might say."

Deek folded the paper and handed it back to Garcia. "The papers look right but there's still the matter of extradition."

Returning the paper to his jacket, Garcia's eyes went cold. "Why waste time with such little details when you can have the money instead? I could give it to you today."

"What's extradition?" asked Monte.

Deek squirmed at bit, causing his saddle to creak. "Extradition is when we give a prisoner that we caught on this side of the border back to Mexico. There's supposed to be a court hearing first, though, and if we figure the prisoner's sure enough guilty we send 'im back to Mexico. Only when Colonel Kosterlitzky was running the rurales we mostly ignored that part of it. We turned them that we caught over to him, no questions asked. And he helped us the same way with all sorts of bad men. That saved everybody a lot of time and helped clean out a passel of gangs and cutthroats.

"So, if it was up to me, Sergeant, I'd hand 'im over. But the prisoner belongs to Monte, here. And I'm goin' along with whatever he decides."

Monte thought for a moment. Something didn't add up. "So why'd you offer us a thousand pesos? Why didn't you just ask for him like you used to?"

Garcia hesitated. "That is my business, amigo. The offer still stands, one thousand pesos of Mexican silver for one filthy, murdering Indian that is worth nothing to you."

A taunting grin creased Monte's lips. "Well my peon is plenty dirty and he's kind of puny. If he was a fish I'd throw him back . . . but I think I'll go ahead and keep him."

"Chingate" blurted Garcia and then spun his horse around, viciously spurring it into a run.

Deek watched Garcia for a moment. "You got a way of makin' trouble, don't ya?"

"It's a gift."

"So," sighed Deek, "who exactly is this fella I got sittin' behind me? And how come he's worth a thousand silver pesos?"

Keeping his eyes on the rurales, Monte answered, "That's Ahayaca. And I have a hunch he's not a murderer like they claim. But they want him mighty bad for something. That's for damn sure."

"I must get to the Yaqui village," Ahayaca said. "Then I will answer your questions."

Watching Garcia rejoin the rurales, Deek said, "The only way out of here now is the train. And there's nothing sayin' those rurales won't get on the train right along with us."

Monte took a long, hard look at Deek. "Not that I'm ungrateful, Deek, but what the hell are you doing out here?"

Deek chuckled. "Yeah. Mighty peculiar, ain't it? Downright lucky I come along when I did."

"Lucky for me and Ahayaca," agreed Monte. "Maybe not for you."

"Well, after what you done to Turk and the boys back yonder at the saloon, the boys turned sour on me. They figured I might have enjoyed watching all of 'em eat crow. And they was right. I could see the way the wind was blowin' after that so I collected my wages and lit out. Naturally, I come down to see if you found them graves you was lookin' for.

"I got to them graves about sundown yesterday and then read the sign. I could see where those horses come up on you and then rode back the way they come. And I could see your tracks got a whole lot deeper when you took off to the north. I knew you was carrying something heavy. I was thinkin' maybe it was gold or silver.

"Anyhow, I rode off after you and kept a goin' til it was close to dark. Then's when I spotted the riders way back behind me and I knowed right off they was followin' after you just the same as me.

"This mornin' I took out soon as I could make out your trail, but those riders was behind me followin' right along. When they got some closer, I seen they was wearing sombreros. I figured that meant trouble for you so I lit a shuck. That's when you saw me."

"What about the extra horse?" asked Monte.

"I bought that mare with some of my wages. I figured you might be tired of walkin'."

"You quit your job," Monte said skeptically, "bought a horse you didn't need, and then followed me all the way down here?"

Deek cleared his throat and stared down at his pommel. "Those boys at the saloon were pokin' fun at me but there was a good reason for it. I used to hit the bottle real hard. I'd run out of money and do almost anything to have me another drink. So, I got to tellin' stories . . . lies . . . to get a drink.

"I give up the whiskey months ago. I drink a beer from time to time but that's all. I been tryin' to straighten up, you might say. But it was hard listenin' to the boys talkin' 'bout my drinkin' days. They never let it go.

"But when you stood up to 'em, when you slammed ole Turk down on that table . . . you reminded me of what I used to be. Used to be, that is, before I was a drunk.

"It made me feel good, real good. It kind of set things right-side up all the sudden. So, I figured I owed you a favor like the one you done me. And like I said, them boys was turning mean on me. It was just a matter of time before there was trouble, so here I am."

Monte shook his head. "Out of the frying pan into the fire."

"We have one advantage," broke in Ahayaca.

Monte glanced over his shoulder. "What might that be?"

"They want me alive."

"Why?"

"They believe . . . they and others believe that I know the location of the Tayopa."

Deek craned his neck around. His eyes flashed with sudden excitement. "The lost Tayopa? The mine?"

"Yes."

"Damn!" exclaimed Deek. "Do you? Do you know where it is?"

"They believe I do. They will torture me to find out."

"What's so special about this Tayopa?" Monte asked.

Looking wide-eyed at Monte, Deek said excitedly, "Why it was the richest silver deposit in all of Mexico. But way back in the sixteen-hundreds, the Indians killed all the Spaniards at the mine and then anybody that come lookin' for it. After a while, the Spaniards forgot where it was exactly. And folks has been lookin' for it ever since. It's worth millions.

"Some say the Indians know where it is but they won't tell nobody. Rich ore and silver bars show up from time to time and there ain't no doubt it's Tayopa silver. Why, everybody down this way, Mexicans and Americans, knows about the lost Tayopa."

Keeping an eye on the rurales who remained clustered together, Monte shrugged indifferently. "At least we know the Mexicans won't take a shot at us. They'd be afraid of killing Ahayaca and losing their treasure."

"Then we'll stick to 'im like white on rice," agreed Deek and then refocused his attention from Ahayaca back to the rurales. "I wonder what they're figurin' now."

Monte looked down the main street of Bernadino. He saw a lone flatbed truck parked in front of a false-fronted mercantile. Next to the mercantile was another large wooden building. A few small clapboard houses surrounded those two structures.

Along with the train station and a single telephone line, that was all there was to the town of Bernadino. And the only vehicle in sight was the truck.

"I've got an idea," Monte said. "But it'll cost some money."

Deek tapped his vest pocket. "I got thirty bucks left of my wages."

"No," Ahayaca said tugging on a greasy thong that was looped around his neck. From under his shirt he pulled out a leather pouch. Opening the pouch he fingered something from it and then tucked the small bag back under his shirt.

Reaching around Deek, Ahayaca held out his closed fist, palm down. "I give you this for your thirty dollars. At least, I can pay."

Deek slid his open hand under Ahayaca's and felt the weight of a coin land in his palm. He looked down expecting to see a silver peso but instead saw a tarnished gold coin the size of a silver dollar. It was an irregularly shaped coin that had been crudely stamped with a number of unrecognizable markings.

"Will that pay for the use of your dollars?" asked Ahayaca.

Staring at the coin, Deek turned it over. There were no markings on the opposite side. "Sure enough it will!"

As Deek pocketed the coin, he glanced at Monte for his reaction but Monte was deep in thought.

"What's your plan?" Deek asked.

"We'll go into town," began Monte, "and get three train tickets going to Globe. The rurales will be sure and follow us to find out what we're up to. Then they'll buy tickets so they can follow us. The train has stock cars so we'll load our horses before we get on and then so will the Mexicans. But when the train starts to move we'll hop off."

"But the rurales will see us," protested Deek. "They won't let us out of their sight. They'll get off as soon as we do."

"I hope they do. Then we'll all be on foot."

"What good would that do?" Deek asked.

"That's the tricky part," Monte said, "but it's easier to think on a full stomach and Ahayaca is going to need his strength. Let's see if we can get some breakfast in town. While we eat, I'll fill you in on the details and you can tell me what you think."

Deek leered at the rurales and then swore to himself. "If this ain't Billy hell, I don't know what is."

"So," Monte said, reining his horse around and starting toward the only street in Bernadino, "we might as well eat."

Spinning his mount, Deek trotted up alongside Monte. "What do you think them Mexicans will do, now?"

Monte huffed. "I suppose they'll ride into town and see what we're up to. I don't think they'll try anything with us on our guard, especially on this side of the border."

The mercantile Monte had seen was not yet open but the building next to it was a saloon and restaurant and its door was open. Dismounting in front of the restaurant, Monte helped Ahayaca to the ground as Deek stepped down and tied both horses. Supporting Ahayaca, Monte paused and glanced back. As he expected, the rurales were starting for town.

Inside the restaurant, Deek knowingly took a table that was next to a wall and away from the bar. All three men took a seat, Monte and Deek with their backs to the wall and Ahayaca with his back to the rear of the saloon.

No one was tending bar but soon a heavyset woman with her hair up in a bun exited a side door near the rear of the building.

"You men here for breakfast?" she asked, her voice deep and throaty.

"We are," Deek answered. "What'ya got?"

"All you get here is eggs, bacon, biscuits, and gravy. Coffee to drink unless you want something stronger."

"Serve it up, ma'am," Deek said. "We're as hungry as an orphaned calf."

The woman nodded and then disappeared through the door she had come out of. The moment she left, the rurales walked into the restaurant, dragging their Spanish rowels across the rough wooden floor. A few feet past the front door the men stopped, their black eyes casually roaming around the room.

Monte glanced at the spurs, noticing the spiked rowels were twice the size of those he had seen in Rodeo. The jingling of the rowels sounded much the same as the Americans' in Rodeo but the men wearing these spurs were not cocky young cowboys. These were trail-hardened and dangerous men.

The woman came out again. Wiping her hands with a white towel, she nodded at the Mexicans. *"Desayuno?"*

The rurales took a table near the front door. "Only coffee," answered Garcia.

As soon as the woman left, the Mexicans began conversing with one another as if nothing was out of the ordinary. When they did, Monte leaned forward and, speaking softly, explained the rest of his plan.

When he was finished, Deek leaned back, a thoughtful look on his face. He glanced at Monte and then stood up. "By damned," he whispered, "I think that'll work." Going to the side door he stuck his head into the kitchen. "Where's your outhouse, ma'am?"

"Out the back door," came the answer.

The rurales seemed to pay no attention to Deek. As he stepped out the back door, the woman brought out a tray loaded with thick porcelain mugs and a pot of steaming coffee. She filled three cups at Monte's table and then served the rurales.

"Plenty of coffee, fellas," she said, heading back to the kitchen. "Just holler if anybody wants more."

Monte immediately took a sip of coffee but Ahayaca hesitated.

"Why do you do this, Monte Segundo? Why do you help me when it puts your life in danger?"

Monte held the mug close to his lips. He suddenly thought of Rosa and Anthony Ortega, something he had not done in several hours. "Hell if I know. Maybe Garcia rubbed me the wrong way or it could be I was just itching for a fight. Who knows?"

Several minutes passed. Monte had finished his mug of coffee and half of Deek's when one of the Mexicans called out, *"Mas café, por favor."*

Both tables were served coffee once again, but it was not until the breakfast plates were being brought out from the kitchen that Deek finally returned.

"Got 'er done," he said, under his breath. "But that mercantile man turned out to be a damned Dutchy, a tight son of a bitch. I had to give up my gold piece to get him to use his truck and play along."

"Did you get the board, too?"

"Yep, measured and cut."

"What about the train?" Monte asked.

Taking out a pocket watch from his vest, Deek said, "Our luck is holdin'. Train's due in at around nine this mornin' and it'll be headin' west. It'll go through a pass in the Chiricahua Mountains and let us off at Cazador. Our horses will be unloaded and waitin' for us at the depot."

Ahayaca turned toward Deek. "You have done well."

Ahayaca's choice of words and his stately tone struck Monte as peculiar but his curiosity was instantly squelched by the thud of a full breakfast plate landing in front of him.

"Gravy's coming," announced the woman as she turned on her heels and hurried off.

Picking up a piece of bacon, Ahayaca asked, "What time is it now?"

Deek took a gulp of coffee before answering, "Ten to eight."

Monte pointed to Ahayaca's breakfast. "Eat slow. If you start feeling sick you better stop. I once saw a starving man eat too fast and it killed him."

"I've heard of that," agreed Deek. "But we all better eat slow. The less time we spend waitin' at the train depot the better off we'll be."

CHAPTER THREE

Deek pulled his watch from his vest, checked it, and then shoved it back in his pocket. "It's ten til."

"Alright," said Monte. "Let's get to it."

Standing first, Deek kept his eyes on the rurales. Monte helped Ahayaca to his feet and then the two of them stepped away from the wall.

"I can walk now," Ahayaca said. "My strength is returning."

Skirting around the rurales, Deek led the way to the front door. Ahayaca was close behind and Monte brought up the rear. As soon as they started toward their horses, Garcia rose from his table. Taking three long strides, he stopped in the open door and watched every move. Deek untied both horses as Monte and Ahayaca waited. Then, together, they proceeded across the street toward the train station where Deek handed the reins to Monte and proceeded to the ticket counter.

Wondering what the Americans had in mind, the rurales casually sauntered over to the station. Overhearing Deek as he purchased tickets for Globe, Garcia immediately sent one of his men for their horses. When he brought them up, Garcia went to the ticket counter and bought tickets for himself and all of his men. He was just leaving the ticket window when, from the east, the lonely wail of a distant train whistle drifted across the desert.

Garcia and his men moved off twenty paces to the right of Monte, Deek, and Ahayaca. When the train rolled in and stopped, Monte was pleased to see not one but two stock cars just ahead of the caboose. The doors of both cars rumbled open. Ramps were lowered and then both slammed down onto the ground. As Deek led his two horses into one car the rurales began loading their five into the other.

There were six passenger cars, none of them overly full. With the rurales still dealing with their horses, Monte selected the last car in line and then he, Deek, and Ahayaca took the back seats that were closest to the rear door.

In minutes, a voice called out, "All aboard!"

Spurs could be heard jingling along the outside of the passenger cars. Garcia's face appeared as he peered through one of the windows. His eyes met Monte's. Garcia said something to his men. They laughed and then all five rurales entered through the front door of the same passenger car.

The train whistle blasted twice and the Mexicans began looking for empty seats. Just as they were seated the train started to roll. When it was approaching the speed of a fast walking man, Monte stood quietly, as did Deek and Ahayaca.

With Ahayaca and Deek close behind, Monte slipped out the door and onto the steps. Stepping down onto the ground but keeping his feet moving, Monte extended a hand back to Ahayaca who hopped down, stumbled, but then caught his balance. Deek jumped next but before he landed, a frantic *"Cabrones!"* erupted from inside the passenger car.

With Monte supporting Ahayaca on one side and Deek on the other, all three started running back toward the restaurant. The rurales, stumbling and swearing, piled out of the passenger car. For a moment they were confused but then, seeing Deek as he reentered the restaurant, they spread out and warily started back across the dusty street.

Inside the restaurant, Monte, Ahayaca, and Deek bounded across the floor to the rear door. Monte went through first and, according to plan, the truck was waiting with the engine running. Ahayaca came out next. Monte lifted him as easily as he would a bag of grain and placed him on the flatbed. Then Deek came through and slammed the door shut behind him. Grabbing a plank that was leaning up against the outside wall, he wedged one end under the doorknob and then, at an angle, jammed the other end into the packed sand.

The doorknob suddenly wiggled and jerked. Then something heavy crashed into the door.

Deek was helping himself onto the truck bed when, on the other side of the door, several shots exploded, splintering the wood near the doorknob.

Monte was about to hop onto the flatbed when Garcia, pistol in hand, came running around the rear corner of the restaurant. In a fraction of a second, Monte's pistol was drawn and aimed directly at Garcia's chest.

The Mexican skidded to a halt, with both hands spread wide and high.

Keeping the barrel of his Colt pointed at Garcia, Monte cautiously stepped up on the bed. As soon as his feet landed the truck rattled away in a cloud of dust.

Deek let out a howl. "Hell's bells, boys. That was slicker than snot!"

Squatting and peering through the haze at Garcia, Monte holstered his Colt. He looked over his shoulder and saw Ahayaca sitting on a bag of grain and leaning uncomfortably against a side panel. "You alright?"

"I am well enough."

Deek excitedly slid over next to Ahayaca. "Did you see how fast Monte pulled his pistol? I ain't seen a quick draw like that in a coon's age!"

Satisfied that they were out of danger, Monte glanced through the back window at the driver and then sat down opposite Deek and Ahayaca.

"Do they teach that kind of gunplay in the National Guard?" asked Deek.

"No. I've used my pistol to hunt since I was seven or eight. It jumps in my hand without much thought."

Ahayaca studied Monte as if seeing him for the first time. "You are National Guard?"

"Yeah . . . at least I used to be."

"From the far north?" asked Ahayaca.

Monte shrugged. "Yeah, Idaho. That's up near Canada."

The truck shifted gears and picked up speed.

"I read in the paper," Deek said, "that President Wilson is sending one hundred and fifty thousand of you National Guard boys down to our border. For him to do that, things must be gettin' mighty hot between us and Mexico."

"I suppose," Monte said, "but it's none of my business anymore."

"How long until we are in Tucson?" asked Ahayaca.

Deek thumbed to his left. "That fella drivin' this Ford says he can make over thirty miles in one hour. If he can do that, we'll be in Casador in no time. From Casador, with Ahayaca and me ridin' double, it'll take two days to make Tucson. But if we could take the train all the way it would only take half a day to get there.

"We got no reason to worry about them rurales now. So, we might as well take the train . . . that is if you got more of that gold to pay for the tickets."

"It is best," Ahayaca said, "that I stay away from trains now. They will use the telephones. The rurales . . . and others, have spies everywhere. They will also be looking for me on the trains and in the cities."

The truck bounced over a rock and then slammed into a pothole, but the driver maintained his speed as the truck clattered through the warm, still air of midmorning.

"Have you got a wanted poster out on you?" Deek asked.

"No."

"Then how's a body to know who you are?"

"There are ways," said Ahayaca. "And many have heard the rumors about me and the lost Tayopa."

Deek scratched at his jaw. "I forgot about that. Yeah, word could spread mighty fast about that sort of thing."

"Do you know how to get to Tucson by horseback?" Monte asked Deek.

"Sure I do. Like I told Garcia, I used to be an Arizona Ranger. Back in eighty-two I was one for a while and when they started up again a few years ago, I was one again. All in all, I rode this country for many a year before I took to the bottle. But, like I said, I mended my ways. Now, I'm on the straight and narrow."

Monte glanced at Ahayaca. "We'll need some supplies, enough food for at least two days."

Ahayaca nodded. "I have a few more pieces of gold. But I believe it will be enough."

"You don't have no silver?" Deek asked. "I figured with Tayopa bein' a silver mine you'd have some silver."

The truck hit another bump and Ahayaca grabbed a side panel to steady himself. "All that I have with me is gold. When I get to my village, I will return to you what it cost for this truck. I am sorry you had to give it up."

Aware that he had said too much, Deek blushed with embarrassment. "Oh, you don't have to do that. Easy come, easy go, I always say."

Monte was hardly listening to the conversation. With all the talk about going to Tucson, his thoughts had once again focused on Rosa. For most of the morning he had been able to put her out of his mind but with the present crisis over, at least for the time being, he began to wonder about her again. And, once more, he felt his gut twist into knots.

"When was the last time you were in Tucson?" Monte asked.

"You askin' me?" questioned Deek.

"Either one of you," replied Monte. "Either of you ever hear of a man there by the name of Anthony Ortega? Or maybe Antonio Ortega?"

"I have never been to Tucson," Ahayaca said. "The name means nothing to me."

Deek took off his hat and wiped his forehead, a band of white skin that had seldom seen the sun. "Name's familiar. It don't have a good ring to it, though."

"He might own a mercantile," prompted Monte.

"That's it," Deek said, nodding. "Yep, I know who he is. He's got a store down on Congress Street. Word is, he's kind of shady, though."

"How's that?"

"Oh, nothin' in particular. Rumors mostly. Some say he makes too much money for just runnin' a store. And I hear he's quite the ladies' man. He's a light-skinned Mexican like them Spaniards that owned all those land grants. And he's been seen drivin' around town with more'n one white woman."

"Driving?" sneered Monte.

"Yep. A Studebaker. One of them long fancy ones. These days, they's more auto-mobiles in Tucson than there is horses and wagons."

Monte felt the heat of jealous anger rising within him but for the first time, it was tempered with a sinking sense of despair. His entire life he had lived from day to day, oblivious to the past and unconcerned about the future. He worked, got paid, and spent his money. Life was simple. If nothing else, it was a comfortable existence. But now he was forced to come to grips with the fact that Anthony Ortega was a Casanova as well as a wealthy businessman. He, on the other hand, was in the middle of nowhere without a penny to his name.

"What's Tucson like?" asked Monte, hoping the town was little more than another Rodeo or Columbus.

"Tucson ain't no little pueblo no more," said Deek. "Not like when I first seen her. No, sir. She was born Spanish, raised Mexican, and then married off to a rich American.

"Hardly any old adobes left. Now, most all the buildings are brick and mortar. A few years ago, they even tore down the Wedge, the whole damn red-light district. Wiped it out.

"They got electricity everywhere and telephones, too. Why they got electric streetcars to get around on and I even seen a shop where a fella could rent an auto-mobile if he had a mind to.

"Now, of course, there's still Old Tucson and the Mexican part of town. That's still like the old days but everything else is blue ribbon."

Monte thought of Rosa, of her long, braided hair, her colorful skirt, loose-fitting cotton blouse and her worn sandals. He wondered how she would feel in such a place. Would she be intimidated by such a city or charmed by it all? Would Ortega's money mean so much to her? Would he buy her new clothes and new shoes?

Blinking hard, Monte tried to stop the questions from coming but it was no use. Of course, Rosa would be thrilled to live in such a city, to wear fashionable clothes and dine in the fanciest restaurants. What woman wouldn't? And Anthony Ortega could give her all that she wanted.

But what did Ortega want with Rosa? Deek said he was a ladies' man. Didn't he have enough women already? But were any as beautiful as Rosa? Of course they were not. That would be impossible.

"Damn her, anyway!" mumbled Monte.

"What's that?" Deek asked.

"Nothing," answered Monte. "Nothing at all."

A little more than an hour after leaving Bernadino, the truck stopped in front of the train depot in Casador. Monte, Deek, and Ahayaca unloaded in a cloud of dust and without a word from the driver, he turned the truck around and speed off back toward Bernadino.

Monte slapped the dust from his shirt and then went to a nearby hitching rail and untied Deek's horses.

Watching the truck drive away, Deek snorted, "Talkative sort, ain't he? And greedy to boot. He took that whole gold coin for doin' one hour's work."

Monte brought the horses up, glimpsing a dry goods store across from the railroad tracks.

"If we've got a two-day ride ahead of us," Monte said, pointing to the dry goods store, "we're going to need some supplies."

Once again, Ahayaca pulled out his leather pouch and this time removed two nickel-sized discs that resembled Mexican *conchos*. The discs, however, unlike the tarnished coin, were polished to a high gloss.

Ahayaca offered the discs to Deek. "I have but one more piece of gold. These must buy enough supplies to get us to Tucson, and all the way to the Yaqui village."

Deek scooped the gold pieces out of Ahayaca's palm. Noticing the temperature of his skin, Deek said, "Your hand is mighty cold, boy. Are you feeling alright?"

"It is an illness that comes and goes," said Ahayaca. "Nothing more. Perhaps if the store has some fruit it would help."

Deek looked Ahayaca over carefully. "Sure thing, son," Deek said, as he started for the store. "I'll see what they have. Mostly though, we'll get jerky and goat cheese. And some hardtack maybe."

Monte led the horses to the dry goods store and then sat in the shade of the porch. Ahayaca followed but stopped short in order to stand in the warmth of the sun.

"Do you think Deek can be trusted?" asked Ahayaca. "He is not like you. His eyes flash at the sight of gold."

Monte looked over his shoulder and through a window of the store. He watched Deek for a moment. "Gold and silver can tempt a man, that's for sure. But so can whiskey. I gather that Deek's been on the wagon for a good while and that tells me he's trying to get back to being the man he used to be. My guess is he'll do right by us."

A moment later, Deek came out of the store cradling a folded wool blanket and a flour sack bulging with supplies. Juggling the sack, he reached inside and retrieved an apple. Handing the apple to Ahayaca, Deek said, "I got a couple of these for you and some dried peaches, too."

Ahayaca accepted the apple. "Thank you."

Deek then reached back in the sack and brought out what appeared to be a small candle wrapped in tinfoil. He offered it to Ahayaca. "I saw your lips was all cracked. This'll fix 'em right up. The storekeeper stays it's called ChapStick. He says it's a kind of lip balm."

Taking the lip balm, Ahayaca said, "Thank you. At first, on my long journey I used earwax to coat my lips but then I had no more wax."

Ahayaca began peeling away the tinfoil.

Deek stepped down off the porch. "Do you want to go to Tucson first or to the Yaqui village?"

"The village," answered Ahayaca as he gently dabbed the balm on his cracked and peeling lips. "I must give them a message. When I have done that I will go to my own people."

Tying the flour sack to the pommel of his horse, Deek said, "That bein' the case and you wantin' to stay clear of towns and all, we can head east from here. We'll camp at the San Pedro River tonight. Late tomorrow, we should cut into the Santa Cruz River south of Tucson. Then we'll head upriver and by dark run right into the village. Goin' that way will save us a few miles."

Ahayaca looked at the apple. He shivered and then took a bite. "Tomorrow night we will be in the village?"

Deek nodded. "With a bit of luck."

After a long, hot ride, the trio camped on the west bank of the San Pedro River. However, that evening Ahayaca took a turn for the worse and began to shiver. His blanket was not enough to keep him warm so Monte and Deek took turns keeping a fire blazing until sunrise.

For breakfast, Monte and Deek filled up on jerky and cheese but all Ahayaca could stomach was a few of the dried peaches. With the rising sun at their backs and Ahayaca's assurance that he was better, the three men rode west. By midmorning, though, Deek could feel Ahayaca's grip weakening. And then Deek felt the dampness of Ahayaca's arms. He was beginning to sweat but it was not due to the sun.

With Deek leading, the men kept a steady pace. Constantly angling to the northwest, they rode at a quick walk hoping to make it to the Santa Cruz River before sundown and then make it to the Yaqui village before dark. But two hours from the river, Ahayaca's arms went limp. He slumped and then began to slide sideways.

"Damn it," snapped Deek, as he grabbed at Ahayaca but missed.

Monte saw Ahayaca falling but too late to be of any help.

Ahayaca landed on his side and then rolled on his back as Monte hopped off his horse and bounded forward. Kneeling next to Ahayaca, Monte bent low, listening for sounds of breathing.

Deek dismounted and then bent over Ahayaca. "How is he?"

"Alive," Monte said and then looked around for some shade. For miles, there was nothing but saguaro cactus and a scattering of brush, none of it higher than the horses' backs. "We'll have to throw our blankets over some of this brush and make some shade. He needs to get out of the sun."

Deek took a canteen from his saddlebags and handed it to Monte. He untied his blanket while Monte dripped water over Ahayaca's forehead and neck.

"He needs a doctor," Monte said. "I don't think he's going to make it."

Bending over for a better look, Deek said, "I don't think we're more'n ten miles from Tucson. But there's no roads and there's gullies and such between here and there. The only way to get a sawbones out here is horse or buggy. One of them motorcars won't never make it."

"You're right about that," agreed Monte.

"It won't be easy to get one of them city doctors on no horse, not these days. And even if you could they'd charge an arm and a leg to come all the way out here."

Monte pulled Ahayaca's shirt away from his neck, exposing the leather thong. "He said he had one more piece of gold."

Monte pulled up the leather pouch. Pulling it open he flipped the pouch over and emptied the contents onto his palm. He felt a solid thud. Taking the pouch away, he glared at what he held.

"Now what in damnation is that?" muttered Deek.

Monte picked up the gold piece with his thumb and forefinger. He turned it back and forth as both men studied it.

The gold had been forged into a pentagon, its five sides as thick as three stacked silver dollars. The top and bottom of the pentagon were flat. One side was smooth and the other had been stamped with what resembled a pitchfork over a half-circle.

"Whatever it is," Monte said, "it's at least two ounces of gold. That's plenty for any doctor. And if it isn't . . . I'll convince him it is."

Deek found two bushes growing near each other and then draped the blanket from one to the other, shading a smooth patch of sand below. Monte spread his blanket over the scorching sand and then laid Ahayaca on it.

"So, you're going for the doc?" asked Deek. "Maybe I should go since I know the country. And the town, too."

Shaking his head, Monte said, "Point me in the right direction. If it's only ten miles, I'll see it soon enough. And then I'll ask about a doctor. If he takes some convincing, I'll persuade the son of a bitch to come."

Deek thought for a moment and then grinned. "Yep. I see your point."

Monte pocketed the gold piece, hopped back on the mare, and gathered the reins.

"First," Deek advised, "ask anybody and they'll tell you where to find Congress Street. There's two or three doctors on that stretch. And there's still a few liveries down in the old part of town. The doc can rent hisself a horse or a buggy down there. But it'll be after dark when you come back. Think you can find your way?"

"By then there'll be a half-moon out and I can see better than most at night. I'll be able to see my tracks. You just do your best to keep him alive. We've come this far with him and I like to finish what I start."

"You and me both," agreed Deek. "*Vaya con Dios, amigo.*"

Trying to save his horse as much as possible, Monte took a full two hours to reach the outskirts of Tucson. By then, the sun was nearing the bleak mountain peaks west of town. At that point, the streets were packed sand but as he rode past a few dozen frame houses his horse's hooves began to clop over pavement. In minutes, two-story brick buildings that had been sandwiched together crowded both sides of the avenue. Noisy automobiles began to pass him. Pedestrians began to stare. A boy on a bicycle rode up beside him. Looking up, the boy smiled.

"You're riding a horse in town, mister."

"Yeah, I am. Do you know where Congress Street is? I'm in a hurry to find a doctor."

The boy nodded excitedly. "Follow me, mister," he said and then stood up on his pedals and pumped his bicycle to full speed.

Monte nudged his mount into an easy gallop and stayed a few feet behind as the boy darted down one street and then another. Motorcars pulled out of the way and let them pass, and startled pedestrians scurried out of the way. The boy pointed ahead and to his right. He slowed and stopped suddenly, causing Monte to veer sharply in order to avoid running him over.

Bringing the horse to a stop next to a panel truck, Monte spun the horse around.

Again pointing, the boy stood on the pavement straddling his bicycle. "That's a doctor's office right there. And you're on Congress Street."

Monte dismounted onto the pavement and then tied his horse to an electricity pole. "You did good, boy," he said, stepping up onto the sidewalk. He started toward a door that had "Horace Helbrand, M.D." painted on it.

The door opened just as Monte reached for the doorknob.

An obese, balding man with a graying beard drew up short. "I'm closed, sir. Sorry, but I must be off."

Monte stood blocking his way. "I got a sick man ten miles

out of town that could be dying. He needs a doctor, bad."

"Sorry, sir. My day is finished. There are other doctors in town and I'm late for my supper. Now, please step aside and let me pass."

"Some doctor you are!" yelled the boy as he rode up Congress and out of sight.

Monte reached into his pocket and brought out the gold pentagon. Holding it in his open palm he said, "Your supper will wait. Meanwhile you take a look at this. It's yours if you're willing to miss a meal. That's a good two ounces of gold."

Helbrand fingered the gold from Monte's hand and looked it over closely. Cradling it in his own palm, he hefted it up and down, estimating its weight.

"Well . . ." Helbrand hesitated.

"Think of it this way, Doc," Monte said icily. "You don't have a choice."

The doctor's eyes flared. He swallowed hard and then shoved the gold deep into his trousers pocket. "I'll get my motorcar."

"No. You'll need . . ." Monte stopped in mid-sentence and eyed the doctor's more than ample girth. "You'll need a buggy. I'm guessing it's been a while since you forked a horse and there aren't any roads to where we're going."

"I'll have to rent one," said Helbrand and then pointed at a parked convertible Ford nearby. "That is my motorcar. I'll drive to the livery. The nearest one is outside of town down by the river."

Monte untied his horse and then retied it to the rear bumper of the Ford. "You drive slow. My horse is tired."

Helbrand stood motionless as if in a daze but when Monte opened the passenger door and glared back at him, the doctor blinked. "My bag. I must get my bag."

"Make it quick."

Turning clumsily on his heels, Helbrand went through his office door and, in less than a minute, emerged with a black leather medical bag. Tossing the bag in the back seat, he cranked the starter. After settling into the driver seat, he turned around slowly in the middle of the street, a street now engulfed in deep shadows from the setting sun.

In minutes, Helbrand pulled up in front of the livery. A deal was quickly made and then a single-horse buckboard with two kerosene lanterns affixed to the side boards was brought out. The doctor stepped up, took a seat, and then gathered the reins.

"I thought my days of doing this sort of thing were over," grumbled Helbrand as he snapped the reins and started off.

Monte rode up beside the buckboard. "You've got sixty dollars' worth of gold in your pocket. It would take me a month to make that much money so quit your bellyaching. Besides, we've got jerked meat and cheese at our camp. You won't go hungry for long."

"It's not consumption, is it?" questioned Helbrand. "Lord knows, we've got more of them in Tucson than we know what to do with. They come here with no money, sick as a dog, and then end up living north of town in that retched Tentville. Pathetic. That's what it is, pathetic."

"You mean, is he a lunger?"

"Yes."

"He gets cold and then sweats," Monte said. "He's skinny as a rail but he doesn't cough."

"You sure he has no cough. None?"

"I'm sure."

"It's going to be dark soon," said Helbrand, "and you said the patient is ten miles out. How will we find him?"

"We'll follow my tracks. I can see in the dark just fine."

Helbrand thought for a moment. "See in the dark? I've read about such cases. Rare, but not unheard of. Years ago, I believe General Crook had a bugler like that."

The two men rode for another quarter mile and then with dusk fading into night, Monte cut sharply to the south.

"Find your tracks?" asked Helbrand.

"Yeah."

"Are you with the army?"

"National Guard."

"I heard President Wilson was sending thousands of guardsmen down to the border. It's as if war with Mexico is a real possibility."

"You better believe it's real. And the Germans would like that, too."

"The Germans?"

"They're down in Mexico stirring things up. My guess is they want us to get into it for some reason or another. Likely to keep us out of their war overseas. But I've done my time in the Guard. Now, all of that's none of my business."

Monte rode on into the night, guiding the wagon around patches of cactus and across dozens of shallow arroyos.

"Mind if I ask where you got the gold?" asked Helbrand.

"I got it from the man that's sick."

"Well then, where did he get it?"

"I didn't ask. None of my business."

His frustration growing, Helbrand asked, "Where does this man call home?"

"I didn't ask," Monte said.

Helbrand huffed. "None of your business, I take it?"

"That's right."

"I must say you don't know this friend of yours very well."

"I don't count him a friend. He needed help and I gave it to him. We crossed paths, that's all there is to it."

The moon rose higher into a star-filled sky. A warm southerly breeze began to drift across the desert. In the distance, Monte saw a tiny light, a flickering light.

"I see the campfire up ahead."

"Fire? Is there someone with the patient?"

"Yeah. A man about your age. His name is Deek. He's from some place near Rodeo."

"And I suppose," quipped Helbrand, "that you don't count him as a friend, either."

Monte nodded, although more to himself than to the doctor. "You learn fast, Doc."

A few minutes later, Monte crossed a deep wash. The buckboard rolled down into the sandy bottom but got stuck coming up the opposite bank. Once the doctor stepped out of the wagon, however, the horse was able to lunge and jerk the buckboard up and back onto the level ground.

Monte rode a few feet ahead as Helbrand lumbered out of the arroyo and back up onto the wagon seat.

"Hello the camp!" Monte called out.

A moment later a faint voice broke the silence. "Come on in."

Quickly crossing the last two hundred yards, Monte dismounted on the edge of darkness and then walked his horse into the firelight. A few seconds later the buckboard pulled up. Helbrand grabbed his medical bag, stepped down, and then lost his footing and tripped. Falling to his knees, he dropped his bag, causing it to pop open and spill.

Swearing in the darkness, Helbrand hastily gathered his supplies, tossed them back into his bag, and then regained his footing.

Ahayaca was wrapped in a blanket lying on his back next to the fire. His listless eyes were open but only halfway. If he was aware that Monte had returned, he made no effort to acknowledge it.

Without a word, Helbrand went straight to Ahayaca, awkwardly knelt down on his knees, and then opened his doctor bag. Taking out a stethoscope, Helbrand clipped it around his stubby neck. He pulled the blanket open. Clipping the stethoscope in his ears, he placed the diaphragm under Ahayaca's shirt and then listened.

Monte and Deek watched and waited.

All Helbrand said was, "Hmmph."

The doctor thought for a moment and then rolled Ahayaca onto his side. He jerked up the shirt and then gasped, "Damn!"

Monte and Deek bent over and glared. Ahayaca's back was covered in scars, scars from being whipped.

"Oh hell, would you look at that," said Deek.

Recovering from the shock, Helbrand placed the diaphragm high up on Ahayaca's back and listened again. He moved the stethoscope and then listened once more. Finally, he took the instrument from his ears and put it back in his bag.

"Well, it's not consumption that's for certain."

"I was wonderin' on that myself," Deek said.

"How long has he been like this?" Helbrand asked.

"Like this?" Deek repeated. "Just a few hours. Before that, he was first sweatin' and then shiverin' like he was about to freeze to death. He told me this sort of thing comes and goes and has for a year now."

"Is that all he said?" asked Helbrand.

"He was mumblin' to hisself some, mostly in a language I didn't get. Not Spanish. That I get mostly. But he did keep sayin' 'henequen.' Over and over he said it."

Helbrand nodded. "That's it then," he announced as he rummaged through his bag and then brought out two bottles of liquid. "He's got malaria. Henequen grows down in the jungles of central Mexico. The malaria causes the sweats and chills. And he probably got those scars down there, too."

Helbrand held one of the bottles close to the fire so that the label reflected the light. He pointed at the label. "That's me.

Doctor Helbrand. The directions are written under my name. It says take one spoonful every eight hours."

Handing the bottles to Monte, Helbrand said, "If you don't have a spoon just give him a swallow of this three times a day until it's all gone. Finish both bottles. It's quinine."

Helbrand closed his bag and then struggled to get his legs under him. "You said you had jerky and cheese. That sounds mighty good. It's way past my suppertime."

CHAPTER FOUR

After leaving New York City, I had to travel a rather circuitous train route, passing through Chicago, St. Louis, Topeka, Oklahoma City, and Fort Worth to finally reach El Paso. Traveling through the northern states was complicated but the El Paso and Southwestern railroad system was quite simple. Basically, it ran back and forth between El Paso, Texas, and Douglas, Arizona. From Douglas there was an extension to Tucson but for my immediate purposes the main east-west route was all that concerned me.

In El Paso, my Pullman car was transferred to one of the El Paso and Southwestern trains and in less than an hour the train pulled out of the station heading west. Then my heart began to pound as I realized that I, William Cabott Weston III, was once again venturing into the untamed and indomitable southwestern desert, into the last vestige of the American frontier.

As soon as the train reached full speed, I excitedly ventured from passenger car to passenger car asking the conductors and porters about Monte and Rosa. It wasn't long before one of the porters recognized Rosa from my description of her. But to my surprise, he had no recollection of anyone that even remotely resembled Monte Segundo.

I kept asking questions and eventually interviewed a conductor who vividly remembered Rosa. He did not recall anyone with her wearing a uniform, but he did remember another man, a man that often traveled on the train. The man's name was

Anthony Ortega and he was a businessman that resided in Tucson. And the conductor was certain, from what he had observed only a week earlier, that Anthony Ortega and Rosa were either relatives or close friends.

I was completely baffled that none of the station agents remembered seeing Monte but with the information I had gathered, I took the spur from Douglas up to Tucson. I was anxious to meet up with Monte and Rosa and it was too complicated to attach the Pullman to a different train, so I bought an economy ticket and rode into Tucson in a passenger car packed with Mexicans, Anglos, Orientals, a few Negroes, and a crate full of obnoxious chickens.

It was midmorning when I stepped off the train and onto an impressive platform of the newly constructed El Paso and Southwestern train station. After plucking a few feathers from my dusty traveling suit, I hefted my small suitcase and strolled through the crowd to the east end of the platform to get my bearings.

The station was on the edge of Tucson, which, to my astonishment, was nothing like the desolate town of Columbus, New Mexico. On the contrary, brick and stone buildings lined Tucson's streets, several of them two and three stories high. Electric streetcars and motorcars rolled down paved avenues. Power poles and electric lines were everywhere, and I guessed the population to be close to fifteen thousand people. Tucson was, in every respect, an oasis in the desert, a city far more sophisticated than anything I had imagined.

Turning around, I saw a pyramid-shaped hill that jutted into the skyline. The hill was barren except for an enormous white letter A near its peak.

I stood there staring at the A until a passerby said, "It stands for Arizona, the university. Last March, the college students carried rocks up there and painted them white. That's Sentinel

Hill. It was a lookout for the Spanish and then the Mexicans back when the Apaches ran through this country. I think it's a damn shame they did that. I don't like it."

The speaker, a middle-aged man wearing a white suit and dark necktie, kept walking and then descended a flight of steps that emptied onto a street. Following after the stranger, I trotted up beside him. "I'm looking for a man named Anthony Ortega. Do you know where I might be able to find him?"

"Sure. Mr. Ortega is a fine gentleman and sound businessman. He runs a mercantile on Congress Street. That's the main business street in Tucson. His store is called 'Pioneer Mercantile.' "

"And Congress Street?" I asked.

Having never made eye contact, the man pointed straight ahead. "Just keep going that way. You can't miss it."

With that exhortation and without breaking his stride, the man abruptly veered to his right and down a side street.

Following those vague instructions, I ventured deeper into Tucson and selected a street that took me in the prescribed direction. After walking under a banner that read, "Vote Against Wilson-Ashurst-Hayden, Their Party Opposes National Women's Suffrage," I continued on a few blocks and indeed found Congress Street. By sheer chance, I decided to go south. Two blocks later, I spotted a large red, white, and blue sign that read "Pioneer Mercantile, Lowest Prices in Tucson."

I crossed the busy street and approached a two-story stone building that had four large paned windows and an impressive brass-framed glass front door. When I entered, a bell above my head was tripped by the door. I stopped next to a glass display cabinet that also supported an ornate cash register.

The first thing that caught my eye was the floor-to-ceiling oak shelves. They lined the walls and much of the floor space and were full of clothing, canned goods, tools, farm supplies, and dozens of other items I did not recognize.

A tall thin man, no older than me, was busy helping a woman in the back of the store. Having heard the sound of the bell, however, another man came out of a rear office. He was well dressed and wore a tailored suit that complimented a slim, athletic build. His skin was olive and he sported a well-groomed mustache. As he approached, I presumed that most women would find the man quite handsome. It was then I felt a wave of uneasiness and I found myself hoping that this was not Anthony Ortega.

The man glanced at me and then his eyes darted down to the small suitcase I was holding. At that moment, I detected a subtle sneer. Instead of coming to greet me face-to-face he stepped behind the display cabinet. Without acknowledging my presence, he opened the cash register drawer, added some bills to it, and then shoved the door shut.

He looked up at me then and forced a smile. "What are you selling?"

"Selling?" I asked. For a moment I was confused but then realized that I did, in some respects, resemble a traveling salesman. "No, sir. I am not a salesman."

I could see the man was not convinced. I must admit, that irritated me but I let the mild insult pass. "I just arrived on the El Paso and Southwestern. I made some inquiries on board the train and was told that Mr. Anthony Ortega was the owner of this establishment. I would like . . ."

I was interrupted by the bell ringing above the front door. A portly man hurried in and very rudely walked right up to the counter next to me. He held a suit coat over his arm, his shirt was sweat-stained, and his dusty pants were held up by black suspenders.

The man behind the counter was clearly surprised. "Dr. Helbrand, is there something wrong?"

The doctor, ignoring me completely, bumped into my shoulder as he bellied up closer to the display cabinet. Reaching into his pants pocket he brought out an object and then clacked it down onto the glass counter in front of him. With a thick finger on top of the object, he shoved it toward the man on the other side of the counter and then took his hand away.

"What do you make of this, Mr. Ortega?"

Realizing the man I had been speaking to was indeed Anthony Ortega, I began to feel even more uneasy. However, I was not distracted enough to miss getting a good look at a small gold pentagon before Ortega picked it up.

Holding the gold piece close, Ortega studied the pentagon. He turned it over and over in his hand. "It's at least two ounces, I would say. Maybe three. I will give you one hundred dollars for it."

"Now that's a fair price, Mr. Ortega, very fair indeed. Your fine reputation is well deserved. I was told that, from time to time, you purchased gold and silver from the Yaqui Indians. That's why I brought that here. And I'm glad I did."

Helbrand wiped sweat from his sunburned forehead. "One hundred dollars for an evening's work. That's far more profitable than delivering babies in the middle of the night."

"Where did you get such an artifact, Dr. Helbrand?" Ortega asked. "This is quite unusual."

"I don't know where it came from. All I know is that it belonged to a patient I was summoned to attend. He was in a camp ten or twelve miles southeast of here in the middle of the desert. The man was sick, a Yaqui as far as I could tell. And he was the one who had the gold. That was the deal, that piece of gold for my services.

"He's resting at the Yaqui village now. We got him there just before sunup this morning."

"We?" questioned Ortega.

"Yes. Two other men were with him. I gather that they found him in the desert and brought him as far as they could. I transported the patient to the village on a buckboard I rented last night. When I left the patient this morning, those two men stayed with him in the village."

The doctor pointed to the gold piece. "Do you have any idea what those marks mean, the pitchfork and the half-circle?"

Ortega shrugged, though I thought unconvincingly. "I've got no idea, Dr. Helbrand. No idea at all."

I had gotten a glimpse of the mark and now I was intrigued. "May I hazard a guess?" I asked.

Noticing me for the first time, Helbrand asked, "Guess at what?"

"The stamp on that gold. I am somewhat familiar with Mexican history."

Ortega's eyes narrowed. After a moment's hesitation, he handed me the gold.

From the library books I had read at home, I had learned about stamps used by the Spanish conquistadors. I knew a bit about what to look for and had a vague idea how to interpret what I saw.

I pointed to the stamp. "This is not a pitchfork. It is a crown. And this is not a half-circle. It is a C as in Charles, King Charles of Spain."

Both Ortega and Helbrand glared at me skeptically.

I smiled. Brimming with confidence and with a modest dash of smugness, I said, "Charles was king of Spain when Hernán Cortés conquered the Aztecs in Mexico City. He plundered their golden idols and jewelry and then melted it all down. King Charles was to receive one fifth of everything, a *quinto*. All the King's gold, his royal fifth or *quinto*, received a stamp. Every piece going to the king, whether an ingot, coin or whatever, was stamped with his mark."

Ortega took the pentagon from my hand and huffed. "A good story. Maybe this is a *quinto* or maybe it is just the mark of a mine. All of the Spanish mines had stamps as well. And there are many lost mines in the mountains of Mexico, each with a different stamp. The Yaquis bring in trinkets all the time. I have seen many such marks. Who knows what they mean?"

"Regardless of the stamp," admitted Helbrand, "I feel a bit guilty for accepting the one hundred dollars. Perhaps I should refund the poor Indian say . . . ten dollars."

"You are a gracious man," Ortega said, softening his tone with a hint of reverence. "But you must be very tired from a long night. Might I be trusted to take the money to the patient? I would like to talk to this man anyway. And, as you know, I am on very good terms with the Yaquis."

"You certainly may, Mr. Ortega, and thank you. I am exhausted and I have not eaten in hours."

The cash register rang and Ortega took out a ten-dollar bill, which he made a great show of putting in his own pocket. Then, handing the balance of ninety dollars to Helbrand, Ortega said, "You are a credit to your profession, Doctor. Not many would do what you did for that poor Indian."

The doctor folded the bill and dropped it into his shirt pocket. "Just part of my job."

As Helbrand left the store, Ortega turned his attention to me. "Would you care to come along with me to the Yaqui village? If there is more stamped gold you might find it interesting. It might even be profitable for you."

"Yes, I definitely would but first, perhaps you could help me. The reason I came here today was to try and locate a woman by the name of Rosa Bustamonte. I just arrived on the train. I am from New York City but I came in on the El Paso and Southwestern. Along the way I made several inquiries and was told that you might know of her whereabouts."

Ortega seemed suspicious, which in turn made me suspicious. I decided, then and there, the less I revealed about my real reason for being in Tucson, the better.

"I don't understand," Ortega said. "How is it that you are asking me such a question?"

"Oh, excuse me. I didn't mean to offend you."

I extended my hand, I said, "My name is Billy Cabott."

We shook hands and then I continued. "I met Rosa in Las Palomas when I was on assignment for the *Chicago Tribune*. I was interested in following up on an article I wrote and investigating her current views concerning the revolution.

"Last week, I saw her getting on the train in Columbus as it headed west. Some of the agents on the train that I spoke with today remembered her. And one remembered that the two of you seemed to know each other."

Seeming to relax, Ortega smiled. "I see. Yes, I know Rosa. We grew up together about sixty miles south of here in Nogales, Mexico. But she is here in Tucson. So you wish to interview her again?"

I hesitated. "Not really. That's what I told the editor of my newspaper." I paused again. "I merely wanted to get re-acquainted. And perhaps take care of some mining business while I'm in town."

Ortega's smile grew into a lecherous grin as he looked me over carefully. "You have come far but I do not blame you. I myself have been trying to get . . . reacquainted . . . with her for several days. But I have had no luck."

The meaning of Ortega's comment did not register at the time. Knowing that my excuse for wanting to see Rosa was weak, my mind was racing to find a better one.

I was still bewildered that no one on the train remembered seeing Monte and yet I had no difficulty finding those who remembered Rosa and Anthony Ortega. And, at that moment, I had the distinct impression that bringing up the name of Monte Segundo would have been a colossal mistake.

"She can be a bit stubborn," I said. As soon as the words crossed my lips I wanted to take them back but to my surprise, Ortega laughed.

"Yes, you do know Rosa. I will take you to her. We will all go to see this Indian that pays his debts with a three-ounce piece of gold. I want to ask him some questions and Rosa will be useful. She has a way of getting men to talk to her. And, along the way, the two of you can visit."

Ortega came from behind the counter. He gestured toward the front door. "I have a Studebaker parked outside. The top is down. It will be an enjoyable drive."

I followed Ortega outside and placed my suitcase off to one side of the rear seat. I then took the passenger seat of his sleek-looking motorcar.

As we drove down Congress, Ortega waved his left arm at the buildings we were passing. "All of this makes Rosa uncomfortable. She prefers the Mexican side of town, the old pueblo district. That is where we are going. And then it is but a few miles out of town to the Yaqui village.

"Are you familiar with the Yaqui?"

"Not at all."

Making a left turn, Ortega said, "They are from Sonora, far south of here. The Yaqui Indians have been at war with Mexico for three hundred years. Some still fight but the *pacificos*, the tame ones, have come here to escape the fighting. They no longer want to fight. No one bothers them and they bother no one.

"The ones that continue to fight are called *broncos* but they remain south of the border. But it is often said that the Yaquis know things about lost mines, things they will never tell a *yori*."

"*Yori?*"

Ortega snickered. "You and me and everyone that is not a Yaqui is a *yori,* an outsider."

"Then what do you hope to gain by questioning this person?"

Making a sharp right turn we left the paved streets behind and entered a section of town that was more of what I originally expected Tucson to look like. Several adobes came into view as did a pack of barking dogs.

"They respect me," Ortega said. "I do business with them. And who knows? Maybe they are changing with the times like the rest of us. Maybe they will talk to me."

We pulled up a few steps in front of a single room adobe with red pepper *guirnaldas* hanging on the front wall. The plank door was closed. Ortega waited for the dust to settle and then got out. I decided to stay seated.

At the door, Ortega knocked. "Rosa, it is me."

Seconds passed. The door jerked open. I heard a familiar voice deliver a blistering streak of Spanish. I heard paper crinkle. I saw Ortega catch something with both hands but all I could see of Rosa was the edge of her skirt. Ortega said something and then there was a sudden silence.

Rosa leaned her head to the side and we made eye contact. I saw a distinct flicker of excitement but that gleeful expression was almost instantly smothered by a mask of indifference.

Rosa came toward me and I got out of the motorcar. I didn't know whether to hug her or shake her hand. When we came within an arm's reach we both stopped and stood there looking at each other.

Despite her attempts to hide her emotions, I could detect a question in her eyes.

"I am here on business," I said. "And since I was here in Tucson, I wanted to see you."

Rosa studied me closely. I had not asked about Monte and

that made her wary. "What kind of business?"

"Mining."

Again I had not mentioned Monte Segundo and now Rosa seemed confused, uncertain. Ortega walked up beside her holding a brown paper package that had been tied neatly with twine.

"Rosa, Mr. Cabott and I are going to the Yaqui village. We would like for you to come along. The two of you can talk on the way."

"Why? Why should I want to talk to either of you?"

I didn't know what to say. I had no answer. I had gotten myself into an awkward situation and knew of no way to get out of it.

"Mr. Cabott wants to interview you again like he did for his newspaper," said Ortega. "But also there is a Yaqui Indian that discovered an interesting piece of Spanish gold. He has been sick but is now resting at the Yaqui village. Mr. Cabott knows something about Spanish gold, so he agreed to come along. And what sick man would not appreciate a visit from a lovely woman?"

Rosa tried to read my thoughts. "Will you be in Tucson long?"

Speaking slowly and choosing my words deliberately, I said, "It all depends on how soon I find what I am looking for."

Her eyes narrowing, Rosa said, "And what is it you look for?"

"First of all," I said, hoping Rosa would understand my meaning, "I would like to get reacquainted with you and ask some questions regarding the revolution. After that I hope to find a friend of mine who was recently in Mexico and ask him some similar questions. My friend is from up north but used to live in this area. I hoped to meet him here in Tucson but he was not where I expected him to be. But if he's within one hundred miles, I'll hear about him soon enough. Trouble seems to follow him. After that, I have some mining business to attend to."

Rosa cast me a knowing look. We both had questions but

understood it was not the time or place to get answers.

Deftly changing the subject, Rosa glanced up at Ortega. "What makes this gold different than any other gold?"

Thinking he sensed Rosa's interest in the gold, Ortega's eyes gleamed with approval. "This gold was cast into a strange shape and then marked with an iron stamp. Mr. Cabott thinks it may be from the time of the Aztecs."

Rosa laughed scornfully. "Aztecs! Next you will tell me it is from Montezuma's treasure or the lost Tayopa mine."

Laughing once more she added, "I will go to see the Yaqui and I will enjoy watching the two of you behave like fools."

Ortega tossed the paper package in the back seat next to my suitcase and then slid behind the wheel. I opened the passenger car door for Rosa but we avoided making eye contact. I then took a seat in the rear next to the package.

I took a closer look at the bundle next to me. It was rounded and soft looking. Whatever was inside had to be made of cloth or very soft leather. Most likely, it was clothing, clothing given to Rosa, a gift that she had vehemently refused to accept.

The Studebaker lunged and we were on our way. Once we were beyond the last adobe Ortega held out the pentagon. Rosa took it and looked it over as we picked up speed. Even from where I sat I could see that she was curious.

Ortega spoke over the engine noise and rush of wind. "I've never seen anything like that. It's almost three ounces."

Rosa turned and looked at me as if asking for an explanation. I shrugged but then silently mouthed, "Where is Monte?"

After casting me a look that could kill, she turned back around to face Ortega. "What do you know of this Yaqui?"

"Only that he is very sick," answered Ortega, "and that two complete strangers, white men, found him alone in the desert. They got a doctor here in town to go out and tend to him and then the three of them brought the Indian to the Yaqui village.

The doctor was paid with the gold. But the two strangers did not leave the village with the doctor. They may still be there in the village and that is why we must hurry.

"Those white men could have stolen the gold from the Indian but they did not, at least not all of it. So they, too, must be hoping to discover where it came from. Why else would they go to so much trouble for a Yaqui?"

From the beginning, I had felt uneasy around Anthony Ortega but I could not say why. Now, after listening to his last comment, I realized that my instincts had been correct. The man was greedy, so much so that he believed everyone naturally behaved just as he did. The thought that some men might simply behave as good Samaritans apparently had never occurred to him.

"Mr. Cabott, what else can you tell me of Aztec gold?"

"I don't know all that much," I said truthfully. "The biggest mystery, though, has to do with the treasure of Montezuma. He was the ruler of Mexico City until Cortés defeated the Aztecs and took over. Only then, the Aztec capital wasn't called Mexico City, of course. It was something else, some other name I can't recall.

"But Cortés plundered all the golden idols and trinkets of the Aztecs. As I said earlier, he then melted it down into bars and such. Or, at least, Cortés thought he had melted all of it. One night, the Aztecs rebelled against Cortés and his men. The Spaniards were forced to flee the city in a hurry. They couldn't carry all their gold but attempted to leave with as much as each man could carry. Many of Cortés's men were killed or drowned with their pockets still full of gold.

"The Aztecs knew Cortés would soon return with more men and weapons so, as the story goes, Montezuma gathered up all the gold from the dead Spaniards and all the gold that he had kept hidden from Cortés and sent it out of the city that very night.

"It is said by some that Montezuma's treasure was sent far to the north and that it was guarded along the way by two thousand elite Aztec warriors. That night was called 'the night of tears' by Cortés and the gold that left Mexico City has never been found . . . if it ever existed."

"That is a lot of *caca*," said Rosa.

Ortega looked over at Rosa. "Does that gold in your hand feel like *caca*?"

Rosa huffed and handed the gold back to Ortega.

"By the way," Ortega enquired, "what type of mining are you interested in? Gold? Silver?"

"Zinc," I said, stifling my contempt for the man.

"Zinc? Why Zinc?"

Thankful that his question did not concern me and Rosa, I answered with feigned enthusiasm. "I am now with Weston Shipping out of New York City. Phelps Dodge is a competitor of ours and, as everyone along the border knows, they have branched out into copper. But we at Weston Shipping are looking past the electrification of the country. We have our eye on the war in Europe and are convinced that President Wilson is ready to join in. When he does, this country will need vast amounts of zinc in order to manufacture brass casings."

Ortega thought for a moment and then nodded. "Very smart. Selling arms and ammunition to Mexico has already made many here in the states very rich. For the resourceful, the war in Europe could be profitable, very profitable."

I didn't like the sound of that. Weston Shipping was, in fact, doing quite well supplying Great Britain and the allies but we were also taking great risks. German submarines were lethal. "Weston Shipping," I said smoothly, "prefers to think of what we do as helping the war effort."

"Sure," agreed Ortega. "But the war in Mexico . . . the war in Europe . . . in the end they are the same. Nothing changes. And, personally, I do not care to die in either one."

Rosa took a long look at Ortega but then looked away. No one spoke again until we were in sight of the Yaqui village, which was nothing more than a few dozen huts, crude dwellings with walls made of loosely stacked stones, and roofs of tangled brush.

I saw a few people milling about but they did not look like Indians to me. In fact, from their sombreros to the sandals on their feet, they looked exactly like Mexicans.

The largest hut was in the center of the village. It had a shaded entrance, a ramada built of gnarled mesquite trunks with woven brush for a roof. Without hesitation, Ortega pulled up in front of it. "This is the meeting house of the village. My bet is the man we're looking for will be inside."

Ortega and I got out of the motorcar but Rosa sat where she was, looking off in the distance. Ortega was first to the door, which was propped open. Instead of knocking he called out into the darkened interior. "It is Anthony Ortega. I would like to speak to the sick man that Dr. Helbrand visited. I have something to give him, something from the doctor."

I approached the hut and stood off to one side of Ortega. An older man appeared, not a Yaqui but an American. "He's asleep."

"And who might you be, sir?" asked Ortega.

"Deek Coleman. What is it you have from the doc?"

Ortega pulled the folded ten-dollar bill from his inside jacket pocket.

Holding out the bill, Ortega said, "Dr. Helbrand felt that his patient overpaid. He wished to refund him ten dollars."

Deek Coleman reached for the money. "I'll give it to him."

Pulling the bill out of Deek's reach, Ortega snipped, "Perhaps I'll wait until he wakes up."

From inside the hut, a hand appeared and eased Deek to one side. Another man stepped into the doorway, filling it from side to side with a pair of broad, powerful-looking shoulders.

"Monte!" I blurted.

Monte's eyes had been on Ortega but then they darted over to me. "Billy?"

"This is," I said, still quite flabbergasted, "why, this is amazing! What a surprise!"

"For you and me both," Monte said dryly. "Are you with him now, too?"

Monte's question confused me for a moment, and then like clues in a mystery novel, things suddenly began falling into place. Monte was referring to Rosa being with Ortega. I knew that could only mean one thing. Shortly after he and Rosa boarded the train out of Columbus, something had gone terribly wrong. And whatever had happened involved Rosa and Anthony Ortega.

"No. No, I'm in Tucson on business. Seeing you here is pure luck."

Ortega looked down at me, his eyes narrowing. "So the two of you know each other?"

More details of the mystery were coming into focus and Ortega was suspicious by nature. I had to think fast. "Yes, we met in Columbus. All three of us actually, Rosa, Monte, and me. We were on the train platform at the same time waiting to leave Columbus. What a day that was."

Ortega shifted his black eyes to Monte. "Now that you mention it, I remember you. You are Monte Segundo, the soldier that was discharged from Pershing's army."

"And you're the one that runs a mercantile in Tucson," Monte said, "and your name is Antonio something-or-other."

Ortega snickered and then turned around to face the motorcar. "Rosa, would you like to say hello to your friend,

Monte Segundo?"

Rosa had been listening and watching the commotion under the ramada and she had immediately recognized Monte's voice. Now, however, she looked skyward as if searching for a non-existent cloud. "Who?"

"You remember, the soldier from Columbus. The one that was on the train with us."

"You mean the deserter?"

Ortega turned back to face Monte. "Deserter? Well, I didn't realize that you were a deserter. You are fortunate not to have been placed in front of a firing squad."

"There are worse things," Monte said. Making no attempt to look at Rosa, he added bitterly, "Like being a turncoat."

I knew that Monte was no deserter and I had a feeling "turncoat" was aimed at Rosa. Before the name-calling escalated, I changed the subject. "When do you think the patient might be able to talk?"

Monte took a deep breath and then let it out slowly. "Maybe tomorrow."

"Does he have a name?" Ortega asked.

"You'll have to ask him," Monte said. "But if you're wanting to find out about his gold, you're wasting your time."

"And you are not?" chided Ortega.

"His gold is his business."

Ortega grinned, his scheming eyes holding on Monte. "Gold is everybody's business, my friend. We shall return tomorrow."

I shook my head. "Thank you, Mr. Ortega, for the ride, but I am going to stay and visit with Monte. Rosa and I can talk tomorrow."

"I see," Ortega said. "And how will you get back to Tucson?"

"He can get one of the Yaquis to give him a ride," offered Monte. "Some of them have carts."

"Yes, they do," Ortega said, and then casually walked back to the Studebaker. He lifted my suitcase from the rear seat and set it on the ground. It was then that I saw Rosa look directly at Monte. Her eyes held steady but they were seething with contempt.

Ortega got behind the steering wheel and took one more look back at us. "Be very careful, *amigos*. The Yaqui Indians are my friends but they do not trust outsiders. At times they can be very treacherous. You are far from Tucson and I have many friends in this village . . . and in Tucson. It is better for you to be my friends than to be my enemies."

As the Studebaker drove away, Monte said, "That sounded like a threat to me."

"It did to me, too," I said as the motorcar disappeared in a boiling dust cloud.

I took a good look at Monte. His face was grim. I desperately wanted to know what had happened between him and Rosa but I also understood that Monte was a man who valued his privacy. I decided to take an indirect approach.

"What is Rosa doing with a man like that?" I asked.

Monte snorted. "Beats the hell out of me," he said and then stepped outside of the hut into the shade of the ramada. He watched the motorcar as it shrank in the distance.

"Did something happen to her?" I asked.

"What do you mean?"

Before Monte could answer, Deek came outside to stand with us. "Ahayaca's restin' now but he was havin' a fit a minute ago. I had to hold 'im down. He was blubberin' all sorts of gibberish. My Spanish is pretty good and I can get by in Yaqui, but I didn't understand hardly a word of it."

Deek glanced at me and frowned. "And who might you be, sonny?"

I put out my hand. "Billy Cabott."

Even though Monte knew my real name was William Weston,

he did not blink. "Billy's alright. He's a friend."

I gushed with pride as Deek shook my hand. To hear Monte Segundo, El Muerte, refer to me as friend was a profound honor, and it was a moniker that I was determined to live up to at all costs.

Looking me over from head to toe, Deek said, dryly, "He shore don't look like much."

"He'll do," Monte said.

Deek scratched the gray stubble on his chin. "Who was the four flusher in the suit?"

"His name is Antonio Ortega," Monte answered. "Sometimes he goes by Anthony. I guessed he was here hunting for gold and it seems I was right."

"Doctor Helbrand told him about the pentagon," I said. "I was in Mr. Ortega's store when the doctor came in this morning. Apparently, the doctor knew Mr. Ortega bought gold and silver from the Yaquis and offered to sell it.

"That was when I recognized, or at least I thought I recognized, the stamp on the gold. I told them it was from the Aztecs, from Mexico City. I must have impressed Ortega because the next thing I knew he invited me out here in case there were more stamps to decipher."

"And Rosa?" Monte asked. "What was she doing here?"

I looked at Monte and sighed. "Well, let me back up a bit. I was anxious to come see the both of you so yesterday I took a train from New York to El Paso. Then I took the El Paso and Southwestern to Columbus and then continued on west. Along the way, I asked the station employees about the two of you.

"To my surprise, no one remembered you, Monte. Several recalled seeing Rosa, though. And one porter remembered seeing Rosa with someone named Anthony Ortega. And since Mr. Ortega is a regular on that line the porter knew he had a business in Tucson. So that's where I went to ask about Rosa . . .

and then hopefully to find you.

"Before we left to come here, I told Mr. Ortega why I had sought him out. He said he would pick Rosa up on the way . . . that Rosa and I could visit while he drove . . . and he said that she might be able to persuade the owner of the gold to talk."

Monte shook his head. "And she came? To find out about the gold?"

"I don't think she would have come for that," I said. "When we first arrived at her adobe, I could see that she was angry with Mr. Ortega about something but then she saw me sitting in the motorcar. If I had to guess, I would say the only reason she came here was because of me. I wanted to ask her about you but we never got the chance to be alone."

A third man appeared in the door but paused to steady himself against the doorframe. He was about my age and height but terribly thin. Dark rings hung below a pair of penetrating black eyes, eyes that locked onto me for several seconds. Then, as if deciding I was no threat, he turned his attention to Monte.

"I am better, now. Please gather the leaders of this village. I must speak to them. When I am finished I will be free, free to go back to my people."

"You sure you feel up to it?" asked Deek. "Just a few minutes ago you was thrashin' around and jabberin' all sorts of foolishness. All I could get out of it was you sayin' somethin' about a snake."

"It was only a bad dream, a nightmare. I am well enough."

Monte pointed to me. "This is a friend of mine. His name is Billy and he can be trusted."

The young man looked at me. He did not extend his hand. Instead he nodded. It was a slow, deliberate motion, one that seemed quite dignified.

"I am Ahayaca," he said graciously yet with a hint of authority.

"Pleased to meet you," I said, sensing an element of sophistication in the man's speech and his mannerisms.

Ahayaca took a few feeble steps outside and then eased himself down onto the sand. He leaned back against the stone wall of the hut. "We will meet out here in the shade. What I have to say will not take long but others in the village besides the leaders may wish to hear my news."

"I'll see what I can do," Monte said. "Do these Indians speak any Spanish?"

"Yes. They speak Spanish almost as well as Yaqui."

As Monte went to gather the Yaquis, Deek and I moved out beyond the edge of the ramada to make room for the Yaquis.

"Do you have any idea what's goin' on with that Ortega fella?" Deek asked in a near whisper.

"Not really," I answered, also speaking softly. "I gather you and Monte found Ahayaca and brought him here."

"Yeah. We got here early this mornin'."

"And Ahayaca paid the doctor with a gold artifact that had a stamp on it?"

"Yep. That's right."

"Well," I said, "Mr. Ortega wants to know where the gold came from. That's about all I know."

Deek grunted. "There's a hell of a lot more to the story than that. Ahayaca is bein' hunted by rurales from Mexico. They want him bad. They're claimin' he kilt somebody important. Monte saved Ahayaca from them Mexicans, even carried 'im on his back for miles doin' it. I come along with a couple of horses just in time for the three of us to outrun the rurales. We lost them greasers in Bernadino but they're still out there somewhere and still lookin'. You can count on that. Men like them don't give up, not when they's a thousand dollar reward out for his head."

"His head?" I asked. "You mean a bounty?"

"I mean both. I was an Arizona Ranger once. Rangers worked across the border time to time with the rurales. They's mostly made up of criminals hired by the Mexican governors to keep order and to do their dirty work. In Mexico, all they tend to bring in is a man's head. Saves a lot of sweat. Totin' a dead body is hard work."

"Rurales?" I said. "How many?"

"Five that we know of. They got a paper on Ahayaca, a paper with his picture on it. All nice and legal as far as Mexican law goes. But they didn't want to wait for no extradition. They wanted him right there on the spot. But Monte wasn't about to hand over our Indian. No, sir. Monte's a dyed-in-the-wool, honest-to-goodness curly wolf. He's smart and he ain't afraid of nothin,' much less a pack of low-down rurales."

I nodded in agreement. "He is one of a kind. And so is Rosa."

"That the woman who was sittin' in that motorcar?"

"Yes. The three of us became friends back in Columbus."

"Well," grumbled Deek, "I can't say much for the company she keeps nowadays."

I heartily agreed. "That has me stumped, too. I do not like Mr. Ortega, not one bit."

With Monte in the lead, a half-dozen older men started for the ramada. They were dressed in the typical white cotton shirt and pants but their raven-black hair was close to shoulder-length. Behind them came a crowd of younger men, women, and children, all dressed in Mexican attire.

Silently the leaders walked under the ramada and then formed a semicircle in front of Ahayaca and then sat down cross-legged. The rest of the village gathered into a tight cluster behind the seated men, most of them in the shade, but some standing in the glaring sun.

Monte came to stand with me and Deek. When everyone was still Ahayaca began speaking in Spanish. As he spoke, Deek translated for me.

"My name is Ahayaca. I deliver a message from Tetabiate Ache. He and his wife, Kelupaina, and their baby son, Kego, were taken captive in the city of Nácori by an *enganchador.* Then they were taken with other Yaquis to Guaymas and put on a ship. The ship took them to San Blas. From San Blas they were put with other men and families and forced to march over the mountains. The journey took three weeks. Many died along the way.

"They reached the village of San Marcos. There, they were held near a train station. It was here that Kelupaina died. During the long walk over the mountains there was not much food but Kelupaina fed her baby from her breast. In this way she gave her own life for Kego.

"Tetabiate buried his wife at San Marcos and then all the Yaquis held there were sold as slaves. Husbands and wives were separated and children, too. Tetabiate could do nothing when they took Kego from his arms and sold him.

"Tetabiate was also sold. He and many other Yaquis and Mexicans were then taken by train to Veracruz and put on another ship. They were taken to the Yucatán, to plantations of the henequen growers.

"There Tetabiate resisted bravely the orders of the *administrador.* He refused to be a good slave. Every day he was beaten but Tetabiate was a strong and proud Yaqui. The beatings did no good.

"One day he and a companion escaped from the plantation. They knew that no one had ever escaped from the Yucatán plantations but still they said to each other, it is better to die as men than to die as slaves. So, they escaped one night by digging through a wall.

"The rurales came after Tetabiate and his friend but the rurales could not catch them for many days. But Tetabiate and his friend had no food, no weapons, no time to stop and rest. Finally, the rurales caught Tetabiate and his friend. But Tetabiate and his friend had made plans for the rurales. They told the rurales that they knew of two lost treasures, lost in the Sierra Madres.

"They told the rurales there was one canyon that branched into two very dangerous *barrancas,* and that one *barranca* contained hidden gold and the other *barranca* contained the lost Tayopa mine. To keep the rurales from killing one and torturing the other, Tetabiate and his friend told the rurales that only Tetabiate knew how to find the silver mine and only his friend could find the hidden gold. In this way, both Tetabiate and his friend would remain alive until they were deep into the canyon that led to the two *barrancas.*

"The rurales believed the story of Tetabiate and his friend. So they did not return them to the plantation. Instead, the rurales took them to the Sierra Madres. Tetabiate's friend led the way to a canyon that he knew well and then led them into a *barranca* that was filled with vines and thick trees. One day they came to a narrow pass between walls of stone, so narrow only one man could pass through at a time.

"It was here Tetabiate and his friend tried to escape from the rurales. Both of them ran fast through the pass but Tetabiate was shot in his leg. The bullet broke the bone and he could not run or walk.

"Tetabiate's friend helped Tetabiate up onto a ledge by the pass. There were many stones on this ledge. There Tetabiate could see down into the narrow pass. He told his friend to leave him, to escape and tell his people how he died, how he resisted the *administradors,* how he bravely endured the beatings and how he fought like a warrior, killing two rurales with only his bare hands and with stones before he himself was killed."

Ahayaca paused for a moment and then finished the message

he had come so far to deliver.

"This, Tetabiate wanted all here to know, to know what became of Tetabiate and his family. And to know he died, not as a slave, but fighting as a Yaqui warrior."

The Yaquis had listened in silence to Ahayaca, not one of them showing the slightest trace of emotion. For a long minute, there was nothing but the soft rush of wind rolling through the tangled branches over our heads. Finally, the eldest of the seated Yaquis spoke.

"You are this friend you speak of, the friend of Tetabiate?" he asked solemnly.

"I am. I am called Ahayaca. I am here today, only because Tetabiate saved my life. He fought the rurales while I escaped. He insisted I go. He only asked that I tell of his family and how he fought to a good death. Now, I have done as he asked."

The old man held his head high and said, "I am the father of Tetabiate. You have done well. You will always be welcome in the pueblos of the Yaqui. You are welcome to stay with us here."

"I thank the father of Tetabiate," Ahayaca said, "but I must go to my people. They will believe me dead. I must go today."

The old Yaqui seem concerned. "You are too sick."

"I am better. The doctor's quinine is working. My people are only one day's ride from this village."

"Then go with our many thanks," said the Yaqui, coming to his feet.

Without a word the rest of the seated Yaquis rose and then the entire village turned and walked away as if nothing had happened.

Once the Yaquis were out of hearing distance, Monte took a few steps toward Ahayaca and then paused. "Was Garcia, by chance, one of those rurales you were talking about?"

"Yes. He and his men work for the governor of Sonora . . . and for the plantation owners. Everyone in the Yucatán is working for the governor or the plantation owners."

"How did you end up in that mess, anyhow?" Deek asked as both he and I returned to the shade of the ramada.

Ahayaca thought for a moment, gathering his thoughts. "This is a year of celebration for my people. As a part of our celebration we perform many sacred rituals. These rituals require objects that must only be gathered from central Mexico. And I was the one selected to gather what was necessary.

"I was on my way to perform my duties when I entered the city of Nácori. Many people were passing through that town and many ate at restaurants as I did. I shared a table with a man that said he was traveling also. We talked as we ate and then he began to argue with me, argue loudly and over nothing.

"Suddenly, two rurales came into the restaurant and I, only I, was arrested and taken before the *jefe politico*. He found me guilty of disturbing the peace and sentenced me to jail. But instead of taking me to a jail, the rurales took me to a house with a large room that was already crowded with other men. It was a *casa de el enganchador*.

"Some of them were Yaqui but most were Mexicans. And then the man that had sat at my table in the restaurant came into the room. I learned that he was paid ten pesos by the *jefe politico* for each man he brought before him to be sentenced. Those that were near me said that man was an *enganchador*, a person who snares. And they told me it was that same *enganchador* that had betrayed all of them.

"I was betrayed and others were kidnapped. Some, though, were tricked into signing contracts to work. After signing the contract, the *enganchador* advanced them five pesos so the workers could buy things they needed, like food or clothing. Once they spent any amount of what they were loaned, they were in debt and then their debt was sold. And the *jefe politico* sold us all for twenty pesos each."

I was astounded. What I was hearing was incredible. I was convinced that I had not heard correctly.

"What do you mean 'the debt was sold'?" I asked.

Ahayaca huffed in disgust. "In Mexico, it is claimed that slavery is illegal. But 'enforced service for debt' is not. But there is no difference because once you are in debt, your 'debt' can be sold from one buyer to the other. Once in debt, the owner pays you only a few centavos but it is barely enough to keep you alive, much less enough to pay off your debt. And the owner of the debt makes certain there is no way you can ever get out of debt. You are then a slave.

"As I was being taken to the casa I saw the *enganchador* and I cursed him. He laughed, and he had a most unforgettable, devilish laugh. The next time I heard that evil laugh was in the San Marcos train station. That is where I met Tetabiate. And that is where I discovered that many others at San Marcos had been betrayed by the same laughing *enganchador*. He was known as El Serpiente and had connections in Mexico City, Veracruz, Oaxaca, and Tuxtepec. And he was becoming very wealthy selling slaves."

"Was Tetabiate tricked the same as you?" asked Deek.

"No. The Yaqui people are not tricked. If they are recognized they are arrested. They have for years been captured and then sent to the Yucatán as slaves. President Díaz wanted their land in southern Sonora but the Yaqui refused to give it up. They have fought for their land since the Spanish first landed in Mexico. To protect their land, they have been at war with the Mexican government for centuries.

"But most have given up and stopped fighting, like those here in this village. But there are some who continue to fight. A few years ago, when Díaz was president, his solution was to arrest all Yaquis, *pacíficos* or *broncos*, men, women, and children, and then send them to the henequen plantations. He called it 'deportation,' but it was not just moving the Yaquis to some other place.

"The rurales were ordered to break up the families along the way. Even children were taken from their mothers. This crushed their spirit. The Yaquis are strong but on the plantations two out of three die before one year is gone."

I was in shock. Nothing Ahayaca was saying made sense to me. I could not accept such barbarity, not in modern times. I tried not to be offensive but I had to find out more. "What kind of people would do such a thing in the twentieth century? What you are telling us . . . to say the least, is very hard to accept."

Ahayaca grunted. "On the Yucatán there are many planters, but there are fifty very powerful families. They form the *Camara*. They are kings of the Yucatán and live in palaces in the city of Merida.

"Tetabiate and his family were arrested by the rurales for being Yaqui but the rurales often take Pimas and Papagos and claim they are Yaquis. In Mexico, no one cares as long as everyone gets paid and slaves arrive for the Yucatán planters."

My head was spinning. Without thinking, I half-mumbled, "But my uncle has a summer residence in Merida."

Ahayaca glared at me, his eyes cold as ice. "Is he a planter of henequen?"

Feeling suddenly trapped, I replied, "No. Absolutely not. He is in shipping."

"Shipping henequen?" drilled Ahayaca.

Panic-stricken, I could not think straight. My uncle, like the rest of the family, shipped all sorts of goods around the globe. I was horrified to think he might very well have shipped henequen. I could not bring myself to face that possibility or reveal that fact so I twisted the truth. "All of his ships are involved in the war effort, helping the allies. He ships food and medical supplies."

For the moment, Ahayaca seemed satisfied. He looked at Monte. "I will leave this village today. I have been away from my people for almost a year. They will think me dead. I am anxious to return to them."

"Are you fit to ride?" Monte asked.

"It is only a day's ride. Maybe two. I am well enough but I invite you, Monte Segundo, to come to my village. I wish to thank you for all you have done."

"You don't need to do that."

Ahayaca seemed pleased with Monte's response. "I would be grateful if you would come."

Monte glanced at me and then at Deek. "I could use some company on the ride."

"I'm in," said Deek. "This village ain't got nothing I want and them rurales is still out there on the prod. You might run into trouble, yet."

"I'll go with you, too, if you don't mind," I said, still fighting off a wave of guilt.

"Well," Monte sighed, "that suits me and I'd just as soon not be here tomorrow when Ortega shows up."

Up until that point, I had forgotten all about Rosa and Ortega. "But I have no horse."

"I'll see what I can do," Deek offered. "With all Ahayaca has done for 'em, these Yaquis likely will loan us an outfit."

As Deek left to find horses, Monte walked out into the scorching sun. He looked past the huts and out into the desert, first toward Tucson and then in every direction. Coming back into the shade he sat down next to Ahayaca. "Tell me about Garcia. When did you first meet up with him?"

"Garcia," explained Ahayaca, "was at one time a well-known but ruthless rurale. Because of his reputation he was hired to be *mayordomo primero* on the plantation where Tetabiate and I were taken. He was made the head overseer because there were many

Yaquis arriving on the plantation. The Yaquis considered themselves warriors and were rebellious. They always fought their overseers . . . at least at first.

"Both Tetabiate and I were very angry when we first arrived at the plantation and we fought with the *capataces*. They were the overseers that beat us with their canes. Since the *capataces* could not break us, one morning Garcia took control and had us tied to posts in front of all the workers on the plantation. Our shirts were torn off."

Ahayaca paused. He seemed entranced for several seconds. I cringed as he again started to speak. "What I say now is not for the Yaqui people to ever know."

"I understand," said Monte.

"You have my word," I said.

"Garcia was also the *majocol* of the plantation, the one who whips the slaves. That day, he reached into a bucket of water and brought out his whip. It had a thick handle and four ropes all made of braided henequen. The water made the ropes heavy so that they would better cut the skin.

"We each got fifteen lashes . . . I quit fighting after that.

"Tetabiate, though, did not stop and the next morning Tetabiate was again given fifteen lashes. This went on for a week. On the last day Garcia gave Tetabiate twenty-five lashes.

"By then, his back was torn to pieces. His flesh was quivering like jelly.

"We all watched and listened to Tetabiate plead for mercy. Garcia had him cut down but he was not finished. He commanded Tetabiate to crawl to him, to beg as he crawled. Tetabiate did this in front of all of us.

"When he got to Garcia, Garcia held out his hand, the hand that had held the whip. Then Garcia commanded Tetabiate to lick his hand with his bare tongue.

"This Tetabiate also did in front of all of us. After that day, he fought no more."

Ahayaca was silent for several agonizing seconds. He inhaled deeply and then said, "But, months later, when we finally escaped, the *jefe politico* of the Yucatán was very angry. He blamed Garcia for our escape and demanded that he return to the rurales. Garcia was then ordered to pursue us immediately."

My blood began to boil. I took one look at Monte and knew instantly that Garcia, whoever or whatever he might be, was marked for certain death. And at that moment I hoped to God that I would be there to see the sentence carried out.

Deek came back to the ramada leading four saddled horses. "I left my two mounts with the Yaquis," he said cheerily. "They loaned us these four. We got saddles, blankets, and gourds full of water. And a sack full of deer jerky."

We did not respond and then Deek looked at each of us one at a time. His brow wrinkled. "Did I miss somethin'?"

"No," answered Monte, coming to his feet. "Ahayaca was just getting ready to tell us about his people. He can do that on the way. The sooner we're out of here the better."

On his way back to Tucson, Ortega drove slowly. Neither he nor Rosa spoke for several miles. Finally, Ortega said, "Do you think Monte Segundo would come to work for me? I think I could use a man like him."

"How should I know?" snapped Rosa.

Ortega laughed. "Because you know men."

"Not that one. I think he is *loco.*"

Ortega laughed again. "Why, because he did not take notice of you?"

"*Chingate,*" snarled Rosa. "I think both of you are *loco!*"

Again, Ortega laughed but this time more heartily. "Oh, my Rosa! What a temper you have."

"Take me to the mercantile," demanded Rosa.

"Why?" asked Ortega, suddenly sober.

"Because I pick what clothes I will wear, not you." Rosa pointed at the package in the back seat. "You will take that back. That is a gringa dress!"

Ortega glanced over his shoulder at the package. "But Rosa, if you come into the better part of Tucson you should dress up. That dress is the latest fashion. Women are wearing it in New York City."

"Fashion?" questioned Rosa. "What is that?"

"That means . . . clothes that are the same as most women are wearing. It means what is in style."

"You mean what gringa women are wearing."

Ortega shrugged. "Times are changing, Rosa. We must change with them. That is progress."

Rosa sneered at Ortega. Taking in his suit and tie, she said, "I like being Mexican. I am not ashamed to be what I am."

Reaching the outskirts of Tucson, Ortega avoided the Mexican district and was soon driving down Congress Street swerving around busy pedestrians and passing dozens of parked motorcars. As he pulled up in front of his mercantile, both he and Rosa took notice of a grizzled-looking Mexican leaning against the outer wall of the store.

Oddly, even in the midday sun the man was hatless. He wore a cheap black suit coat above Mexican style riding pants and heavily worn knee-high boots.

Ortega got out of the Studebaker and grabbed the package from the back seat. Rosa exited the motorcar and scampered to the mercantile door, which she opened and darted through, but did not close. As Ortega stepped onto the sidewalk, he glanced at the hatless man. "Good afternoon, sir," he said and then walked through the open door of the mercantile and up to the glass counter.

After placing the package next to the cash register Ortega

looked around for Rosa and saw her rummaging through a stack of clothes. His clerk started toward her.

"She is with me," Ortega said, waving off the clerk.

Ortega was watching Rosa when he heard footsteps behind him. Turning, he found himself face-to-face with the hatless Mexican.

The Mexican stared at Ortega for several seconds and then said icily, "Good afternoon to you . . . Señor Ortega."

Instantly, Ortega sensed this was no ordinary Mexican. In fact, he had an idea that this man was dangerous. "May I help you, sir?"

"Hablamos en Español, sí?"

"No. On this side of the border I speak only English."

"As you wish," replied the Mexican.

"How may I help you?" Ortega asked.

The man reached inside his coat and pulled out a small bottle. "I am Sergeant Garcia, a rurale of Sonora. I have been following the trail of a murderer for many, many miles. I lost his trail in Bernadino. It was very hard to find once more but I did. I followed the trail and it was coming straight to Tucson. Then I lost it in the roads outside of town. You know, too many motorcars like yours. Too many tire tracks."

Garcia paused. His eyes roamed around the mercantile. He focused lustfully on Rosa for a moment and then turned back to Ortega.

"Tucson is a big city, Señor Ortega. There are many places to hide."

"What is that to me?" questioned Ortega.

Garcia smiled, showing a row of large white teeth that contrasted sharply with his thick black mustache. He held up a bottle. "On the trail I found this bottle of medicine. It is from a doctor here in Tucson. And the man I have been trailing for many, many miles was also a very sick man. His name is Ahay-aca."

Instantly, Ortega knew why Garcia had been waiting outside the mercantile but he stalled to gather his thoughts. "Ahayaca. I have never heard that name."

Unimpressed with Ortega's claim, Garcia continued, "So, the doctor of this sick man was paid in gold and the doctor told me you bought that gold. He also told me you would know where to find this sick man."

"Wouldn't the doctor know that better than me?" returned Ortega. "Why don't you ask him?"

Garcia grinned again. "I think maybe the doctor was scared to talk too much to me. He told me to ask you. But he did tell me something more."

"Like what?"

"The doctor told me that you think the gold you bought from him is not just any gold. He said maybe you think it is gold from a lost treasure."

"That's nonsense. I buy gold form the Yaquis all the time," quipped Ortega. "And silver. I have heard many stories of lost treasures and mines. I don't believe in childish legends. I have no idea where they get their gold or their silver and I don't care. I am here to make a profit. I am a businessman and there is no profit to be had in chasing after make-believe stories."

Garcia's eyes hardened. "Yes, you are a businessman and maybe you make lots of money. But if something happens to you, señor, and you cannot spend your money, what good is it?"

Understanding the veiled threat, Ortega had had enough. "You take me for a fool, Sergeant. Bu you are not in Mexico now and you have no idea who you are talking to."

"And you," countered Garcia, "have no idea who *you* are talking to. Do you know what is the *acordada* or what they can do to you . . . even in Tucson?"

"You speak of the *acordada*," Ortega said snickering. "I *know* the *jefe de acordada* of both Sonora and Chihuahua."

Garcia's eyes flashed with surprise but then narrowed as he studied Ortega. "Few men outside of the government know what is the *acordada*. But maybe still you are bluffing."

"Only the very well connected know of the *acordada*," replied Ortega. "And you are looking at one of them."

Garcia gave Ortega a complimentary nod. "Then it would be better if men like us work together and do not kill each other."

Ortega smiled shrewdly. "It would be more profitable . . . and involve less risk. As I said, I am a businessman. A partnership would serve us both."

"So it will be, then," agreed Garcia. "Now you can tell me, where is this Indian?"

"He is in the Yaqui village," admitted Ortega. "And you know as well as I, if you go in there and they suspect you are a rurale they will kill you on sight. But they trust me. I was there today but the Indian is guarded by two *Anglos*. They would not let me see him. They said he was too sick to be disturbed.

"I will go back tomorrow, though. He should be able to talk by then."

"I know of these two gringos," said Garcia. "The big one is very clever. By now he will know of the gold the Indian has been carrying."

Ortega nodded in agreement. "I have come to the same conclusion."

"The big one carried the Indian on his back for miles to get away from me. He saved the Indian's life so the Indian will be grateful, very grateful. Maybe grateful enough to tell the gringo about the hidden treasure."

Raising an eyebrow, Ortega asked, "What makes you believe there is a treasure? Maybe he had only one piece of gold."

"No," grumbled Garcia, "when he first escaped he had no

gold, no nothing. Later, he used bits of gold to buy food all across Mexico. That is one reason he has kept ahead of me. He knows where there is gold. I am sure of it."

"Then we have two American competitors," Ortega said. "Maybe even three, now. Another *Anglo* is curious about the gold. He thinks the gold the Indian had was Aztec."

"Aztec!" Garcia blurted.

"He was just guessing," cautioned Ortega. "He saw the gold piece that I bought from the doctor. There was a stamp on it, a stamp he thought was from the time of the Aztecs."

Garcia reached into his pants pocket and brought out a crude coin. "Did the stamp look like this?"

Ortega took the coin and looked it over. "No. It was much different. Where did you get this?"

Taking the coin from Ortega, Garcia shrugged indifferently. "I found this on a dead man near Bernadino . . . after he told me all that I wanted to know about the escaped Indian and his two gringo friends."

"It is good," said Ortega thoughtfully, "that you did not catch the Indian. He is Yaqui. He would die before he talked about the gold and his secret would die with him.

"For now it is best that we go slowly. I will find out what I can tomorrow. If the gringos should find out about the treasure they will have to be convinced to join us. If they do not join with us we will have to make them tell us what they know."

"In that case," Garcia said, as he turned to leave, "the big one will be mine."

"How will I get in touch with you?" Ortega asked.

Starting for the door, Garcia answered, "It will be me that gets in touch with you."

"Alright," relented Ortega, "I live above this mercantile. There are outside stairs in the back of the store that lead up to my door."

After Garcia was gone, Rosa came up to Ortega. "And what is an *acordada*?"

Ortega's lips tightened with irritation. "You have good hearing, Rosa. Maybe too good."

"I didn't hear everything," said Rosa, "but I heard enough. Would you rather me ask the rurale what is an *acordada*?"

"The *acordada*," sighed Ortega, "are secret assassins that work for the Mexican government. I have only heard of them, that is all. Garcia was too confident. I was bluffing when I said I knew them.

"Forget about that. Tomorrow morning we must talk to the Yaqui. I mean the Indian no harm, Rosa. All I wish to know is if he has more gold to sell."

Rosa started to ask more questions but then thought better of it. Instead, she merely stared up at Antonio Ortega. How, she wondered, did the penniless boy she grew up with come to know about the existence of secret government assassins?

Rosa could not imagine what had happened to her childhood friend, but after eavesdropping on his conversation she had no doubts about one thing. Monte Segundo and Billy Cabott were in serious danger.

CHAPTER FIVE

Riding close together, we were a mile south of the Yaqui village before Ahayaca said another word. I was still trying to figure out the best way to hold onto my suitcase when Ahayaca broke his silence and pointed to a mountain range a few miles ahead of us.

"Centuries ago, my people came to these mountains. We were farmers and lived at peace with all the tribes, even the Apaches. In the early seventeen-hundreds Jesuit missionaries came. They built a large adobe building with thick walls that was used as a trading post and church. They were good men and tried to convert us but we had our own religion. Even though we did not convert, we lived peaceably among the Jesuits and learned many things from them. We respected the priests. They left us alone in our village and we left them alone at their trading post. The Jesuits were decent and wise men.

"One century later, the Spanish came to where the Jesuits once were and started a large rancho. The Jesuit trading post still stood, so, next to it, the Spanish built a hacienda with walls four feet thick but also with many shooting portals. They even covered the roof with dirt so that it could not be set on fire. This they did to protect themselves from the raiding bands of Apaches.

"The Spanish raised cattle on the land that surrounded our village but we also lived in peace with them. We left their cows alone and they left our crops alone. Later, other owners of the rancho arrived, also Spanish. Some of my people then began to work for the hacienda. We are good, strong workers and the ranchers enjoyed having my people work for them and my people enjoyed working for the ranchers. Even though the ranchers told us that we lived on their land, they were wise and left us alone in our village. This way of living became a tradition. It is a tradition that has been passed down from rancher to rancher, from generation to generation. And so it is to this day."

"How in hell," blurted Deek, "did you live at peace with the Apaches? I never heard of any tribe in these parts the damned Apaches didn't raid, especially the farmin' kind of Indians."

Ahayaca shrugged. "They showed no interest in us."

Deek shook his head. "Mighty peculiar," he mumbled. "I never heard of that before."

"Well, there is an old story," offered Ahayaca, "that says when our people first came to this area centuries ago, the local Indians believed us to be shape-shifters, that we could turn into jaguars. Then, as jaguars, we would hunt people down and then eat them.

"Perhaps that superstition is what kept the other tribes from bothering us."

Thinking for a moment, Deek scratched at the stubble on his neck. "Now I've heard of shape-shifters before. The Navajo up north believe in that sort of thing to this day. Some of what they believe is downright spooky, if you ask me. And the Navajo and Apaches are cousins.

"So offhand, I'd say that shape-shiftin' nonsense was the reason your tribe was left alone all these years. Injun superstition is mighty powerful."

We began to veer to the west. "We will go through a valley the white man calls the Altar Valley," Ahayaca continued. "Not far from my village is a small town called Sasabe. The Rancho de la Osa hacienda is the home of the rancho whose land we share. We will go out of our way to see the *jefe* of the rancho before we go to my village. It is the custom to do this before we cross his land."

"One thing I been wonderin' about," Deek said. "Back at Bernadino, Garcia said there was a thousand dollar reward out on you. Working as a Ranger, I come in contact with lots of rurales that was hunting fugitives. The going price for an escaped prisoner was ten pesos or ten dollars.

"How is it, especially since you didn't murder nobody, that you're worth ten times that much?"

Ahayaca smiled. "It was ten dollars for me and Tetabiate when we first escaped. But it took many days for Garcia to catch us. After we convinced Garcia and his men that we could guide them to lost treasure, he telephoned the *jefe político* and told him he could not find us but that he would keep looking.

"The *jefe político* then explained to the planter that we had not been caught. So another week passed as we traveled farther away from the Yucatán. At another city, Garcia telephoned again with the same story. It was then Garcia learned the planter had raised the reward to one thousand pesos apiece, dead or alive. The planter and all the families of the *Camara* became fearful. They did not want anyone to learn the slave trade still existed in Yucatán. The planters were becoming desperate, so to ensure our capture the price on our heads went higher."

"Makes sense," Deek said. "So, how long did it take you to get all the way up to Arizona?"

"I was at the plantation for four months. It took me almost eight months to get to the border, to the graves where Monte found me."

"The graves?" I asked, and then turned to Monte. "Did you find the graves of your mother and father?"

Monte nodded. "With Deek's help, I did. He remembered about the Apache raid and what had happened. He even knew where the Apaches attacked my home. And he told me how to get there. That's where I found Ahayaca. He was hiding under the rocks that covered one of the graves."

"He was what?"

"I was being pursued by Garcia and I could go no farther," Ahayaca said. "There was no place to hide and I knew the rurales were very near. I saw the graves and chose one. I covered myself with the sand and the stones. It was all I could do.

"I was lying there thinking that the stones covered me. But I could still see out of one eye. I saw Monte coming. And then I heard horses, those of Garcia and his men. After that I passed out."

"What happened then?" I asked.

Scanning the desert to his left and right, Monte said, "I convinced Garcia to turn back. It was a bluff but it worked."

Knowing Monte to be a master of understatement, I asked, "What kind of bluff turned back five rurales?"

Monte glanced at Ahayaca, and smiled, "I told them I had a platoon of itchy-fingered sharpshooters hidden in the brush."

I chuckled. "That would do it."

Deek chuckled along with me. "Monte's not only a damn good bluffer, he's the walkin'est man I ever seen. The day we met, he'd already walked all the way from Hermanas to Rodeo. When I told 'im where the graves was to be found, he took off again and walked clear down to the border."

"Hermanas!" I said. "You got off at Hermanas? But that's just a few miles west of Columbus."

"I suppose that's where I got off," was Monte's subdued response.

I shook my head in disbelief. "So that's why no one on the train remembered seeing you. For the life of me I could not figure that out."

I shifted my suitcase for a better grip, which gave me time

enough to gather the courage I needed to pose a question that had been gnawing at me for days. "Can I ask *why* you got off the train?"

Monte turned and checked our back trail for half a minute. "Do you remember when we were on the train platform in Columbus?"

"Yes."

"Did you hear me, plain as day, ask Rosa to come with me on the train?"

"Sure I did. I'll never forget that moment."

"Well, as soon as I stepped inside that passenger car I saw her sitting with another man. They were smiling at each other and chattering like pine squirrels. Rosa didn't even look up to see if I was on the train."

"And that other man," I surmised, "was Antonio Ortega?"

"You got it," affirmed Monte.

"I'll be damned," snorted Deek.

"Well, anyway," continued Monte, "I went ahead and sat down across from the two of them but Rosa acted like she barely knew who I was. I got so sick of listening to the two of them that I had to get as far away as I could. So, the first chance I got, I got off that train."

Deek squinted at Monte. "This Rosa, she was somethin' special to you?"

Monte grunted and then said, "I thought she was."

We rode on for several minutes without speaking. Ahayaca began to doze in the saddle but I was busy trying to make sense of what had happened on the train. Suddenly a thought occurred to me.

"Wait a minute," I protested but keeping my voice low. "Something is wrong here. Rosa likes you very much, Monte. I have no doubts about that. None whatsoever."

"Women is just fickle," Deek said, keeping his voice low.

"That's the problem. And that Ortega fella looks like he's got money. I got a look at that Rosa lady while she sat in that fancy-dan Studebaker. She's a looker for damn sure.

"Now, did you ever see a rich man with an ugly woman? No, you never did and you never will. Women is to money like steel is to magnets. That's what happened, if you ask me. That Rosa lady just up and went for the money."

I shook my head. "Not Rosa. She's different."

"You're still wet behind the ears, Billy," Deek said. "Wait 'til you're old as me. You'll see. Women can't help it. Just the way they're put together. Like steel and magnets."

"Not Rosa," I repeated, but admittedly my confidence had been shaken. Why, after all Monte and Rosa had been through together, would Rosa choose to ignore him on the train? She knew as well as I did that it was extremely difficult for Monte to express his feelings. She also knew that asking her to come with him on the train was, for Monte, a major step forward.

"And those good-lookin' women," continued Deek, "Lord, do they like to torture a man. Like a cat does a mouse. Can't none of 'em handle the power God give 'em. First thing Eve did to old Adam was twist 'im around her little finger and get 'im in a pile of trouble. Nothin's any different nowadays.

"Nope. This country's right not to let women anywhere near the ballot box. Give 'em the right to vote and that kind of power would go straight to their heads. Women has got too much power over a man as it is."

As we rode on, I thought about what Deek had said. There was a grain of truth to his sentiments. On several occasions I had witnessed Rosa battling Monte's physical might and emotional detachment with her extraordinary cunning and beauty.

Then it hit me.

"That's it!" I whispered.

"What?" Deek asked.

"Monte," I said, "when you were on the train with Rosa, she was only trying to make you jealous. She was using Ortega in hopes that you would admit how you felt."

Monte turned and glared at me with eyes full of skepticism.

"Oh, they'll do that, alright," agreed Deek. "That's one of their favorite tricks. They love to bait a man, snare 'im and then sit back and watch 'im twist in the wind."

Monte slowly shook his head. Whether in disagreement or disbelief, I could not tell.

For an hour we kept riding on a course just south of due west. Once we got past a range of barren hills, we headed due south. In minutes we began to see tufts of parched grass growing between the cat's claw and the prickly pear. Here and there we saw tracks of cows and where they had been lying in the shade under the mesquite and palo verde trees.

The farther south we rode, the fewer and fewer saguaro we saw, but the grass grew denser. As we were crossing a rock-strewn plain, Ahayaca caught sight of a wagon trail and we rode over to it. The road, if it could be called that, meandered north to south and we followed it, riding directly toward Mexico.

Near sundown the heat began to dissipate. Ahayaca, seemingly refreshed from his napping in the saddle, picked up the pace. A few minutes after the sun had set we came to a Y in the road. To my surprise, instead of taking the southern fork, we took the one that abruptly veered to the northwest.

"Sasabe is three miles to the south," Ahayaca informed us. "Soon we will be at the hacienda of Don Carlos Cruz. Perhaps he will have enough food prepared to invite us for supper. I am hungry and I have had my fill of dried jerky."

"You'll get no arguments from me," Deek said.

We had just broken into a trot when a voice erupted a few feet behind us.

"Stop right there!" was the order and it was punctuated with the blast of a rifle.

A few yards in front of us a man pointing a Winchester lunged out of the fading light and into the middle of the road.

We reined in, our eyes searching the sides of the brush for any other guns.

The man with the Winchester started walking toward us. "Who are you," he demanded with a distinct Mexican accent, "and what do you want here?"

Ahayaca answered calmly. "We are here, Fernando, to see Don Carlos."

Behind us came another question. The voice was firm but unquestionably feminine. "Who are you?"

"Señorita Angelina, it is good to hear your voice," Ahayaca said. "Does your father know that you now play with guns?"

The one called Fernando took another step closer. "Who the hell are you? Tell me now or I will shoot you!"

"I am Ahayaca."

It was getting dark fast. I could see Fernando straining to see Ahayaca's face. "Ahayaca is dead."

"If that is so, how would I know that Señorita Angelina once tried to smoke a cigar behind the corrals when she was ten years old and that it was I who told her father what she had done?"

A woman, wearing a broad-brimmed hat and riding pants, ran forward. She swerved wide around us but when she got in front of Ahayaca, she edged a half step closer. "Who has a match?" she asked. "I need to see his face."

Monte was closest to Ahayaca. "Don't get itchy with those rifles," Monte said as he slowly reached into his shirt pocket to finger out a match. "I'm just reaching for a light."

Dragging the match across his pant leg, it burst into flame. He held the match up high illuminating Ahayaca's gaunt face.

"I have been sick and have not eaten well," said Ahayaca, "but it is me."

Señorita Angelina gasped and put a hand over her mouth. "It is you. My God, it *is* you! We all thought you were dead!"

"These men with me are friends, Angelina. We have come far and are hungry."

Angelina waved her arm. "Fernando, get the horses. Father will be so pleased. And your people, they mourned for so long. I can't wait to see their faces. I can't believe this! Oh, this is wonderful. It's a miracle."

I watched Fernando come out of the brush leading two mounts. He brought them close.

Even in the near darkness, I could not help but notice how gracefully and yet how athletically the woman bounded into her saddle.

She rode up beside Ahayaca and, as if they had practiced it, both kicked their mounts into a gallop, and rode down the road together. We followed at a short distance with Fernando bringing up the rear. I glanced back and was surprised to see that he still held his rifle at the ready and was glancing back over his shoulders as if he still expected trouble.

In a matter of minutes we dropped down a slight grade and rounded a tree-lined bend in the road. Then, as if springing out of the desert sand, we were confronted by the bulky shadow of a chest-high adobe wall. It was too dark to see the length of the wall but the road we were on led straight through it. We passed under a gate frame constructed of three massive beams. Burning lanterns on each of the vertical beams illuminated a small white cross carved deeply into the wood.

Beyond the adobe wall, lanterns were flickering from the porch posts of several low-lying buildings, all of which faced an open plaza of trimmed grass. In front of us, however, was a sprawling hacienda with large windows that glowed with soft yellow light. Leading up to the hacienda and illuminated by torches was a set of stone steps that merged with a flagstone walkway. On opposite sides of the steps, steel hitch-rails had been sunk into the sand. Off to the right of the hitch rails, almost invisible in the darkness, was a Ford motorcar.

We rode to the hitch rails and dismounted. We were tying our horses when the heavy wooden door of the hacienda opened wide. A gray-haired man, silhouetted by lamplight, called out, "Angelina, is that you? You are late. I was beginning to worry."

Angelina jumped the steps entirely and ran to the man. Taking him by the arm she coaxed him out of the doorway and toward the burning torches. He was dressed in expensive-looking Mexican style clothes.

"Wait 'til you see, Father," Angelina said, excitedly, "wait and see who is here, who Fernando and I met on our way home this evening."

We stayed in the shadows as Ahayaca walked up the steps and into the firelight.

Angelina brought her father to within an arm's length of Ahayaca and then stopped.

The warm night air was still. The flickering glow from the torches danced across Ahayaca's gaunt features. A horse stomped and then blew. Other than that, there was complete silence.

Angelina's father leaned closer. "It cannot be. It cannot be!"

Angelina giggled as she bounced up and down on her toes. "But it is, Father. It is him. It's Ahayaca!"

I was immediately impressed with the young woman standing next to her father. It had been a long, difficult day and I found her effervescence quite refreshing. I tried to get a better look at her but the brim of her hat shielded her face from the torchlight. All I could see was one side of her cheek but even that was enough to prick my interest.

Angelina's father tentatively extended his hand. "Is it really you, Ahayaca?"

Ahayaca shook hands. "It is I, Señor Cruz."

Still shaking hands, Señor Cruz squinted and tilted his head as he gazed at Ahayaca from different angles, "I still can't believe it. How can this be? All this time we assumed you were dead."

"I have a long story to tell, Señor Cruz, but I am anxious to be home. Tomorrow we can speak but those with me have come far. They are tired and hungry. Would you be so kind as to care for them this evening?"

Letting go of Ahayaca's hand, Señor Cruz peered into the darkness. "Certainly, certainly. Your friends are my friends."

"Thank you, sir," said Ahayaca as he spun around and then hurried back down the steps. "It is good to be home!"

Stepping back into his saddle, Ahayaca waved and then galloped north past the hacienda and disappeared into the night.

"Isn't it wonderful?" Angelina said to her father. "Finally, we have some good news."

Señor Cruz nodded while straining to see us better. "Come in, gentlemen, come inside. Fernando will care for your horses.

"*Mi casa es su casa.* We have only stew this evening but our cook, Kim Lee, always prepares more than enough."

Before anyone went forward, Monte and Deek began slapping the dust from their shirts and pants. Realizing what they were doing and why, I set my suitcase down and did the same.

They were finished dusting before me. When I looked up, they were following Señor Cruz through the open front door of the hacienda. Angelina, however, had politely stayed behind to wait for me.

Feeling a bit like a fool, I picked up my suitcase. I went up the steps but avoided Angelina's eyes. When I came up next to her, she started walking alongside me. I could feel her looking at me.

"What are you selling?" she asked as innocently as a child.

Now feeling like a complete fool, I cleared my throat. "I'm not a salesman though I must appear to be one. You are the second person today who has asked me the same question."

"It's nothing to be ashamed of," Angelina said.

I felt my face flush with heat. "No, miss. You misunderstand. I arrived just today on the train. I've been traveling ever since. This is my suitcase."

When we got to the open door, I extended my arm, allowing Angelina to go first, which she did without hesitation. Inside she paused, once again waiting for me to come alongside her.

"I'm from New York City," I offered feebly.

"Now, you don't have to be ashamed of that either," replied Angelina. "I'm sure you do the best you can."

Embarrassed and confused, I continued walking with Angelina until we entered a well-lit, large rectangular room. It had a high ceiling and walls decorated with large paper murals, some depicting matadors and others lovely women singing on stage. In the center of a red tile floor was a long dining table surrounded by ten sturdy wooden chairs.

I glanced up to see Monte and Deek standing near the table. Monte was staring at me and Deek wore a sarcastic grin.

It did not register that they had taken off their hats.

Angelina took the suitcase from my hand. Before I could protest she set it against a wall. "Your things will be safe here. Don't be offended, but I doubt very seriously that we would be interested in buying anything from New York City."

I heard Deek chuckle. I clenched my teeth and decided to let the subject drop.

Señor Cruz was nowhere to be seen. Angelina approached Monte and Deek. She extended her hand to Monte. "I am Angelina Cruz. And you are?"

Monte shook her hand. "Monte Segundo, miss."

Angelina put out her hand to Deek. "And you, sir?"

Shaking her hand Deek said proudly, "Deek Coleman, former Arizona Ranger."

"Pleased to meet you both," Angelina said and then pointed to some chairs. "Please sit there."

Turning, she looked at me with the greenest eyes that I had ever seen. She came toward me. I tried to look away but I was mesmerized.

She paused and then extended her hand. In her high-heeled riding boots she was almost my height. Suddenly, I was very conscious of the fact I was wearing shoes made for walking on city sidewalks, shoes with a very low heel.

I took her hand, thankful that my hands were still calloused from being in Mexico for the last several weeks. Her hands, though, were surprisingly soft.

"Well?" she said. "Do you have a name?"

Finally, I was able to blink. "Will . . . ah . . . Billy Cabott."

Angelina frowned. "Are you sure?"

I heard Deek laugh and then the squeaking of chairs sliding up to the table.

"Where would you like for me to sit?" I asked, unaware I was still holding her hand.

"If you let go of me, I'll show you."

I pulled my hand away. "Sorry. It has been a long day."

"Sunstroke?" questioned Angelina in all seriousness.

"Maybe a little," I said.

Angelina's eyes glanced upward. "With a hat like that, I'm not surprised."

I merely closed my eyes. Taking off my fedora, I slumped. "Please excuse me. I have totally forgotten my manners."

"It's quite alright, Billy Cabott. We weren't going to buy anything from you anyway. Money is tight on a cattle ranch."

I sighed. "Where should I sit?"

"Sit across from Deek Coleman, former Ranger. I will sit across from Monte Segundo. And you will sit next to me."

Hanging my head, I walked over to the table and pulled out a chair for Angelina.

"No," Angelina said. "You sit. I'm going to help Father."

As I sat, I heard Angelina's footsteps behind me and then I heard them fade away. I glance up at Monte. He was looking at the murals as if nothing had happened. I glanced at Deek, who was smiling and shaking his head.

"She's trouble," Deek said. "Didn't you listen to what all I said earlier about women?"

"I heard. I'm just trying to be polite."

Deek snorted. "The hell you are. You about come unglued the minute you saw her."

"That's nonsense," I said, lying the best I knew how.

I heard footsteps again but dared not look up.

"You must excuse us," said Señor Cruz, "we are shorthanded on the rancho and must sometimes make do for ourselves."

Lifting my eyes, I saw Señor Cruz coming toward us carrying a white porcelain pitcher in one hand and, in the fingers of his other hand, four matching mugs. He set the mugs down in front of us and then filled them with water from the pitcher.

"You must be thirsty from your long ride. Where did you come from?"

"The Yaqui village up by Tucson," Deek answered.

Setting the pitcher down, Señor Cruz said, "Yes, I know of that village. So, you have come far."

Monte was still studying the murals so Deek again answered. "One day's ride, that's all."

Señor Cruz nodded and spun on his heels. "I will get the plates."

"May I help?" I asked.

Walking back toward the kitchen, Señor Cruz said, "No, no.

You are our guests. Please make yourselves comfortable."

Angelina passed her father in the kitchen doorway. Catching sight of her, I quickly averted my eyes, grabbed my water, and started drinking.

After placing a rolled napkin down in front of Monte and Deek she came around the table and placed one beside me. Again, I felt her eyes on me. I kept drinking but she did not step away. Finally, the mug was empty and I eased it back down on the table.

"You must have been thirsty, Billy Cabott," Angelina remarked. "You drink like a horse."

"Angelina!" scolded her father. "Remember your manners, child. These are our guests."

I wearily turned my head to see Señor Cruz coming toward me holding a wine bottle and five long-stemmed crystal glasses.

Setting the glasses and bottle down on the table, Señor Cruz said, "Please excuse my daughter. She forgets her manners. I fear she has lived too many years out here on the rancho. Perhaps I should send her to charm school."

A tinny male voice came from the direction of the kitchen and reverberated across the tile floor. "Charm school no take her! No money enough to take her."

I looked up to see what appeared to be a stoop-shouldered peon carrying a large double-handled pot, but when I looked closer I saw that his eyes were slanted.

Angelina sat down on my right. "Kim Lee is right, Father. Besides, I would never go."

Taking a seat to the left of Angelina, Señor Cruz said, "Gentlemen, this is our cook, Kim Lee. He is Chinese but cooks the best Spanish food I have ever tasted. And his stew is also excellent."

Kim Lee set the pot in the center of the table and then took a ladle from his hip pocket and handed it to me. "I cook better

Chinee," he grumbled taking the lid off the stew, "but Angelina no like!"

With me awkwardly holding the ladle by its handle, Kim Lee muttered to himself and then ambled back toward the kitchen.

Even though I was staring straight ahead, I could see Angelina slowly leaning toward me. She paused and then said, "Are you going to lead a band, Billy Cabott, or dish out the stew?"

Deek hung his head. "Oh, Lordy."

"Never mind," Angelina said, taking the ladle from my hand. "You're the guest."

Monte was the first to respond. He held out his bowl as Angelina filled it. "Thank you, miss."

"You are quite welcome," Angelina said, pleasantly, and then filled Deek's bowl.

She filled her father's bowl next and then it was my turn. I nudged my bowl a few inches in her direction and to my relief she filled it and said nothing more to me for several minutes.

I watched Monte for a clue what to do next but both he and Deek sat motionless. I glanced past Angelina to Señor Cruz and then saw him and Angelina bow their heads and make the sign of the cross. After that Monte and Deek picked up their spoons and started to eat.

Following their lead, I began as well. The stew was hot and delicious. The instant I tasted it I realized just how hungry I was and, for a moment, forgot who was sitting next to me.

We ate in silence for a brief moment and then Angelina stopped suddenly. She looked from Monte to Deek and then to me. She filled her spoon but then put her spoon back into her bowl. She again looked the three of us over.

Pointing to Monte she said, "You're a soldier."

Pointing next to Deek she said, "And you're a cowboy."

And then she pointed to me, "And you look like a salesman."

Angelina thought for a moment. "How is it that a soldier, a

cowboy, and a salesman came riding in from Tucson with Ahay-aca?"

Señor Cruz cleared his throat, "Angelina, you know it is impolite to ask such questions, especially at the table."

Angelina flushed. "I was just curious."

"I found Ahayaca three days ago," offered Monte. "He was in a bad way. The next day Deek happened along. With Deek's help we got him to the Yaqui village. I met up with Billy in the Yaqui village this morning and then we all rode here. And I'm not a soldier. I was mustered out of the army a week ago."

"So, you just met Deek two days ago?" asked Angelina.

"Four. I met him the first time in Rodeo, over near the New Mexico border."

Angelina waited for Monte to say more. But she didn't know Monte Segundo. She soon grew impatient.

"So is Billy Cabott a friend of Deek's or a friend of yours?"

Monte didn't hesitate. In fact, I think he had already anticipated the question.

"Billy and I rode together hunting renegade Apaches down in Mexico."

At that moment, having been paid the highest compliment imaginable, my heart soared. I felt a surge of confidence and my insecurities vanished. Inwardly, I was howling like a wolf. It no longer mattered that I was a Weston from New York City or that I wore an expensive suit and ridiculous hat.

As Billy Cabott, I had ridden through the heart of the Mexican Revolution with Monte Segundo and for the first time, I knew that I had earned his respect. I was now one of the few, a westerner tried and true.

Angelina glared at me in stunned disbelief. I raised my eyebrows and flashed her an I-told-you-so smile.

Deek almost choked on what he was eating. He swallowed hard. "I'll be damned."

"*You* . . . hunted Apaches?" scowled Angelina.

"Well, yes," I said, with only the slightest hint of sarcasm, "but I wore a different hat."

For a moment, Angelina was speechless. Finally, a bewildered "humpf" passed between her lips.

I began to eat my stew and then so did Angelina.

"What kind of Indian is this Ahayaca anyhow?" Deek asked. "I heard him talking while he was asleep and I didn't recognize none of the words. It wasn't Apache or Papago. I know that much for a fact."

Señor Cruz shrugged. "No one knows. A small tribe, no doubt. All anyone knows is that they are peaceful and hardworking farmers. Like many of the Yaquis, they still hunt with bows and arrows. I don't believe there is a single firearm in their entire village.

"In some ways they are like the Mormon *colonias* in Mexico. Like the Mormons, Ahayaca's people have their own religion and they keep to themselves. Except when they come here to work, of course."

"How far away is the village?" Deek asked. "Ahayaca took off like it was close by."

"Only five or six miles," answered Angelina, recovering from her recent shock. "But the men that come here to work, come on foot. They run."

Feeling vastly more at ease, I glanced at Angelina and asked, "What do you mean they run?"

"Like the Tarahumara Indians. Have you heard of them?"

"Yes," I answered, "they are the Indians that live up in the Sierra Madres, the ones that can run well over one hundred miles in a single day."

"That must be how Ahayaca escaped," Deek said. "Bein' able to run like that would give him an edge."

"Escaped?" questioned Señor Cruz. "What do you mean, 'escaped'?"

"He'll have to tell you about it, himself," Monte said, indicating that Deek and I should hold our tongues.

"Yes, of course," agreed Señor Cruz and then politely changed the subject. "Are you gentlemen able to stay with us for a while? We get few visitors being so far from Tucson. We would very much enjoy your company."

Monte looked at Angelina and then at me. "I finished what I set out to do. I'm in no hurry to leave."

I felt a fluttering in my stomach. "Well, I mainly came to Tucson to find Monte."

Deek chimed in, "I just quit my job, so I'm in."

"What job was that?" asked Angelina.

Deek sheepishly answered, "Workin' cows on a ranch north of Rodeo. I didn't like the foreman so took off to give Monte a hand."

"We could use some help here on the ranch," admitted Angelina. "Most of our *vaqueros* have disappeared without saying a word. Others have outright quit."

"How come?" Deek asked.

"Rustlers," sighed Señor Cruz. "We have had cattle stolen. The *vaqueros* were afraid, I think. Some claimed they were going to join the revolution in Mexico, but I do not believe it."

"How bad is the rustlin'?"

Señor Cruz sighed. "Bad enough that when the banks heard of it, they would not loan me money to replace what I had lost. Even though I explained that I desperately needed more cows for my bulls, they told me that I was a bad risk.

"If it had not been for a businessman in Tucson who gave me a loan, I would have been ruined already."

"Yes," agreed Angelina. "Thank God for Mr. Ortega. He is so generous."

"This is true," said Señor Cruz, "And he's also very intelligent. Someday he could be mayor of Tucson. He might even run for governor."

Monte eased his spoon into his bowl of stew. "Antonio Ortega?"

"Why, yes," beamed Angelina. "But most know him as Anthony Ortega. Do you know him?"

"I met him a couple of times. He sure seems to get around."

Angelina smiled and then said dreamily, "Oh, isn't he wonderful?"

"Gentlemen," cautioned Señor Cruz, "you will have to excuse my daughter. She is but seventeen."

Angelina stiffened. "You were much older than Mother when you got married."

"That was another time, Angelina, a different country and a different life."

Knowing how Monte felt about Ortega and feeling a twinge of irritation myself, I steered the conversation away from Anthony Ortega. "How many men do you need here on the ranch?"

"Five more," Señor Cruz said. "Maybe six to make sure the next shipment of two-year-olds gets through."

"And Ahayaca's people," I asked, "are you unable to use them as *vaqueros*?"

"Most do not ride. They work here in the gardens and care for the horses. And, as I mentioned, they are peaceful Indians. Contending with rustlers can be dangerous. I could not ask them to deal with cattle thieves."

I tried to make eye contact with Monte but he was deep in thought. And I knew Monte well enough to know he was thinking of Rosa and Anthony Ortega. So, I decided to play a hunch.

"I would be glad to help out," I said. "How about you, Deek? Do you want to work cows with me?"

139

"If they'll have me, I sure enough would."

Monte blinked. His eyes narrowed as he spoke, "If you lose the next shipment of cattle, what happens then?"

"If that should happen," groaned Señor Cruz, "I would have to borrow more money."

"In that case," said Monte as he picked up his spoon, "I'll hire on and work your cows for you, Señor Cruz, as long as you understand one thing."

"What is that, Mr. Segundo?"

"If I run into trouble, I want you to know that this pistol I'm wearing isn't for decoration."

"Mine ain't either," agreed Deek. "Like I said, I was a Ranger once and we didn't take kindly to rustlin'."

Señor Cruz glanced thoughtfully at Angelina. His eyes filled with uncertainty but then, a moment later, they suddenly hardened.

"It is understood," announced Señor Cruz, his tone grim. "Would the three of you care to start tomorrow?"

"What's the pay?" Deek asked. "Not that it matters much."

"Fifty dollars a month, payable on sale of the cattle. We feed you well and we have a very comfortable bunkhouse."

"Then, tomorrow's fine with me," Deek said.

"Fine with me," added Monte.

"I must go to Tucson tomorrow," I said. "I have a bit of business to attend to but it should only take a few hours. As soon as I am finished I will come back."

"That business wouldn't have nothin' to do with gold, would it?" Deek asked.

I resented the implication of Deek's question but then, giving him the benefit of the doubt, allowed that he did not know me well and perhaps that afforded him the right to be suspicious. However, his question did serve to remind me that there was much more going on at the Rancho de la Osa than just cattle rustling.

"Not gold but zinc," I said casually. "I represent some New York interests that want to invest in zinc mines."

"You have come to the right place," Señor Cruz said. "There are many fine mining companies in Tucson that can help you. This land is rich with minerals."

"Excellent. Then I should be able to return to the ranch in a day or two."

"Allow me," offered Señor Cruz, "to use my automobile and drive you into Tucson tomorrow. It will save you much time."

"Thank you. If it is not too much trouble."

Angelina broke in excitedly. "I want to come. Please, Father? I haven't been to town in so long. Fernando can show Mr. Segundo and Mr. Coleman the rancho."

"If it is alright with Mr. Cabott," said Señor Cruz.

Bowing to Angelina, I confessed, "It would be a pleasure, Miss Angelina."

"Very well!" affirmed Señor Cruz. Reaching for the bottle of wine he pulled the cork. "Shall we celebrate with a glass of Vega Sicilia?"

Everyone nodded except Deek. He put a hand over his crystal wine glass. "Me and John Barleycorn come to an agreement a while back. I leave him alone and he leaves me alone."

"Good for you, Mr. Coleman," said Señor Cruz as he filled our glasses. "It is a wise man who avoids that which would entrap him."

Angelina raised her glass to make a toast. "To the Rancho de la Osa and an end to the cattle rustling."

CHAPTER SIX

Rosa did not sleep well and was up before dawn. The day before, she had overheard enough of the conversation between Ortega and Garcia to worry her. Garcia was clearly a savage and she hardly recognized the Antonio Ortega she once knew. Both men were after gold and would apparently do anything to get it. Somehow, Monte had become involved and then, purely by accident, so had Billy.

Ortega told Rosa he would pick her up at daybreak and that he wanted her with him when he spoke to the Yaqui. Rosa was well aware that Ortega was using her but she also knew that by pretending to go along, she might discover what he and Garcia had planned. It was the only way she could think of to determine how much danger Monte was in.

Rosa slipped into a loose-fitting cotton blouse, one that would slide down a bare shoulder if she so desired. To guard against the cool morning air, however, she covered her shoulders and arms with a wool shawl.

She thought of Monte. How would he react when he again saw her with Ortega? And if she attempted to coax information out of the Indian, Monte would immediately know she was after the gold. What would he think of her then?

On the train out of Columbus she had only wanted to make Monte jealous, to force him to show his true feelings. But instead of fighting for her, instead of grabbing her and kissing her right in front of Antonio Ortega, Monte Segundo had abandoned her. He did not so much as lift a finger to hold on to her. That day, his actions made her angry but now, waiting in the dark for Antonio Ortega, she was uncertain. She questioned whether what she had done on the train was appropriate, even admitting to herself that her behavior might have been cruel and selfish.

Rosa was wrestling with her doubts when she heard the engine of a motorcar.

Flinging open the door of her adobe, Rosa stepped out into the murky predawn light. Without a word she walked in front of the beaming headlights and opened the passenger door.

"It's good that you were ready and waiting," said Ortega as Rosa settled onto her seat and slammed the door. "I want to be there when the Indian wakes up. We will talk with him today no matter what the gringos say."

Ortega stepped on the accelerator and the Studebaker lunged away from the adobe. Rosa wrapped the shawl tightly around her neck. "The sooner we talk to him the better," she said, feigning impatience. "I don't like wasting time."

Turning a sharp left onto a narrow dirt road, Ortega said, "I went to the Carnegie Library last night and did some reading. That kid from New York was right about the conquistadors. There *was* a Spaniard named Cortés and he did conquer the Aztecs. Mexico City used to be called Tenochtitlan and there was gold everywhere. Tons of it.

"And the kid was right about the royal fifth being stamped and set aside for the king of Spain. That gold piece the Yaqui had might very well be part of the Aztec treasure. And Garcia had another piece of stamped gold that also came from the Indian. Who knows how much this Yaqui had with him before he got sick? What we need to find out is where he got it."

"So," asked Rosa, "how are you going to get him to talk? I can only do so much."

Ortega chuckled. "Today, Rosa, you are only window dressing. A distraction for the gringos. We must appear harmless. But there are those in the village that I trade with for rifles and ammunition. Perhaps, now, they will be willing to trade information about the gold for those rifles."

"You supply the Yaquis with guns?"

The sun rose off the east and Ortega turned off his headlights. "They need them to fight the government of Mexico."

"You mean fight for the revolution?"

"No, Rosa. They only fight for their land. It is a hopeless dream but some still fight. But not long ago the Americans made an agreement with Mexico. They refused to sell arms and bullets to the Yaqui. So, I trade with them for what they need."

"What do the Yaquis have that they could trade for rifles and ammunition?"

Ortega looked at Rosa and grinned. "That is a secret, dear Rosa. One I may reveal to you when you are . . . more attentive to me.

"But I will tell you that someday soon I will not live above the store. Instead, I will own a large rancho, one that borders Mexico. Then I will have my own private trade route into Mexico. I can smuggle whatever I want across the border and all of it right under the noses of the gringos. I can make big profits off of cattle, guns, gold, silver, liquor, you name it. My mercantile, you see, allows me to deal in all sorts of merchandise with no questions asked. Someday, I will be a *haciendado* and in control of an entire region of borderland."

"Then why do you go after this Yaqui's gold? Why not be satisfied with your plans to own your big rancho?"

Catching sight of the Yaqui village, Ortega began to slow, allowing time for the dust to settle. "Because I have even bigger plans."

"Bigger? How much bigger?"

"Like becoming the *jefe político* of southern Arizona."

Rosa scoffed. "There are no *jefe políticos* north of the border."

"Not yet. And that is why I will succeed. I will be the first to bring Mexican politics to the United States. All I need is enough money. Then I will have the power to do whatever I want."

Ortega pulled into the village with the brilliant rays of the rising sun casting long black shadows beyond every hut. Only a few Indians were up and about when the Studebaker stopped in front of the meeting house.

Not waiting for Rosa, Ortega hurried to the door. He glanced back at Rosa and then knocked impatiently. "It is Anthony Ortega. How is the patient this morning?"

Rosa came up beside Ortega. She felt uneasy about loosening her shawl, but knowing it was expected, she did it anyway. There was no answer from inside the meeting house. Ortega knocked again and raised his voice.

"Good morning, Ahayaca. We are here to see you. We have some money for you, money from Dr. Helbrand."

"They are gone," said a distant voice.

Ortega and Rosa turned but the blinding sun was directly behind the speaker. All they could make out was the bent form of a man.

"What do you mean 'gone'?" asked Ortega. "Do you know who I am? Do you know what I do for the Yaquis?"

"I know you," answered the Yaqui. "That is why I tell you. They are all gone. We gave them horses and they rode away to the south. They rode yesterday before the sun was high."

"Do you know where they were going?"

"No. But I will tell you one thing. He is not one of us. He is not Yaqui."

Ortega was stunned. "Not a Yaqui?"

"No."

"What is he then?"

"No one knows," said the Yaqui and then ambled off past the huts and out into the desert.

Now able to see the Indian was an old man, Ortega said, "That is one of the head men. I have seen him many times. He is a *pacifico*."

"What do we do now?" Rosa asked, hoping that now Ortega would give up his quest for the gold.

Ortega started for the Studebaker. "If they went south on four horses it should not be hard to circle the village and pick up the tracks. I'll tell Garcia. If I cannot find Garcia when we get back to town, I will trail them myself."

With Monte and Deek mounted on fresh horses and Fernando leading the way, the trio left the ranch bunkhouse before dawn to take a tour of the rangeland. The open desert where they had been riding for the last hour was strewn with rocks and cluttered with thorny mesquite, cat's claw, and white thorn, yet it also held a surprising amount of grass.

As the warming rays of the sunrise crested the eastern mountain range, Fernando pointed down. "It takes one hundred acres of this grass to feed one steer. That is why the ranchos in Arizona are so big. But the grass is good grass. The rains will come soon and then the grass will grow green again."

Unimpressed, Deek said, "Hard to believe it ever rains here."

"When the rain does come," Fernando said, "you will think the sky is falling. The desert will flood with water. Every low place will become a river. You will soon see."

Monte had been riding behind Fernando since they left the hacienda but after dropping into a shallow arroyo, he suddenly dismounted, pretending to tighten his cinch. He scanned the desert as he tugged on the latigo strap and waved for Deek to pass him by. When Deek was well out in front, Monte took a few steps out of the wash. Going to one knee he quickly examined a set of tracks that Fernando had ridden past without noticing. After one more look out into the desert, he remounted.

With Monte in the rear, Fernando continued riding in a wide arc, lazily pointing out landmarks as he rode. Since leaving the hacienda, the *vaquero* had seldom even bothered to check if Monte and Deek were still behind him. As the sun began to rise, however, Monte saw the Mexican suddenly sit up in his saddle. He then reined his horse sharply to the north.

When Monte got to where Fernando had altered course, he held up and studied the ground below him. A moment later he caught up to Deek.

Casually riding alongside, Monte asked, "Have you noticed anything peculiar about our *vaquero*?"

"You mean, like him takin' us away from them horse tracks back yonder?"

Nodding, Monte spoke softly. "That was the second time he did that. The first set he missed, I thought maybe he just wasn't paying attention. But now I know better. Both times there was an unshod horse pushing a cow."

Keeping an eye on Fernando, Deek said, "Them horses the Yaquis loaned us yesterday was all unshod."

"Yeah," agreed Monte. "I thought of that. But I would imagine lots of Mexicans ride horses without shoes, too."

"They do," Deek said. "And the border's just a hoot 'n' a holler to the south of us. Whoever's doin' the rustlin' wouldn't have far to go. It wouldn't take much to ride over, steal 'em, and then run 'em back to Mexico and sell 'em."

"Right now," Monte said, "I'm wondering what Fernando is up to. He saw those tracks. They weren't fresh but they weren't all that old either. We should have followed them."

"I say we ask 'im."

"I was thinking the same thing," Monte said. "First though, tell me what you know about the Yaquis."

Deek huffed in disgust. "Hell, they ain't much different than any other Indian, only the Yaquis is twenty years behind the times. They're wild yet. And I don't care what anybody says, there ain't no way to tell a tame one from a wild one. Just like twenty years ago there weren't no way to tell the good Apaches from the bad ones.

"These Arizona Yaquis started showin' up about ten years ago, the same time that I was a Ranger. At first folks around here felt sorry for 'em. But then they started gettin' robbed and murdered by them same Yaquis and things turned around.

"Back then Teddy Roosevelt was president and he ordered the U.S. marshal of Arizona to crack down on selling the Yaquis any guns or ammunition. And then the territorial governor did one better and come out and made it illegal to sell, give, barter, or rent any guns to *any* Indian *anywhere*.

"He done that 'cause we couldn't tell an Opata or Pima from a Yaqui. We even started catchin' Yaquis and then deportin' 'em back to Mexico like their President Díaz wanted. Then the revolution come about. Now, nobody's in control of nothin' down there anymore. And the Yaquis is still fightin' the Mexicans. But they always need more guns and ammunition. They come across the border to steal anything they can get their hands on so they can trade for guns."

Monte rode for a while thinking about what Deek had said. Most of it was likely true enough but if it were the Indians rustling the cattle, why had Fernando turned away from the tracks? Was he afraid of the Yaquis or was he trying to protect them?

"Have the Yaquis ever been known to torture a man?"

Deek sneered. "Damn straight! Not as much as the Apaches, though. Onliest Indians that come close to them Apaches was the Comanche."

"Do you think Fernando turned off because he's afraid of the Yaquis?"

Staring ahead at Fernando, Deek said, "Them tracks was days old. I'm thinking they might've led to a camp or a holdin' pen maybe. I seen that sort of thing many a time. Seems to me he might be coverin' up for the rustlers, makin' sure we don't find their holdin' pens."

"I think," Monte said, "it's time to get some answers."

"I'm game," Deek said. "Let's ease up on 'im. I don't favor a chase across this desert."

Monte and Deek picked up their pace but did not break into a trot. In a few minutes they rode up on opposite sides of Fernando.

"Getting hot," Deek said, taking off his hat and wiping his face with the back of his sleeve. "Are there any water holes out here?"

Fernando nodded. "There are some tanks but not close. The water is good, though."

"Say, Fernando," Monte said easily, "back there by those tracks, why did you turn away? Shouldn't we have followed after them to see where they went?"

Fernando froze in his saddle; his eyes did not blink.

"Funny thing," added Deek, "you actin' like you didn't even see that an unshod horse was pushin' a cow off somewheres. That seems a might peculiar, don't it?"

"I did not see any tracks," said Fernando. "What tracks?"

Deek reached over and pulled Fernando's rifle from its scabbard. "How about we go back and show you?"

Fernando glared at his rifle now in the hands of Deek with the barrel pointing at his gut. "Sure, *amigos,* I think maybe I was asleep and then my horse, it took a wrong step. That must be what happened."

"That could be, Fernando," Monte said, his tone friendly,

"but we don't know you from Adam and we hired on to catch rustlers. You understand that, don't you?"

Fernando tried to relax. He forced an unconvincing smile. "*No problema, amigos.* I understand. We just misunderstand each other."

Deek pointed at Fernando with the rifle barrel. "You lead off, *amigo.* Follow our tracks back up the trail. We'll tell you when to stop."

Spurring his horse, Fernando took off at a trot with Deek and Monte close behind. In less than a minute Deek bellowed, "That's far enough."

All three horses came to a dead stop. Monte dismounted only a few feet from where Fernando had ridden only minutes before. Letting his reins fall, Monte followed the unshod horse tracks uphill to a ridge and then disappeared over the far side. A few minutes later he returned.

Picking up his reins, Monte glared up at Fernando. "Three riders held the cows in a little box canyon just over that ridge. Then they headed due south pushing the cows."

"Damned Yaquis!" blurted Deek.

Monte's eyes were still locked on Fernando. "They weren't all Yaquis. Some of them wore boots, boots with big pointed spurs."

Deek looked down at Fernando's boots and then his spiked rowels. "You mean like them there?"

"Yeah. Mexican spurs just like Fernando's."

Fernando began to shake his head. "I swear I did not see those tracks. I swear on my mother's grave."

The irony of Fernando's words swirled in Monte's mind. Only days had passed since he knelt beside his parents' graves. Even though he could not tell which was his mother's and which was his father's, the ground where they lay was hallowed, sacred beyond words. And here was a man desecrating his mother's grave with a filthy lie.

Monte reached for his pistol. His wanted to put a bullet through Fernando's heart, to kill him for blaspheming the memory of his mother.

Fernando's hands flew up. "No, señor, no! I will talk."

Monte checked his impulse to kill but his eyes still blazed with fury. "Start talking!"

"The rustlers are *bronco* Yaquis. I am paid to look the other way, not to follow after the cattle. That is all I know."

"Who pays you?" demanded Deek.

"I do not know, only that one of the rustlers gives me money."

"What happened to the other *vaqueros*," Monte asked, "the ones that used to work for the rancho?"

"One refused the money. Later, we found what was left of him tied on top of an anthill. Then the others took the money. But afterwards they ran away. The Yaquis told me to stay or they would find me and kill me. I was to tell Señor Cruz that the other *vaqueros* had gone off to join the revolution. And I was told to watch Señor Cruz and tell the Yaquis what things he did."

Deek thought for a moment. "Where are the cattle?"

Fernando shrugged. "I do not know. They take cows and calves only. No bulls. They drive them across the border and sell them, I think. The inspectors at Sasabe are also paid to look away. This much I know."

Monte took his hand away from his pistol. "Did you know that if Señor Cruz loses any more cattle he'll go broke?"

Clearly surprised, Fernando exclaimed, "No, señor! This, no one told me. I thought he was rich, that losing a few cows would not matter so much."

"What do we do now?" asked Deek. "It wouldn't be right to hang 'im . . . or would it?"

"What kind of rifle are you holding?" Monte asked.

Deek looked at the printing on the barrel of Fernando's rifle. "Winchester thirty-thirty smokeless."

"Fernando, how many rounds do you have?" Monte asked.

"Only what is in the rifle. Five cartridges."

Monte put out his hand and Deek handed him the Winchester. Monte levered the breech open just enough to see that a cartridge was in the chamber.

"You take Fernando and have him show you every nook and cranny of this country. I'm going to follow the rustlers' tracks and see where they lead. I'll meet you back at the hacienda, hopefully around sundown.

"Don't let him out of your sight. If he steps out of line, kill him and leave him for the coyotes and buzzards. I'd rather the Cruzes believe he ran off than for them to find out he was a traitor."

Deek sneered, "It'd be my pleasure. Just like old times."

"Fernando," said Monte.

"Sí, señor."

"You're working for us now. You don't say a word about what happened out here today. You just tell anybody that asks that you showed us the rancho, that's all. Do you understand?"

"Yes," said Fernando. He hung his head. "I am ashamed for what I have done."

"You should be," Monte said, as he stepped into his saddle. "But know this. If you ever swear on your mother's grave again, you better pray to God I don't hear it. If I do, I'll shoot you where you stand."

Kicking his horse into a gallop, Monte rode back up and over the ridge. He slowed when he reached the box canyon where the rustlers had held the cattle. From there, a half-dozen cows and three unshod horses had headed south. With a trail deep enough for a blind man to follow, Monte followed at a fast walk.

Near noon, the tracks passed near a single concrete marker and Monte rode over to investigate. The cement post was six feet tall and resembled a four-sided beam with a pointed top. Painted on the north side of the marker, and partially blocked by an ocotillo cactus, was "United States." On the south side, "Mexico" had nearly been obliterated by the elements.

Monte stood in his stirrups looking as far as he could to the east and to the west, but no other markers were to be seen.

"Hell of a border," grumbled Monte and then, aware that he was entering Mexico, resumed his tracking.

Late in the afternoon, his horse was startled by the sudden rush of heavy wings as a vulture flew up from behind a shelf of broken rocks. The horse had spun halfway around before Monte could check him with the reins. Then a second and third vulture flapped up from the rocks, each gaining altitude until they spread their wings and began to float in the heated air.

The horse, ready to bolt at any second, faced the rocks. With its ears forward, it blew nervously and then blew again.

"Easy now," Monte said, rubbing the horse's neck. "Easy."

Monte studied the desert in every direction and continued to calm the horse. The wind shifted slightly, carrying with it the unmistakable stench of death.

Nudging the horse, Monte eased around the rocks and was relieved to see nothing more than a dead cow. He was about to ride away when he noticed an oddly shaped patch of hide on the flank of the carcass was missing.

Dismounting, Monte went to take a closer look. When he did, it was easy to see that the cow had been killed by a large cat. But it was also clear that the missing patch of hide had not been ripped away by any animal. It had been cleanly cut off with a knife.

Searching the ground around the cow, Monte found a partial boot track. He was looking for another when he pulled aside a palo verde branch and discovered, not another boot print, but the largest cat track he had ever seen.

Feeling the hairs on the back of his neck stand on end, Monte palmed his pistol and then warily searched for more sign. In minutes he was able to piece together what had happened.

Perhaps a week before, a huge mountain lion had killed a steer and then partially eaten it. Later, someone riding an unshod horse had come along, discovered the dead animal, and then cut the brand off its flank. Reading that from the sign was simple enough.

What puzzled Monte was why anyone, especially a rustler, would cut the brand off of a dead range cow, a cow that most likely belonged to the Rancho de la Osa.

Relieved to leave the cat tracks behind, Monte remounted and then followed the southbound tracks of the rustled cattle for another hour. On a ridgeline he caught a slight breeze and paused to cool off. He was wiping sweat from his eyes when, a half mile down a slow descent, he spotted a partial clearing. It was surrounded by a thicket of spindly mesquite trees, trees that were full of vultures and ravens.

From where Monte sat he could see for miles in every direction. The brush was heavy enough to hide a small army so he searched for any disturbance of dust that might be rising in the heated air. When he was satisfied that no one was near, he worked his way down the ridge. As he neared the clearing the smell of rotting flesh was enough to make him choke.

Dismounting fifty paces from the birds, he crouched and listened for several minutes but all he heard was the raspy squawking of the ravens. Leading his horse upwind, he studied the ground around him and saw more unshod horse tracks.

When he rounded a big mesquite he expected to see piles of guts from butchered cattle but what he saw sickened him.

A dozen or more bloated cattle lay sprawled in the sand.

Each one had been shot in the head. Some were cows and some steers but there were no calves. None of the cattle had been butchered but every brand had been cut off, just as was done on the lone steer the cat had killed.

Circling the carnage, Monte discovered more sign, enough to know that the men who had killed the cattle and taken the brands had continued riding deeper into Mexico. The calves, none of which likely had a brand, had been loaded onto trucks and driven away.

With nothing more to be gained from following the tracks of the rustlers, Monte rode back to the boundary marker and then turned due east. Meandering through the cactus and mesquite, he attempted to stay as close to the border as he could but with boundary markers set miles apart it was anyone's guess where the line actually was.

Several times he cut old trails of what had to be Cruz cattle being driven south but the herds were always small, never more than ten. He concluded that the theft of cattle was intentionally being carried out in small increments, likely a strategy designed to arouse no attention. But it appeared that only the calves had been taken to sell or to eat. And yet, with the revolution going on in Mexico, brands on stolen cattle would be meaningless. So why would anyone kill cattle that could easily be sold to hungry armies with no questions asked? Why were Cruz's cattle worth more dead than alive?

An hour before sundown, Monte rode through the front gate of the hacienda. He knew Deek would be waiting to find out about the rustlers but Deek was a talker. Something about the missing brands was very unsettling and Monte's gut told him it was best to play his cards close to his chest. So, for the time being, he decided to keep what he knew about the dead cattle to himself.

Directly in front of the hacienda, on a carpet of green grass, he saw a small table had been set up. Angelina, Billy, and Señor Cruz sat around it looking his way. At the feet of Angelina, a small boy, dressed in white cotton pants and shirt, sat with his legs crossed.

Monte rode up to the hitch rails, dismounted, and tied off his horse. He looked again at the table. All eyes were on him but no one said a word.

"Is there something wrong?" Monte asked. "Where's Deek?"

Señor Cruz pointed to another adobe. "He is in the bunkhouse with Fernando. They have been together the whole day. Come, have some tea with us."

Seeing no empty chair, Monte approached the table. Angelina took a glass, filled it, and handed it to Monte. She then nodded, indicating the boy. "This is Pedro. He has a message for you."

Monte looked at me for some sort of explanation. I merely shrugged.

The boy, no more than seven or eight years old, sprang to his feet.

"I have come from the village of Ahayaca. This night we wish to honor you. I am to invite you to come. You are to bring one trusted friend and one only. There will be a feast and a celebration for you."

Monte stared down at the boy and then took a long drink of tea. He looked at me and raised an eyebrow. "I guess that means you're invited too, Billy."

Bursting with pride, I grinned. "It would be an honor."

"I don't get it," Angelina protested. "No one is *ever* invited to their village. No one. I've known Ahayaca my whole life and he never once invited me."

"This is true, Señor Segundo," agreed Cruz. "This is quite remarkable."

Pedro spoke with the tone of a military officer. "Come, we go now."

"Where's your horse?" Monte asked.

"I run," Pedro said. "I need no horse."

Monte glanced down at the boy's feet. He was barefooted.

"I'll get a horse," I said and then hurried off to the corrals.

Instead of taking my empty seat, Monte continued to stand. "I saw a cat kill today. It got one of your steers, Señor Cruz. I've never seen puma tracks that big."

"No puma," said Pedro. *"Jaguar."*

"Jaguar?" Monte repeated.

"Jaguar," Angelina said, pronouncing the J. "It's like a leopard. There are several in these mountains."

"The *jaguar* is lord over the puma," Pedro said. *"Jaguar* means 'one who kills in one leap.' *Jaguars* are the greatest warriors. Their jaws crush even the strongest of bones."

Monte finished his tea and set the glass down. "Did you run here all by yourself?"

"Yes."

"And you're not worried the . . . *jaguar* . . . will eat you?"

"I am to be a warrior," bragged Pedro. "I fear nothing. Soon, I will be like the *jaguar!*"

"How is it that you have been invited to the village?" asked Angelina. "What did you do? What did you do for Ahayaca that was so great?"

"Didn't the boy tell you?"

"No. I asked him but he refused to answer me."

"Did you ask Billy?"

Angelina frowned. "He's not much better than Pedro. Billy said I would have to ask you."

"Well, he was wrong about that."

"What do you mean?"

"I mean, you'll have to ask Ahayaca."

Angelina let out an exasperated groan. "So much modesty!"

Changing the subject, Monte asked, "How was the trip to Tucson?"

"We accomplished much," said Señor Cruz. "Mr. Cabott spoke with some mining companies and then sent a telegram to his father telling him of the progress. Angelina did some shopping as did Mr. Cabott. The three of us had a fine lunch together and a pleasant drive back to the ranch.

"We had only just arrived when Pedro came in. That was hardly a half hour ago."

With the rustling operation no longer dominating his thoughts, Monte asked, "Did you run into Anthony Ortega while you were in town?"

Still irritated, Angelina snipped, "I went by his mercantile. I was going to go in but I saw him taking to another woman, talking and laughing."

"Was she a Mexican?" asked Monte.

Angelina flushed. "Yes. And she was beautiful."

Monte clenched his jaws and rotated his head to work the stiffness out of his neck. "He does get around."

Before I went to the corral to saddle a horse, I ducked inside the bunkhouse. While I was in Tucson I had purchased some items and I was anxious to put them to use. Changing out of my suit I slipped into my new clothes, a cotton shirt, denim pants, and hunting boots that laced up to the knee. To top off my outfit and bolster my new image, I took my leather shoulder holster and thirty-eight Smith and Wesson from my suitcase and slid my shoulders through the straps. I then covered my hideout gun with a wool vest and donned my brand-new, tan-colored broad-brimmed hat.

Feeling completely at home in my rugged attire, I selected a horse from the corral, saddled it, and then I rode back up to the hacienda. I was confident that I looked more like a westerner but then, for the first time, I realized that I actually *felt* like one. It was as if I had become another person. I truly was Billy Cabott.

Hearing me ride up, Monte mounted his horse without giving me so much as a second glance. Angelina, on the other hand, gave me an appraising head-to-toe once-over.

"Billy Cabott," she said, coming out of her chair, "You're like Theodore Roosevelt without the glasses."

I didn't know if I had been complimented or insulted but I was feeling too good to care. "I'll mention that to Teddy the next time Father has him over for supper."

Angelina huffed. "Oh, I am sure you will. And next week I'm having tea with the Queen of England."

I flashed Angelina a confident smile. "Miss Angelina, which is more difficult to believe, that I hunted Apaches in Mexico or that I know Theodore Roosevelt?"

Angelina wrinkled her nose, frowned, and then shook her head. "Apaches, maybe. But Teddy Roosevelt . . . that's too far-fetched."

Pedro sprang to his feet and then started trotting toward a dirt road just north of the hacienda. Monte let him gain some distance and then followed after him. I, however, took a moment to take one last look at Angelina. With a cavalier smile on my lips, and all the showmanship I could muster, I tipped my hat and spurred my trusty steed into a gallop.

Just beyond the hacienda, however, I caught up with Monte and slowed to a walk.

We had ridden less than a minute when we discovered, that to keep pace with the little Indian, we had to put our horses into a slow trot.

It was then, I opened up my vest to reveal my pistol. "What do you think?" I asked.

Monte glanced over at me, then his eyes dropped to my

shoulder rig. "What caliber is it?"

"A thirty-eight Smith and Wesson. It's a bit small but it fits my hand."

"That's plenty," said Monte. "I'm glad you're armed. Especially out here."

Pleased that Monte approved, I let go of my vest.

"Do you want some advice?" Monte asked.

"Sure."

"If you ever have to use that pistol, I mean if you *have* to use it, don't think about it. Don't think about it before or after. Just do it. Afterwards, shut the door on it and move on."

I mulled over Monte's words for a moment, wondering if I could truly follow his advice. Could I actually shoot a man? Would I, if I *had* to, or would I hesitate? Would I second-guess myself or do what needed to be done?

"Is it hard?" I asked. "Is it hard to shoot a man?"

Monte took a deep breath and let it out slowly. "It's easy. Way too easy. Putting it behind you is the tricky part. But it gets easier as you go along."

We rode on in silence for a few minutes. I was imagining all of the ways I might react in a deadly situation when I realized I was doing the opposite of what Monte advised. I was thinking too much, analyzing too much. I finally decided that if the situation arose, I would know it then and there. With no reason to engage in a game of endless what-ifs, I put the matter out of my mind.

I looked out at Pedro. Leaning toward Monte, I asked in a soft voice, "Do you think he can keep this up for five miles?"

"I bet he can," answered Monte. "Look how he's running mostly on his toes. I've never seen anybody run that way. He's not even straining. If we were to keep up this clip we'd cover eight miles in one hour.

"I'll bet we'll reach the village before the sun sets. Wait and see."

Sure enough, Pedro kept up his amazing pace for the next two miles. Then, when the road veered sharply to the west, he slowed but only long enough to make sure we were behind him. After a quick glance over his shoulder, he turned off the road onto a well-worn path, a trail so narrow that Monte and I had to ride single file.

Maintaining a northerly direction, we followed Pedro as he snaked his way around rocky bluffs, between patches of cactus, and across sandy arroyos. But at no point along the way did I see a single stone on the path. Pedro was running on nothing but sand.

Finally, just as the sun was setting, we dropped into a deep arroyo. We rode across it and when we bounded up the opposite bank we came out onto a flat plain, a plain that was checkered with fields planted in corn, beans, squash, tomatoes, peppers, and several other crops I did not recognize.

Astonished by what we saw, Monte and I drew up. When we did Pedro stopped. He was breathing easily.

"We farm here," Pedro said. "The rains will come soon and then we will have water for the next year's crops."

I looked closer. I saw ditches everywhere. "They use irrigation!"

Monte looked back at the sunset and then again at the fields. "I would say there are close to thirty acres out there."

Pedro waved. "Come. We go now. The village waits for us."

"Lead the way," Monte said, and we were off again riding at the same pace we had kept up for the last five miles.

Following a path through the middle of the fields we approached a range of low-lying hills that rose abruptly out of the desert. The peaks of the hills were no more than three-hundred-feet high but each terminated in a relatively sharp point that was covered in cream-colored boulders. Beneath those boulders, every hillside was blanketed in a dark green thicket of what appeared to be palo verde and mesquite trees.

In seconds, an opening between the hills came into view, a deep and narrow pass that would have been difficult to see even in broad daylight. Near the entrance, two flaming torches burned a halo of light into the black shadows. We rode directly toward those flames until we were within a stone's throw of the torches. Then Pedro slowed to a walk.

In a low tone, I asked Monte, "Did you notice how green these hills are?"

"I did. I think they're covered in thorny mesquite. But they'd have to have been planted. Trees out here wouldn't grow natural like that. Not that close together."

Pedro climbed up on a rock face at the entrance of the pass and took one of the torches. Climbing down, he led us into the darkness. Monte rode in the lead and I followed close behind. The mouth of the pass was fairly wide and V-shaped but it soon turned into two perfectly smooth walls of solid rock that took us in an erratic, weaving course. At any point along the way I could have stretched out my hands and touched both walls.

About the time I was beginning to feel claustrophobic, we rode into a more open space. And what Monte and I saw on the other side of the pass astonished us.

Dozens upon dozens of people lined both sides of a wide flagstone street, a street that stretched out in front of us for several hundred feet. Standing in attentive silence, every man and woman held a burning torch in their right hand. Interspersed among the adults, the older children held baskets that were decorated with various patterns of red and green.

Behind the people, on both sides of the street, a continuous wall of stone buildings rose two and three stories high up both sides of a narrow canyon. Flowing white cotton awnings covered every door and window while the awnings themselves were adorned with hanging baskets of multicolored flowers.

At the far end of the street, the buildings came to an end but the street continued on until it reached a large circular plaza. In the center of the plaza was an elevated stone platform. The four walls of the platform were slightly angled and no more than four feet high. In the center of each wall a flight of steps led up to a patio of stone on top. There, a burning torch lit each of the four corners.

Pedro stepped to his right. We sat our horses, waiting for further instructions but at the same time taking a closer look at the villagers. The children were dressed the same as Pedro but the adults wore white ponchos that had been embroidered along the edges with every color imaginable. Most of the women and some of the men had earrings. Several of the adults wore necklaces. And barely visible beyond the bottom of the ponchos of every man and woman, we could see strings of deer hooves that had been tied off just below the knee.

Suddenly, drums sounded from the darkness beyond the plaza, their ominous rhythmic beats echoing off the canyon walls and down the street.

Two Indians then stepped out of the crowd and onto the street. One said in perfect English, "Please, gentlemen, dismount and follow us."

Monte and I glanced at each other and then stepped down. As soon as our feet hit the flagstones the villagers on both sides of us stepped into the street, each side walking toward the other until both sides formed a human alleyway six feet wide.

Side by side, the two Indians started walking down the alleyway. Without a moment's hesitation, Monte and I followed after them. Immediately, the children nearest us reached into their baskets. Their clenched fists came out quickly and, with a brisk backhand, they began flinging flowers at our feet.

The adults began to step in place, their feet lifting and falling in unison as thousands of deer hooves rattled with each beat of the pounding drums.

I looked left and right. Amber flames lit up hundreds of smiling faces but not one word was uttered, not one infant cried out.

With flowers carpeting our path, the drums pounding, and the deer hooves rattling, we made our way to the plaza. It was then I noticed the top of the platform was a perfect square with sides close to thirty feet in length.

The two Indians leading us stopped in front of the stairs. One stepped aside and the other led Monte and I up onto the elevated stone floor. On our way up, we caught a glimpse of movement in the shadows. Behind the platform, another Indian came into view. Behind him, another figure emerged from the blackness and before I recognized who it was, I guessed correctly that it had to be Ahayaca.

The Indian leading Ahayaca was making his way toward the set of stairs opposite the ones we had used. He was dressed in a white linen poncho that had been embroidered with solid green all along the edges. His hair, pointing straight up, was tied on the top of his head.

As Ahayaca walked into the light, I noticed that he was barefooted and wore a green cape that tied just below his neck. When he followed the first man up the stairs, I was bewildered to see that under the cape, the only article of clothing covering Ahayaca's body was a heavily embroidered breechcloth.

The Indian in the white poncho came and stood directly across from me. Then, Ahayaca stepped onto the platform and took his place next to Monte.

At that instant, everything stopped. There was complete silence.

"Montesegundo," began Ahayaca, blending both names

together as one, "you saved my life. I wish to honor you by making you my blood brother. Do you know, Montesegundo, what it is to be a blood brother?"

"I understand the general idea of it," answered Monte. "I lived with the Kootenai Indians for quite a few years."

"That is as it should be," said Ahayaca. "Do you accept?"

Monte nodded solemnly, "I do."

The Indian wearing the white poncho turned toward the crowded street and raised both hands high over his head. He called out a single word, a tongue twisting word I could never hope to pronounce.

Erupting with exuberant cheers and whistles, the villagers abandoned the alleyway and began flooding into the plaza. As they crowded close to the platform an Indian woman walked up the steps and handed a cloth-covered bundle to the Indian across from me.

Ahayaca untied his cape and then ceremoniously handed it to me.

"Montesegundo," Ahayaca said, "Please remove your shirt."

I detected a slight hesitation in Monte but then he unbuttoned his shirt. Without being directed, as if he already understood what to do, he also handed his shirt to me.

The Indian holding the bundle removed the cloth, which was covering a simple brown gourd that had been hollowed out to make a shallow bowl. In the bottom of the gourd was small knife. It had a handle of polished jade but a glistening blade of razor-sharp flint.

Taking the knife, the Indian handed the bowl to the man who had led Monte and I up the stairs. I took a step back as the Indian holding the bowl stepped closer to Monte.

Ahayaca held out his right arm and made a fist.

The Indian with the knife touched Monte's left arm. Understanding what was intended, Monte held out his left arm and also made a fist.

The drums again began to beat but this time more rapidly than before.

The tip of the knife punctured a vein just above Monte's elbow on the inside of his arm. The blood rushed out. It flowed down his arm and then dripped off his elbow into the waiting gourd. After a long minute, the bleeding stopped.

Next, Ahayaca's vein was opened. His blood was collected in the bowl and then the gourd was held high by the Indian. After a brief but boisterous chant, the gourd was offered to Ahayaca. He took a drink of the mixed blood and then handed the gourd to Monte, who did the same.

The two Indians then turned to the villagers. The drums ceased as one Indian held up the gourd and the other the knife. They spoke two unintelligible words and then the entire village bent down on one knee, bowed their heads, and placed their left palm flat down on the flagstones.

A moment later the drums started up again but this time they seemed to thunder.

Hearing the drums, the villagers sprang to their feet cheering and whistling. Somewhere, deeper in the canyon and completely out of sight, I heard what sounded like trumpets.

Ahayaca nodded graciously. Taking Monte's shirt from me, he handed it to Monte. "We are now blood brothers. Your blood is in me and mine is in you."

"I am honored," Monte said as he put on his shirt. "Truly honored."

I handed Ahayaca his cape. "And I am honored to be here," I said sincerely. "Extremely honored to be a part of such wonderful celebration."

Ahayaca tied his cape. "We will feast now. And dance. All until the sun rises. This is to show our thanks, our thanks to El Muerte."

Monte stopped buttoning his shirt. We both stared at Ahayaca waiting for an explanation.

Ahayaca smiled. "It took many months to get from Yucatán to Arizona. I met many people on my journey and I heard many stories. Until I saw for myself, I did not believe them."

At first, I was astonished that Ahayaca had discovered that Monte was also El Muerte but then I realized how simple it was for him to figure it out. The uniform and moccasins, the physical strength, the ability to see in the dark and the indomitable courage all pointed in only one direction. Anyone who had heard of El Muerte, the legendary man-killer, and then seen Monte Segundo in action would have no trouble coming to the same conclusion.

All of us on the platform descended together, and as soon as we were clear of the last step, branches started sailing through the air and landing in the center of the raised patio. In a matter of seconds there was a pile of wood six feet high. Torches were then thrown onto the branches and the brush burst into flames, spewing swirling sparks high into the star-filled sky.

In twos and threes, the villagers approached Monte. Gently touching his arms, they repeated the same simple greeting over and over. "*Bienvenido.* Welcome. *Bienvenido,* welcome."

Logs were added to the bonfire and as the flames grew hotter the crowd backed away, eventually forming large a circle. The drumbeats softened and then slowed and the villager's exuberance mellowed.

On some signal that I never was able to figure out, the Indians began a rhythmic sidestepping type of dance. Stomping left-right, left-right, they circled in a clockwise direction as the deer hooves rattled to the beat of the drums. A half-minute later, the entire group changed directions and began circling counterclockwise.

"Come," Ahayaca said to Monte and me, "It is time to feast."

Leading us through the dancers, Ahayaca took us from house to house where we were fed meats of venison, rabbit, poultry, and wild pig. For vegetables, we were given corn soup, chili and bean soup, zucchini, squash, and pumpkin bread. Desserts consisted of various types of cobblers made from the fruit of the prickly pear and saguaro cactus.

We drank mostly what was called *atolli*, a mixture of corn, chili peppers, and lime mixed with water. We were offered an alcoholic drink, the name of which I could not master, but both Monte and I found it too bitter to consume very much of it.

The celebration and the dancing continued until daybreak. By then, Monte and I were more than ready to leave our gracious hosts. We were exhausted and had eaten so much that neither of us wanted to even think of food.

As the villagers began to break into small groups and then disperse to their homes, Ahayaca escorted us to the pass and had our horses brought to us.

The three of us stood there in the cool of the morning. A few stars could still be seen in the west but a dingy yellow glow was creeping into the eastern sky. A breeze flowed through the pass and down through the canyon of the Indian village.

Ahayaca put out his hand. As Monte took it, Ahayaca said, "You are a brother. Our people have always guarded our privacy and our traditions."

Monte shook Ahayaca's hand. "I understand. I'll say nothing about any of this."

Ahayaca shook my hand next. "And you are Montesegundo's trusted friend."

I nodded. "It has been an extraordinary experience. But as long as you guard your privacy, so shall I. You have my word."

"Now that the celebration has come to an end," Ahayaca said, his demeanor hardening, "I will tell you that my sentinels and runners have informed me that Garcia and his men followed our tracks. They are now watching the hacienda."

"Sentinels?" I asked.

Ahayaca nodded. "When I first arrived back at the village I sent out sentinels to watch the desert. I also sent runners to backtrack us. Garcia and his men have followed me for months. I was never able to lose them for long. I knew it was only a matter of time until they came here."

"Do they know you are here in the village?" Monte asked.

"No. They seem to think I stayed at the hacienda. They arrived there yesterday after sundown, after you and Billy had come here."

"Then they'll see us ride in," Monte said. "They might get curious and then circle and find our tracks. That would lead them here."

Strangely, Ahayaca seemed pleased. "I am home now. I am no longer in danger. It is the two of you who must be careful."

"We'll do that," Monte said as we both stepped into our saddles.

"One thing," Ahayaca said, "If El Muerte, my brother, goes out in the desert tonight, all I ask is to have Garcia returned here to me . . . alive."

Monte's eyes flickered with a devilish light. "If it's possible, I'll have him here tomorrow morning."

With that chilling declaration, we turned our horses and rode back through the narrow pass. Alone with our own thoughts, we followed the road through the empty fields in total silence and did not speak until we were back on the desert trail.

"I still can't believe what happened last night," I offered. "It all seems like a dream,"

"That about sums it up," agreed Monte. "But we can't tell a soul what we saw."

"I know. But, no doubt, we're going to be asked about it. They won't be happy when we don't answer their questions."

"That Angelina sure won't," Monte said. "She's a handful."

I thought for a moment. "I kind of like her."

"Are you sure?"

I looked to my left. The horizon was now a blazing lemon-yellow. "Well, it doesn't matter anyway," I confessed, and then without thinking, I added, "It appears that she's infatuated with Anthony Ortega."

Monte huffed. "Yeah. He sure gets around."

"Speaking of that," I said. "What about Garcia?"

Nodding as if to himself, Monte said, "There's only one way to stop a man like that. I know it and so does Ahayaca."

Monte thought for a moment and then said, "But there's another problem."

"What's that?"

"What would you say, if I told you that yesterday I found of bunch of dead cows just over the border? And they'd been shot and left to rot."

I shrugged and said the first thing that came to mind. "I'd say they were sick cows and someone had to destroy them."

"Alright," continued Monte, "now let me add one more thing. Every single brand had been cut off of the cows."

Thinking along the same vein as I had before, I said, "I would say that the rancher that owned those cows didn't want anyone to know he had diseased cows. So he removed the brand."

Monte thought for a moment. "I hadn't thought of that. What you say makes sense."

"Did you find cows like that?"

"Over a dozen of them. And they'd been driven from Cruz's land over the border. And Fernando claims rustlers are doing the work."

I squirmed uncomfortably. My saddle creaked. "You don't think Señor Cruz is trying to cover up something? Do you? Something like anthrax?"

Monte sighed. "Billy, ever since that court-martial trial, I don't know what to think about anything anymore. It seems like everything around me is going to hell in a handbasket."

"What do we do, now?" I asked.

"I say, we keep our mouth shut about those cows. I've got a bad feeling about all of this. None of it's adding up. None of it."

CHAPTER SEVEN

For the second night in a row, Rosa had slept poorly. Worrying about Monte had kept her awake most of the night. She rose before dawn with the conviction that the only way she could protect Monte was to find out what Ortega and Garcia had planned. And to do that, Rosa knew she had to play along with Ortega and win his absolute trust. If that did not work, she was prepared to do whatever was necessary, regardless of the cost.

Anticipating another early visit by Ortega, Rosa prepared by unbraiding her hair, brushing it straight, and tying it back with a single red ribbon. Then, shrewdly, she put on an American dress, the one she had selected for herself while at the mercantile. It was a fashionable mid-sleeved afternoon dress, blue in color with a tight-fitting waistband. However, with no shoes to wear, she slipped her feet into the only pair of sandals she owned.

Ortega had been awakened before dawn by one of Garcia's men pounding on his door. He was then given the urgent message that Ahayaca had been located. Wiping the sleep from his eyes, he selected one of his best suits and then shaved and dressed as rapidly as he could.

Hurrying down the stairs and out the front door of the mercantile, Ortega glanced at the eastern sky. Only minutes remained before the sun crested the mountain peaks and he wanted to catch up with Ahayaca before he had a chance to leave the Rancho de la Osa. And he also wanted to find out how much Monte had learned about Ahayaca's gold.

He knew that prying that kind of information out of Monte Segundo would take time but he also assumed that Rosa would have no problem extracting from me everything that I might have discovered.

Jumping into his Studebaker, Ortega sped down the empty streets and in no time was sliding to a stop in front of Rosa's house. He rushed to the door and was about to knock when the door opened wide.

Holding the door open, Rosa scowled at Ortega. "What did you find out about the gold?"

"It is good that you are an early riser," Ortega said, hardly noticing the new dress. "Garcia trailed the Yaqui and the gringos to a rancho near Sasabe. I know the owner of the rancho. If we hurry we may find them still there."

"I will get my shawl," Rosa said, this time leaving her door wide open.

When Rosa came outside, Ortega was waiting in the automobile with the engine running. The sun was cresting the mountains.

Rosa hopped in the Studebaker but before she slammed the door the automobile was already plowing through the chilled morning air.

"How will you explain us showing up at the rancho?" Rosa asked. "You can't just drive in there without a good reason. And how will you explain me?"

"Oh, my little Rosa," Ortega said, "You have so much to learn."

"Like what?"

"Where we are going, the *haciendado* is a man like any other. Beauty such as yours needs no explanation. And as for me, it is a matter of good business."

"What kind of business? You are a storekeeper, not a rancher."
Ortega snickered and shifted gears. "Do you know what is
. . . 'collateral'?"

Rosa shrugged indignantly. "You know I do not."

"The owner of the rancho is named Cruz. He needed money
to buy cattle. He was a bad risk so the banks would not loan
him any money. So, I loaned him the money. Now, if he does
not repay me, I get his rancho. That is 'collateral.' "

"So you go to the rancho to collect your money?" Rosa asked.

"Not yet. But you see, I know Cruz and I also do business in
Sasabe at the border crossing. I will simply tell Señor Cruz that
I was in Sasabe on business and decided to stop by and pay
him a friendly visit. I will introduce you as a childhood friend.
They will think nothing of it."

"Who is 'they'?"

Ortega grinned. "Señor Cruz has a daughter."

Rosa shook her head and rolled her eyes. "And how old is
this daughter of Señor Cruz?"

"Old enough," chuckled Ortega. "But she is not as beautiful
as you."

Rosa thought of Monte and wondered what she would do if
he were still at the ranch with Ahayaca. She wanted to warn
him about Garcia but would she have the chance? And even if
she did, would he believe anything she had to say? But she
knew her biggest problem was that she still did not know exactly
what the rurale and Antonio Ortega had planned or how far
they were willing to go to get the gold.

"Where is Garcia?" Rosa asked. "I do not trust him. Perhaps
he has already gone to the rancho and taken the Indian away."

Ortega slowed and then turned southwest onto a narrow and
bumpy dirt road. "Garcia is no fool. With five thousand
American soldiers after Pancho Villa for his raid on Columbus,
Garcia would not dare attack an American rancho. If he did

that, even the Mexicans would kill him. And he knows it.

"No, Garcia is there watching the hacienda. He will meet us on the road when we get near."

Bouncing down the dusty road, Rosa thought long and hard. There was no question that Garcia was ruthless but Antonio Ortega had not hesitated to join forces with him. Both were after gold, gold that belonged to someone else. No honest man would do such a thing. But why would a dishonest man like Antonio loan money to an honest rancher? Or was Señor Cruz a man like Garcia, a man that would soon fall prey to the lust for gold? Would the rancher become another accomplice in the theft of Indian gold?

"Why did you give Señor Cruz money? Is he your friend?"

"Friend?" exclaimed Ortega. "I hardly know him. He is just another fool."

Rosa stared at Ortega. "You say you are a businessman and yet you give your money to Señor Cruz, a man you call a fool? What does that make you?"

Ortega laughed. It was a high-pitched hideous laugh that Rosa had never heard. "It makes me rich. Very rich. I love fools!"

Rosa scoffed. "You are loco, Antonio. Loco."

"Am I? Do you not remember that I told you I would soon own a rancho? The Rancho de la Osa is such a rancho and it controls all of the Altar Valley. Sasabe is the only unguarded border crossing for miles. When I own that rancho, I will have my own highway into and out of Mexico. My profits will soar."

"But you do not own the rancho!" countered Rosa. "The *haciendado* will pay back the money and you will have nothing."

Ortega laughed again but this time his tone was deeper with a diabolical ring to it. "I will have the rancho for myself. And soon."

Rosa's eyes narrowed with suspicion. "What makes you so sure?"

Ortega swerved to avoid a pothole. "You have already forgotten what I told you about collateral, my dear. Just accept the fact that you know nothing of business. That is all you need to know."

"And all of this helps the revolution?" Rosa asked.

Without a moment's hesitation, Ortega answered. "Of course. How else can I so easily smuggle guns and ammunition to Villa and his army?"

Glancing at Rosa, Ortega grinned and started to speak when the Studebaker slammed into a deep pothole, almost jerking the steering wheel from Ortega's grasp. After bounding out of the hole, the front end of the automobile began to vibrate.

Ortega swore bitterly and hit the brakes.

"What wrong?" demanded Rosa.

"A damn flat tire," roared Ortega. "That's what is wrong!"

Flinging his door open, Ortega jumped out and went to the front of the automobile. Swearing under his breath, he unlatched the T-jack from the driver's side of the running board. Sliding it under the front axle, he began frantically pumping it up and down.

"Rosa," barked Ortega, "on the running board on your side there is a toolbox. Inside there is a wrench. Bring it to me."

Rosa got out, thumbed open the latches to the toolbox, and flipped the lid open. It was full of small gauges, bulbs, and electrical wire. "What does it look like?"

"It's the only long tool in there. It is round at one end."

Rosa rummaged through the box and saw the wrench near the bottom. Shoving the clutter aside, she grabbed the wrench and jerked it free. It came up and out of the box but, along with the wrench, came a cylindrical roll of what appeared to be leather. The roll bounced on the running board and then onto the sand.

"I have it."

"Go to the rear of the automobile," Ortega ordered, "and start unscrewing the bolts that hold the spare tire and rim."

The front of the Studebaker started to rise as Rosa went to the spare. She placed the wrench on one of the lug nuts but it would not budge.

"I'm not strong enough," Rosa said.

Ortega swore again and stopped pumping the jack. He scrambled to the rear of the motorcar. Snatching the wrench from Rosa's hand, he bellowed, "Just stay out of the way, damn it! And don't touch anything!"

Struggling to suppress a wave of rage, Rosa walked back around to the toolbox. Glancing down, she saw the cylindrical object that had fallen out of the toolbox and then rolled to the side of the road. As Ortega yarded on the nuts, she nudged the roll with the tip of her sandal. Bending down, she picked it up.

The roll was indeed leather and about five inches wide. She turned it on its end and saw several curled-up layers of leather and hair. Curiously, she unrolled the leather partway. It was stiff but not from age. This was rawhide.

Turning away from Ortega, Rosa peeled back the edges of the curling leather. She saw a brand, a cross with a bar at the bottom. Separating the leather further, she counted three hides, all with the same brand.

Ortega was lifting the tire from its frame and paying no attention to her. Allowing the leather to curl back on itself, she stepped close to the toolbox. Dropping the roll back inside, she walked a few steps out into the desert. At first, Rosa could see no reason for having the brands but then a thought swept through her mind.

The owner of the Rancho de la Osa was named Cruz and Cruz was Spanish for cross.

Having returned from the village, Monte and I wearily

unsaddled our horses. We put them in the corral with the other horses and then went to the bunkhouse hoping to get a few minutes of sleep before heading back out on the range. When we went inside we saw Deek and Fernando sitting at a small table drinking coffee.

Deek looked up. "You two look like you been rode hard and put away wet. That must have been one hell of a shindig last night."

"It was," I said.

"I'll bet," Deek said snidely.

Monte and I went to our bunks and laid down.

"Mostly," I said, "we just watched them dance and then we ate. A few minutes sleep is all I want now."

"Lucky for you," continued Deek, his tone distinctly sour. "Today's Sunday. Fernando was just telling me that nobody works around here on Sundays."

I closed my eyes. "That's good to hear."

"I guess," Deek said, "Ahayaca forgot who it was that come up with the horses that saved his life."

"He didn't forget," said Monte. His voice was calm but I detected a subtle warning in his tone. "I could only take one man along and I've known Billy a good while longer than you, Deek. That's all there was to it."

I had almost dropped off to sleep when Deek asked another question.

"What about the gold? Did you find out anything?"

If Monte answered, I didn't hear it. The next thing I knew, I was being shaken.

Forcing my crusty eyelids to crack open, I saw Deek standing beside me. "Time to get up."

I rolled on my side and saw Monte sitting up on his bunk and rubbing a hand over his face.

Yawning, I asked, "What is it, Deek?"

"Señor Cruz is having his own shindig here at the ranch. Company's come to visit."

I groaned. "What time is it?"

"One. Two maybe," Deek answered, now seemingly in a better mood. "You two done slept for six hours.

"As soon as you get cleaned up come over to the hacienda. That's where everybody is at."

I sat up trying to focus my eyes. "Who's here?"

"You'll see," answered Deek and then slammed the bunkhouse door on his way out.

I walked to the window and pulled back a linen curtain. Peering through the clouded glass, I saw Ortega's sleek Studebaker parked alongside Cruz's Ford. Then I got a glimpse of Rosa. I swore. "Rosa is here. And Ortega."

I expected to hear Monte swear as well but I heard nothing but the squeak of bedsprings. I turned to see Monte stand up and start unbuttoning his shirt. "This shirt's got to be washed first. And I need a shave. They can wait 'til I'm done or do without me."

I staggered to my feet. "I need to wash up, too, but I've got an extra shirt in my suitcase. I'm too tired to do laundry."

Tossing his shirt into a metal bucket, Monte emptied a pitcher of water over it. Taking a bar of soap he began to scrub. "Anybody else out there that could pass for 'company'?"

"Not that I can see."

"It didn't take those two long to smell us out, did it?"

I went to my bed and slid my suitcase out from under it. "Ortega must have gone back to the Yaqui village after we left. Maybe one of the Yaqui followed us and then told him how to find us."

Monte dipped his shirt in and out of the bucket and then wrung out the water. "They're not looking for you and me. All they care about is Ahayaca and his gold. But they're looking down a dry well. Ahayaca is twice the man they think he is. No matter what they try and pull, he won't tell them anything."

I was about to pull off my vest when Deek stuck his head back inside the bunkhouse. "Angelina says not to wear no hardware. She wants to impress that Ortega fella with our good manners, so she says to leave our pistols here."

Again, Deek slammed the door.

Monte unraveled his damp shirt and flapped it up and down. "To hell with that. I'm not going anywhere, especially anywhere around Ortega, without my pistol."

"No one but you has seen my shoulder rig," I said.

"Then, wear it. Ortega is a snake. I'd bet my last dollar he has a hideout gun on him."

"What will you tell Angelina about your pistol?"

"I'll tell her it's army regulations. As long as I wear the uniform I have to go armed."

I chuckled. "Clever. Very clever."

Not having much of a beard, it took me little time to shave, wash up, and then change into my new white shirt. Sliding the leather straps of my holster over my shoulders, I put on my vest and then, to make certain nothing was visible, fastened two of the buttons.

"How do I look?" I asked.

"Dapper and unarmed as ordered," Monte said lightheartedly. But then he grew more serious. "Billy, just be yourself out there. You've got nothing to prove to anybody. And besides, it won't be long until Angelina finds out about Ortega. Then, things will look different to her. After that, she'll be looking for a decent sort of man, a man she can count on."

"I'll do my best," I said and then opened the bunkhouse door and stepped outside. Closing the door behind me, I stood for a moment taking in the activity across the plaza on the front lawn of the hacienda.

Everyone was standing in the shade of some eucalyptus trees, each with a glass in one hand. Ortega and Angelina were standing off to one side. Señor Cruz, Rosa, and Deek were conversing a few feet away.

Taking a deep breath, I blew hard and then started walking. I intentionally gazed off to the east as if something of importance commanded my attention. As I walked, I began planning my grand entrance, how I would sweep past Angelina as if she weren't even there, how I would stand, how I would smile, how clever I would be.

And then I remembered Monte's advice. Passing by the motorcars, I laughed at my own stupidity. I simply walked up the steps and over to Rosa. I extended my hand.

"Rosa," I said, giving her hand a gentlemanly shake. "I'm so glad to see you."

Señor Cruz was surprised. "You know each other?"

"Yes," I said. "We met in Columbus, New Mexico. We recently met again in Tucson but unfortunately, we had no time to visit."

"How are you, Billy?" Rosa asked.

I noticed that Rosa seemed uneasy. In that instant, I realized that if Señor Cruz was unaware that Rosa and I knew each other, he very likely knew nothing of what had transpired at the Yaqui village two days earlier. That meant that Rosa, Deek, and Ortega were all deliberately concealing information from Señor Cruz and Angelina.

"I'm doing well," I said. "I'm a cowboy now. I work here."

Rosa squinted in disbelief. "You *work* here?"

I turned to Deek. "You didn't tell her?"

Deek frowned. "It slipped my mind."

"Yes," said Señor Cruz, "I hired Deek and Billy and one other to help me gather my cattle. They came along at a most convenient time. I was shorthanded, you see."

Before Rosa could react, I said, "You remember Monte Segundo, I'm sure. He is also working here. He'll be along shortly."

Again Cruz registered his surprise. "Señorita Bustamonte, do you also know Monte Segundo?"

Rosa flashed a beautiful, disarming smile. "Yes. I met both Billy and Monte in Columbus, New Mexico. The revolution brought us together at the train station. And now a twist of fate has brought us together once again. Is that not strange, Señor Cruz?"

Señor Cruz chuckled. "It is the twentieth century, señorita. The world is growing smaller and smaller."

"That must be it," I said, amazed at how easily Rosa distracted Señor Cruz and diverted his attention.

"Come, Billy," Señor Cruz said, placing his hand on my back. "Allow me to introduce you to Mr. Ortega."

Uncertain how Ortega would handle the introduction, I decided to try and continue the charade that was in progress. As we approached, Ortega made eye contact. Hardly moving a muscle, I shook my head "No."

"Mr. Ortega," Cruz said, "I would like to introduce you to Mr. Billy Cabott, one of our new *vaqueros.*"

With our eyes locked, I pushed out my hand, "Nice to meet you, Mr. Ortega."

Ortega nodded and then smiled. "Nice to meet you also, Mr. Cabott."

Feeling the undeniable sting of jealousy, my first impulse was to avoid making eye contact with Angelina. But again, Monte's words echoed in my head. Instead of being petty, I tipped my hat. "Good afternoon, miss."

Angelina smirked. "Did you forget my name already?"

Without missing a beat, I answered, "Angelica, isn't it?"

Señor Cruz laughed. "As you can see, Mr. Ortega, my daughter is quite pert. However, she has met her match with

Mr. Cabott."

Ortega smiled but his lips were flat. "Yes. He seems very adept."

"It is nice to meet you, Mr. Ortega," I said and then started back toward Rosa. When she saw me coming she said something to Deek and then met me in the middle of the lawn.

In a near whisper, she said, "We must talk."

With a laugh she put her arm through mine and gave me a tug. We walked off of the lawn and onto the walkway. Rosa leaned into my arm and I was suddenly aware that I felt the soft warmth of her breast rubbing up against me. She pretended to giggle.

"What are you doing?" I asked softly. We walked down the steps and began strolling around the outer edge of the plaza.

Rosa spoke softly. "Antonio Ortega is not the man I once knew. He wants the Indian's gold and now has joined with a Mexican rurale named Garcia. You and Monte are in much danger. And the Indian, too."

"Ortega and Garcia are working together?" I asked. "How did that come about?"

"Yes. Garcia is a very bad man. He came first to the mercantile two days ago. That is when they met.

"Today Garcia and three other rurales met us on the road not far from here. Antonio talked with them but I could not hear what they said. Antonio thinks I also want the gold. I only pretend to want it. He wants me to tempt you, to get you to tell me what you learned of the Indian's gold.

"He will be watching us, Billy, so I want you to laugh. Act as if we are having a good time. Do it now!"

I laughed but it was a weak performance.

"Ahayaca is not here, Rosa. And Monte and I know nothing of his gold. I didn't ask about it. And you know Monte wouldn't."

183

Glancing down at Rosa as we walked, I saw her smile. "Yes," she said, "Monte would not care about the gold. Not him."

Seeing the look on Rosa's face was all the encouragement I needed to broach a different, if not equally precarious, subject.

"Rosa, Monte is convinced you betrayed him. But I don't believe it."

We walked a full minute before Rosa spoke again.

"Antonio has not touched me. Not once. I have not allowed it."

"Then why are you with him?"

"Because."

"Because?"

Rosa huffed. "On the train when we left Columbus . . . Monte said . . . he said that he might come to Tucson. Antonio gave me a house to sleep in and money for food. He is expecting something in return but that is his fault. I never told him to expect anything."

At that point, we had skirted most of the plaza and were on our way back to the lawn. There wasn't time enough to tell Rosa everything so I simply said, "Monte will be very pleased when I explain all of this to him."

"No. You cannot tell him. Not yet. Not tonight. You know Monte, and bad things could happen. Wait until Antonio and I have gone back to Tucson."

Noticing that Ortega was watching, Rosa laughed and flirtatiously rubbed up against me.

"I saw you look at the daughter of Señor Cruz," she whispered. "Do you like her, Billy?"

I swallowed hard. "Is it that obvious?"

"Then I will tell you something else, something I do not understand."

"What's that?"

"Antonio says he will soon own the Rancho de la Osa and

today I found three brands in Antonio's motorcar. They were on hides from cows. The brand was of a cross, the same as I saw on the gate driving in here today."

I thought for a moment and then recalled the dead cattle Monte had found. And then, in a flash of cognition, I remembered the loan Señor Cruz had accepted from Ortega.

"Of course!" I said in a raspy whisper. "Who would make a loan without collateral?"

"That is it!" Rosa said. "Antonio says he has a collateral and it will get him this rancho."

"Now it all makes sense," I groaned. "The ranch itself is the collateral. Monte was right."

"About what?"

We were too close to continue talking. "Not now, Rosa," I said with a big grin. "I'll explain later."

Rosa and I were making our way back up the walkway steps when Monte exited the bunkhouse and started across the plaza. Halfway across, however, he caught a flicker of movement off to his left. Looking just past the old trading post, he saw Ahayaca, now dressed as a typical peon, riding toward him.

Monte abruptly changed his direction. Walking toward the ancient adobe, Monte shook his head trying to signal Ahayaca not to come any closer. But it was no use.

Ahayaca rode past the adobe and in full view of everyone at the hacienda. He continued riding until he dismounted next to Monte.

Monte glared at Ahayaca, trying to read his expression, but a glimmer of light drew his attention to a circular pendant that hung down from Ahayaca's neck. It was a round piece of black glass the size of a man's palm and it was rimmed with yellow metal.

"Garcia will see you," whispered Monte, making no attempt to hide his irritation.

"Yes, Montesegundo, this I know. But I have come with a warning."

"Warning? What kind of warning?"

Ahayaca looked over at the gathering in front of the hacienda. He saw Angelina and Señor Cruz break away and start walking toward him. "I came to tell you to beware of the man and woman that arrived in the motorcar. They are in league with Garcia."

Monte was only mildly surprised. "What makes you say that?"

"I told you of our sentinels and runners but we also have . . . what you might call, spies. These are invisible spies that keep watch all around our village. We have had them for centuries. On the road to this hacienda, one of our spies witnessed the meeting of Garcia with the man and woman. The spy was close enough to hear that Garcia is soon to be joined by nine Yaquis, *bronco* Yaquis. The Yaquis work for the man in the motorcar. His name is Ortega. All are after gold. They believe I know where a treasure is hidden."

Monte thoughtfully scratched his jaw. "Ortega found out about your gold from the doctor that brought you the quinine. Ortega came out to the Yaqui village. He wanted to talk to you but we told him you were too sick. But I can't imagine how Garcia came to hook up with Ortega."

Ahayaca lowered his voice as Señor Cruz and Angelina came closer. "Did Ortega come to the door of the adobe that day at the Yaqui village? Did he speak?"

"Yeah. He was at the door. That's where him and me had a few words. Why?"

"It is nothing. I heard voices that morning . . . in a nightmare that I had. That is all."

Indicating the pendant, Monte said, "That's quite a necklace. That's not gold around the edges, is it?"

"Does it look like gold?" asked Ahayaca.

"That or brass, maybe? Nobody's going to miss seeing it, that's for damn sure."

"Good," said Ahayaca, stepping away from Monte.

Ahayaca shook hands with Señor Cruz. "I have come at a bad time. Forgive me."

"Nonsense," replied Señor Cruz, "it is the perfect time, isn't that right, Angelina?"

"It certainly is! You're just in time, Ahayaca. We're going to have an early supper and we'll have Kim Lee set another place. I have so many questions to ask you."

"But you have guests," Ahayaca said.

Angelina took Ahayaca's arm and gave it a tug. "Come on. We'll introduce you."

Señor Cruz extended his hand, indicating the hacienda to Monte. "We wish to introduce you to our guests as well."

Monte took the reins of Ahayaca's horse. "I met your guests a couple of days ago. I'll put the horse up first and give him some grain. He's put in a lot of miles. Then I'll be along."

"You met Anthony Ortega?" asked Señor Cruz.

"He can tell you about it," Monte said and then led the horse down toward the corrals.

As Angelina escorted Ahayaca to the lawn, the pendant caught my eye, as I'm certain it did everyone else's. It was uncharacteristically reckless for Ahayaca to wear such a piece to the hacienda, especially knowing Garcia was somewhere nearby. In an attempt to discern Ahayaca's reason for showing himself, I watched his every move. Whatever his motive for coming to the hacienda, whatever message he brought, I knew it had to be of the utmost importance.

Approaching with Angelina on his arm, Ahayaca took us all in with one sweeping glance. He seemed confident and relaxed but then, taking a second long look at Ortega, his eyes suddenly narrowed. He glanced away from Ortega only to look back for a moment and then quickly glance away. When Ahayaca came up the steps with Angelina, I noticed a subtle change in his demeanor. He suddenly seemed uncertain, perhaps even perplexed.

Angelina directed Ahayaca toward Rosa and me. "Señorita Bustamonte, may I introduce you to Ahayaca? He and I grew up together on the rancho."

Rosa extended her hand. Ahayaca took it and to my surprise bowed just as any gentleman would have done. "It is a pleasure to meet you, señorita."

It was then that Ortega and Señor Cruz walked over. Not waiting for a proper introduction Ortega offered his hand. "And I am Anthony Ortega."

Ahayaca looked curiously at Ortega. I detected the faintest hesitation before he shook hands. "And I am called Ahayaca."

"Ahayaca was born on the rancho," offered Angelina, "and he has lived here all of his life. He was gone for almost a year and we thought he was dead. He has just returned to us and we have been waiting on pins and needles to hear all about what kept him away for so long."

Before Ortega could offer a response, Kim Lee burst out of the hacienda and waved both hands. "Come, come. Food is hot now. You all come to table while food is hot."

Angelina peered over her shoulder at Kim Lee. "I hope you don't mind, Mr. Ortega, if Ahayaca tells us his story while we have supper. I am so anxious to hear it."

"Not at all, Angelina," smiled Ortega. "It sounds most interesting."

"Wonderful!" Angelina said, and then added excitedly, "Wait one moment, Father, before you all come inside. I must rearrange the names and set a place for Ahayaca."

Señor Cruz grinned as Angelina scampered into the hacienda. "She is very excited but she also has a taste for formality."

"She is a fine hostess," I said.

Ortega shot me a dismissive glance and then said to Ahayaca, "That is an interesting piece you are wearing. Do you mind if I ask what it is?"

With a lingering question still in his eyes, Ahayaca said, "It is obsidian, formed and polished into a mirror. It has religious meaning for my people."

Casually eyeing the pendant, Ortega asked, "It seems to be rimmed with gold."

Ahayaca shrugged indifferently. "Gold or brass. It is very old so no one in my village remembers. The meaning is all that is important to us."

"Are you Papago?" asked Ortega, "Pima perhaps?"

Señor Cruz was clearly uncomfortable with Ortega's rude questions but before Ahayaca responded, Angelina emerged from the hacienda. "Time to eat, everyone. The table is set."

"Shall we?" invited Señor Cruz, extending his arm and then escorting Rosa toward the hacienda.

I wanted to do the same with Angelina but I knew better, and sure enough, at the door of the hacienda, she walked inside with her arm in Ortega's.

Anxiously, I looked back in the direction of the corrals, but Monte was nowhere to be seen. I desperately wanted to explain to him about Rosa but I also needed to tell him what she had learned about Ortega and his designs on the ranch.

Ahayaca put his hand on my shoulder. "We should go in, Billy. All is well."

I peered into Ahayaca's eyes. "Is it? I saw how you were looking at Ortega. Do you know him from somewhere?"

Urging me toward the hacienda, Ahayaca said, "We will see. But for now . . . we must finish what this day has begun."

With Ahayaca at my side, I entered the large dining room. The table had been formally set with china dishes, polished silverware, and crystal glasses. Everyone was seated.

Ortega sat on one corner. Next to him was Angelina, then an empty seat and then Rosa. There were two empty seats across from Ortega but I could see Ahayaca's name on one and Monte's on the other. Deek was sitting next to Monte's seat and Señor Cruz sat beside him and across from Rosa.

Rosa pointed to the empty chair between her and Angelina. "Here, Billy, you sit here."

Realizing I would be sitting with Angelina on my right, my stomach turned over.

"And Ahayaca," Angelina said, "You are on the corner across from Mr. Ortega."

As soon as Ahayaca and I took our seats, Kim Lee began serving the food. He began by setting a large pot in the center of the table and then returning to the kitchen. It was to be another help-yourself-and-pass-it-on ranch style of service to which I was slowly getting accustomed.

The pot was filled with a steaming soup called pozole. Then Kim Lee brought out a type of corn salad, which was promptly followed by an assortment of enchiladas, empanadas, taquitos, tamales, corn tortillas, various-colored chili peppers, and finally a chicken casserole.

Placing my white linen napkin in my lap, I fought down a smirk. It seemed quite comical to be serving Mexican food on fine china and eating it with expensive silverware. However, the moment I noticed the innocent glee on Angelina's face, I felt a twinge of guilt. Then, I found myself wondering if my lessons on proper etiquette might not have included a modicum of Anglo-Saxon prejudice.

There was a moment of silence as the Catholics among us, including Ortega, made the sign of the cross. Angelina was first to uncover the steaming pozole and grab the ladle.

Filling her bowl with the soup, she commented, "Ahayaca, I

have never seen you wear jewelry."

Ahayaca nodded. He stared across the table as Ortega accepted the soup ladle from Angelina and started filling his bowl. "Our people only wear jewelry like this once in a century. Our century, though, is only fifty-two years long. And this is the end of our century. We will soon celebrate the beginning of a new century. When we do, everyone in the village will wear their jewelry."

Unaware of Ahayaca's cold stare, Ortega continued filling his soup bowl. "Mr. Coleman tells me you had a celebration last night, Ahayaca. Was that to begin your new century?"

"No," Ahayaca answered. "That was to make Montesegundo my blood brother."

"Blood brother!" blurted Deek.

"Yes. He is now a member of our tribe, an honored member."

Ortega looked up but then he merely handed the ladle back to Angelina.

Angelina, dumbfounded, slid the soup bowl and ladle down to me but I slid it to Rosa. "You first," I said.

"That is a high honor for Mr. Segundo," admitted Señor Cruz. "You are full of surprises, Ahayaca."

Over the shoulder of Ahayaca, Ortega caught sight of Monte coming through the front door. "Speaking of surprises, here comes Mr. Segundo."

Uncertain how Angelina would react to Monte wearing his pistol, I held my breath. Watching Angelina from the corner of my eye, I saw her head snap up.

Monte paused outside the entrance to the dining room and hung his hat on a peg. As soon as he stepped into view Angelina asked, "Are you planning to shoot our cook?"

Most of us laughed but Ortega bellowed. It was a distinctive laugh, one that filled the room and reverberated off the adobe walls.

Glancing down at his pistol, Monte said easily, "It comes with the uniform, miss. Army regulations."

Ortega smirked. "I understood you were no longer in the army."

Monte gave Ortega a look that made me nervous. I had seen that look before and knew all too well what it meant.

"That's a matter of opinion," Monte said. "I'm still National Guard and President Wilson has called us all down to guard the border."

Angelina disapprovingly rolled her eyes. She indicated the seat across from her with a sweep of her hand. "Please sit. The soup will get cold."

Monte pulled out his chair. I watched his eyes shift from Angelina back to Ortega. He glanced at me and then, for a moment, his eyes held on Rosa.

"We just learned," Angelina said, "that you and Ahayaca are now blood brothers."

"That's right," Monte said. "And that makes him the only family I've got."

Angelina took a lid off of another bowl and took out a tamale with a pair of silver tongs. "Help yourselves everyone, whatever you like."

As we started filling our plates, Ortega glanced at Ahayaca. "I did not know anyone still believed in blood brothers, at least, not in the twentieth century."

Inexplicably, Ahayaca now appeared to be immensely pleased. He smiled broadly. "We are a very traditional tribe. We keep to ourselves and hold to the old ways."

"Times are changing," countered Ortega. "You won't be able to stay isolated for much longer."

"I don't know," Deek said. "Them Tarahumara up in the *barrancas* of the Sierra Madres are still wild as can be. Nobody can even find 'em. Anybody goes to look for 'em don't ever come back. And there's *bronco* Apaches back in them mountains, too."

"Yes, I have heard as much," Ortega said, "but the *barrancas* are deep and narrow. At the bottom of those canyons it is like a dark jungle."

"So, you have been to a *barranca,* Señor Ortega?" asked Ahayaca.

Ortega's face was unreadable. "No, I have only read about them. But *barrancas* are far different than our open desert."

I thought of the mesquite trees planted in the hills above Ahayaca's village and the hidden pass leading into it. There was no way a stranger could approach the village from the outside but I knew Ortega was right. And I thought it best that Ahayaca knew the truth.

"As a matter of privacy," I said, "I have to agree with Mr. Ortega. When Monte and I were in Mexico, we saw several airplanes. General Pershing was using them to deliver messages but also to search for Pancho Villa and his men. Those airplanes will change everything."

After thinking for a moment, Ahayaca asked, "How high can these machines fly?"

It pained me to respond for I knew what effect my answer would have on Ahayaca and ultimately his people. "Higher than the mountains."

Ahayaca looked to Monte for confirmation.

Monte gave him a regretful nod. "It's true. Now any two-bit pilot can fly wherever they have a mind to and look down on whoever they want. And there's nothing you can do about it. I suppose, though, if one of those airplanes was in range a fella might be able to hit it with a rifle."

Seeming a bit deflated, Ahayaca admitted, "We have no firearms."

"No firearms," questioned Ortega. "No one in your village has any?"

Ahayaca regained his composure. He smiled, although not as broadly as before. "We live at peace with everyone. It has always been so. That is why we can exist as we have for so long. Since we fight no one, we are able to trade with all the tribes, Pima, Papago, Opata, Yaqui, and even the Apache."

"So," I said, "you are what we call 'neutral.' A country called Switzerland is like that."

Angelina glared at me. Reacting to my trifling comment, her brow wrinkled with disapproval, but she said nothing.

"Who do you see crossing the ranch most often?" asked Monte.

"These days, Yaquis," answered Señor Cruz. "Wouldn't you agree, Ahayaca?"

"Yes. They come to our village from the south. They trade with us or get water and then go farther north. When they return, we often see them with new rifles."

Monte picked up a yellow chili pepper and looked it over.

"I would not eat that if I were you," cautioned Rosa. "They are very hot."

I was amazed that Rosa had decided to speak to Monte. It seemed to stun him also.

"Oh, they are not that hot," Ortega said, picking one from the dish and popping it in his mouth. "See. Not so hot."

Deek then reached across the table and took one. He took a bite and said, "No, a little spicy but not bad."

Monte, still gazing at Rosa, seemed undecided. So, on a hunch that something was not right, I helped myself to one. As I took a bite, I saw Angelina lean forward and stare at me.

At first there was merely a slight tingling. And then my eyes began to water. The next thing I knew my entire mouth felt like it was on fire.

I grabbed my glass of tea and gulped but it had no effect. Everything was a blur. The pain was so intense I wanted to scream. And then I felt someone's hands on my lips, and fingers shoving something in my mouth.

I heard Angelina saying, "Chew, Billy. It's butter. Chew!"

With tears rolling down my cheeks, I chewed as fast I could manage. The burning eased somewhat. With my scalded tongue, I rolled the butter out onto my lips and more of the fire went out. I wiped my eyes with my napkin but still could not focus on anything.

I felt a hand patting me on the back and then realized it was Angelina's. "Not bad," she said, "not bad at all for your first one."

Monte looked at Ortega waiting for him to say something.

Ortega grinned. "It is a joke we play on gringos. It is all in fun."

My eyes cleared. I saw the hate in Monte's eyes but I saw something else in them as he twirled the pepper between his fingers. And then I remembered that not only was Monte's mother a Mexican, he had been close to seven years old before his parents were killed.

Peering across the table at Ortega, Monte dropped the entire pepper in his mouth and started chewing. Everyone waited for his reaction but all Monte did was pick up a tamale and take a bite.

I looked at Señor Cruz and saw his relief.

"Monte," asked Señor Cruz, "is Segundo perhaps a Spanish name?"

"My mother was Mexican."

Ortega sneered and then took another chili.

"Well then, that explains it," Deek said. "I ain't any part Mexican but I grew up on the border. Eat enough of them chili peppers and you get used to it."

"Señor Cruz," asked Monte, "when do you plan on selling off your cattle?"

"Within a week or two at the latest. Soon we will gather them and drive them to Tucson. I want to avoid the rains."

Monte took another bite of his tamale. Wiping his lips with his shirtsleeve, he asked, "What happens if you don't get a good price or you've had more losses than average?"

Señor Cruz expelled an artificial laugh. "In that case, I would have to beg Mr. Ortega for an extension on my loan."

Ortega held up a hand. "God forbid that should happen. No, it has been a good year for cattle. I expect the price of cattle to be up as well."

I saw my chance and I took it. "I think Monte is asking, if you had to put up any collateral for your loan."

"Well," admitted Señor Cruz, "Mr. Ortega did not request it, but I insisted that I put up the rancho as collateral. It was the least I could do in light of his very generous offer."

Acting as if I knew nothing about the rustled cattle, I said, "Certainly. That is a standard business practice."

"Yes," agreed Ortega, "a needless formality among honest men."

Monte gave me a faint but knowing nod. I knew then he understood that Ortega was somehow involved with the slaughtered cattle and missing brands. But Monte also understood that without the brands, there was no proof the dead cows belonged to the Rancho de la Osa. And without that proof, the ranch would soon belong to Anthony Ortega, the same man that took Rosa from him and then joined forces with Garcia to steel Ahayaca's gold.

"I don't want to hear about business," Angelina said. "I want to hear all about what happened to Ahayaca. I've been waiting for two whole days, now."

"As have I," added Señor Cruz. "Please tell us everything. Leave nothing out."

Ahayaca wiped his lips with his napkin and laid it beside his plate. "Where shall I begin? Let me think."

"Ahayaca!" demanded Angelina. "You are stalling. I know you. Now tell us."

Smiling at Angelina, Ahayaca began.

"Our tribe is small but our blood is pure. There is only one other such tribe with our blood and it is in Mexico near Malinalco. Last year I left our village to go to Malinalco because we had received word that a wife had been selected for me."

"Oh, that sounds romantic," chided Angelina.

Offering Angelina a patronizing smile, Ahayaca said, "Royalty is not concerned with romance."

Angelina's face twisted with disbelief. "What do you mean, 'royalty'?"

Señor Cruz frowned with disapproval. "Angelina! Please do not interrupt."

"Angelina," said Ahayaca, "you are like a sister to me . . . but there is much about me and my people that you do not know. I want you to understand that I never deceived you. But on many occasions, I did withhold the truth. I am sorry for that but I had no choice."

Angelina looked deep into Ahayaca's eyes for several seconds. "You are serious!"

"Yes. Unfortunately, I am."

Crossing her arms, Angelina leaned back in her chair. "Go on. I apologize for interrupting."

Ahayaca gazed at Angelina. For a moment he seemed distant, almost sad. But then he blinked and once again looked around the table.

"Centuries ago," explained Ahayaca, "the Jesuits taught us that *Jesús Christo* was king of kings. That may be so, but I am king of my people, the *Ocelomeh*. It was the same with my father and his father's father. It is our tradition and there is no choice involved.

"And it is the same in Malinalco with the *Cuayumeh.*

"I was on my way to visit the *Cuayumeh* but I had gone no farther than Nácori when I was tricked by an evil man and arrested. This evil man and the *jefe politico* of Nácori worked together and ensnared many men and families. Mainly they were after Yaquis but they took many Pima and Opata. In fact, they took anyone that was poor and dark-skinned and could not protect themselves.

"Those of us that had been arrested were held prisoner by the *jefe politico* and guarded by rurales. In time, we were taken to Hermosillo and then to Guaymas where some of the families were broken up."

"What do you mean, 'broken up'?" asked Rosa.

"Wives from husbands, children from father and mother," answered Ahayaca. "Some were sent one way, some another. They were never reunited.

"I, and the people that I was with, were then put on a steamer. We sailed south for four days and then landed in San Blas. From there we were forced to march over a rough mountain road for three weeks to San Marcos. But on the way many died.

"It was at San Marcos that I again saw the same evil man who had tricked many of us. The people said he was an *enganchador,* one who traps."

Ahayaca had been glancing at each one of us as he spoke but then his eyes rested squarely on Ortega.

"And because he was so well known to so many, the people named that *enganchador . . .* El Serpiente."

There was a long silence and then Ahayaca's eyes again began to roam around the table. "At San Marcos, El Serpiente broke up more families and then sold us once again to others in the slave trade. Eventually, we all ended up on henequen plantations.

"It was at San Marcos that I first heard El Serpiente laugh. I heard him many times after that. I will never forget that awful sound."

Sitting across from Ortega, Monte had been keeping an eye on him and, though his expression had not changed, Monte could see Ortega's skin beginning to flush red.

"What do you mean you were sold?" snipped Ortega. "You keep saying 'sold.' There is no slave trade in Mexico. The Mexican constitution has never allowed slavery."

"In Mexico," countered Ahayaca, "debts can be sold . . . And the people along with their debt. It is called 'enforced service for debt' and it is perfectly legal. Once the plantation owns the debt, they own the worker. And debts can be bought and sold."

Ahayaca looked up at the ceiling as if he were gazing into the sky. "This is the year the *Ocelomeh* and the *Cuayumeh* begin our new century. We have rituals to perform, traditions to pass on. If we do not do this, we believe the Black Sun will come. If that happens, the Black Sun will destroy all that is left of our race. Then, we would cease to exist. And it is I, and I alone, that must perform some of our most sacred rituals.

"So, you can see how fortunate it is that I escaped the henequen plantation and was able to return to my village in time for our ceremonies. Very fortunate."

"What about this El Serpiente?" Monte asked. "He sure seems to get around."

Even though Monte and I had already heard most of Ahayaca's story, I noticed there was something different about this version and I guessed that Monte had noticed also. And when Monte used the phrase *he sure gets around* I knew exactly what he was thinking.

"Yes, El Serpiente became very wealthy. He bought and sold men, women, and children in Oaxaca, Tuxtepec Veracruz, Mexico City, Merida, and many other places. To the government, he was known as a 'labor contractor' but since he was mainly selling Yaquis and bribing the government officials, El Serpiente was treated as a respected businessman."

"But why was he called a 'labor contractor'?" asked Señor Cruz. "I do not understand."

Ahayaca looked at the tattoos on the back of his hands and smiled. "El Serpiente is a clever man and he uses many tricks. One of his favorites was to approach poor men that were looking for work. He would tell them he had a good paying job for them and then convince them to sign a contract to work. El Serpiente then gave them five pesos, five pesos he said they could repay after they worked at their new job.

"The men were grateful for the money and in a hurry to buy food for their families or badly needed supplies. So they spent the money. Only when they got to their new job, they were never paid what they were promised. They barely made enough to survive, much less pay off their debt. So they were forever in debt. And this is how they were sold."

"That is awful," gasped Angelina. "Unthinkable."

"What happened after San Marcos?" asked Señor Cruz. "How did you get to the plantations?"

Ahayaca thought for a moment, his eyes focusing on something unseen. "From San Marcos we were taken by train to Mexico City. From there we were herded onto another train and taken to Veracruz. At Veracruz, we were put on another steamer. This one was named the *Sinaloa*. On that vessel we were forced into a filthy hole in the belly of the ship. There, we stayed for three days, until we were taken ashore at Progreso. From Progreso, we were taken to the plantations where the planters took over.

"We were worked during the day. At night we were imprisoned in an area surrounded by high adobe walls that had broken glass on top. And there were guards outside the walls, as well."

"And what was it like on the plantation?" asked Angelina.

"They worked us hard all day every day. They beat us often and fed us tortillas, beans, and rotten fish. Most of the workers died within six months."

Angelina gasped and put her hands over her mouth. Señor Cruz somberly shook his head.

Oddly, Ortega seemed to have regained his composure. "How did you manage to escape?"

"Ah yes," said Ahayaca, "Let us move on to more pleasant matters." Ahayaca took a long drink of tea and then set his glass down. "Just thinking of it makes me thirsty.

"At the plantation, I became friends with a Yaqui, a Yaqui that had been beaten very severely. In time, we discovered that each of us knew certain secrets, secrets guarded by our tribes over the centuries. And we decided that the only way we might escape was to use our knowledge."

"What kind of knowledge?" Deek asked, suddenly taking an interest in the story.

"The Yaqui, Tetabiate, was familiar with stories of lost silver mines. I knew of many rumors that told of the lost Aztec treasure. But we both knew details that no one else familiar with the legends had ever heard, convincing details.

"We finally managed to escape but were soon caught by some rurales. Then, as we had planned, we told the rurales that for our freedom, we would reveal the location of the treasures. But we also convinced them we would have to guide them there. We explained that no map could ever be drawn well enough to show the way, that the paths to the two treasures were too old and too treacherous."

"Along the way, in a narrow pass, Tetabiate gave his life so that I could get away. And because I was a runner, I kept ahead of the rurales. I kept ahead of them even when I got out of the jungle and they got back to their horses.

"They almost caught me many times but I always managed to escape. Since the planters became fearful that I would expose their slave trade, a large reward was offered to make certain that I was captured. Those that came after me never gave up. They were all experienced trackers. When they questioned any that had helped me along the way, the rurales were merciless and brutal. They never failed to get the answers they sought.

"I was starved and weak when Montesegundo found me. He protected me from the rurales and brought me here. He brought me home."

Deek squirmed in his seat. "Aren't you forgettin' a few things?"

"I have forgotten nothing. I do not want to bore the guests with a longer story than is necessary."

"Well," sneered Deek, "they might find it interestin' how I come along with two horses just in time to save both your hides from them rurales."

"That's right," agreed Monte. "Without Deek, the rurales would have had us for sure. He came along in the nick of time and helped us get to Bernadino. That's where we got clear of the rurales."

"And what about the gold?" Deek asked. "You left that part out, too."

Expecting Ahayaca to take great offense to what Deek had said, I took a good look at Ahayaca but saw no indignation. In fact, I saw no expression at all until, inexplicably, he began to smile.

"As I said, our tribe has certain secrets, secrets that are sacred to us and to us alone."

Angelina looked across the table at Deek. "What gold are you talking about?"

Deek snorted. "One piece was a big round coin with stamps on it. A gold coin big as a silver dollar but twice as thick. It was mine for a while. I held it in my own hands and it was heavy. But then I give it up to a man in Bernadino so we could get outta town and away from them rurales once and for all by ridin' in a motor truck."

Rosa remembered a coin that matched Deek's description. She saw it in the mercantile but she also recalled that Garcia claimed to have killed the man that owned it. She was trying to decide if she should say anything when Monte interrupted her thoughts.

"You did the right thing in Bernadino, Deek. But Ahayaca's gold is none of our business. What is our business, all of our business, is this ranch. And I think now is as good a time as any to talk about it."

Señor Cruz extended a hand toward Ortega. "It is up to our guests. Perhaps this is not the time to speak of such matters?"

"No," Ortega said, glancing at Rosa. "Do you mind, Rosa?"

Rosa shook her head.

Ortega grinned amiably. "In a manner of speaking, the rancho does concerns all of us, so I think now is an excellent time to discuss it."

"Good," Monte said, shifting his weight and leaning his forearms on the table. "When I was out on the range yesterday, I followed the tracks of a couple dozen cow-calf pairs that were being driven south by riders on horseback. The horses had no shoes so I knew they weren't from the ranch.

"I followed those tracks for several miles. I crossed the border and followed the tracks on into Mexico. I kept riding and after a while I found all the cows. The calves had been loaded onto trucks and taken away but the cows had all been shot in the head and left to rot."

Monte let his news sink in for a moment. Ortega seemed concerned but Angelina and Señor Cruz were stunned.

"Shot!" blurted Señor Cruz.

"That's right."

Angelina was angry. "Who would do such a thing!"

I glanced at Rosa and saw her eyes harden. She suddenly seemed rigid.

"Señor Cruz," Monte asked sternly, "do your cattle have anthrax or anything like that?"

"No!" answered Señor Cruz. "We bought healthy stock, healthy bulls. We bought only the best. All came from reputable cattlemen."

"Well," Monte said, "then I can't think of too many reasons to kill your stock. Anybody else have any ideas?"

Seeming to be genuinely perplexed, Ortega suggested, "It sounds to me like the work of Yaqui Indians. Perhaps they killed the cattle for meat but were discovered before they could butcher any of them."

Monte shrugged. "Could be." He turned to Ahayaca. "You got any ideas?"

Ahayaca studied the back of his hands as he thought. "Perhaps it was a Yaqui ceremony, maybe one that required animal sacrifice."

"Could be," Monte said.

Deek frowned. "I never heard of no Indians sacrificing animals. And they'd never waste meat. Lots of 'em even eat their dogs."

"One other thing about those dead cows," Monte said easily. "Every last one of them had their brand cut off. Now why would a bunch of Yaquis do a thing like that?"

Ortega huffed disdainfully. "That could be explained as being some sort of superstition."

"How's that?" challenged Monte.

Ortega was prepared. He leaned back in his chair and answered confidently, "The Yaqui have just recently come into this area. They have resisted the advance of civilization for decades. The tribe is backward, but like so many Indians, they are partially Christianized. They blend their primitive beliefs with those of the Catholic church.

"It is very likely that some of the Yaquis entering from Mexico saw the brand of the cross on the cattle and took great offense. Their reaction to such sacrilege was to kill the cows and destroy the brands. That could easily explain what happened to the cattle."

Rosa sprang to her feet so suddenly that her chair skidded backwards across the floor with a piercing screech. She pointed a finger at Ortega. "Liar! Antonio Ortega, you lie!"

Caught between Rosa and Ortega, I scooted my chair back and out of the way.

Wide-eyed, I asked, "What is it, Rosa?"

Rosa was so furious she began to tremble. "You have done nothing but lie to me."

Ortega glared at Rosa, his eyes beginning to smolder.

Deek broke in, "If you got somethin' to say, lady, spit it out!"

Pulsating with fury, Rosa burst out, "I found three brands of this ranch in his toolbox today. They were on rawhide cut from cows."

Monte's hand instantly flashed across the table. He grabbed Ortega's necktie and jerked him halfway across the table.

Just as quickly, Deek lunged to his feet. Knocking his chair over, he pulled his pistol that had been hidden behind his belt. He pressed it against Monte's ribs. "Hold it Segundo!" he demanded. "Let go of 'im."

Monte opened his hand. Ortega, red in the face and gasping for air, fell back into his chair.

"Deek," I demanded, "what are you doing?"

"Shut up, kid," Deek snapped, as he eased Monte's pistol from its holster and stuck it behind his waistband. "Doin' good deeds got me nothin'. Gold is what I'm after now. I'm throwin' in with Ortega."

"But you can't," I said, slowly coming to my feet.

Deek was then directly across from me. He was facing Monte and Ortega was coughing, still trying to breathe. As I reached for my pistol, Deek caught the movement from the corner of his eye. He turned his head and glared at me but my pistol was already aimed.

I saw my target, the center of Deek's rib cage just below his shoulder. I did not see the pistol in my hand. I felt it there but only as an extension of my arm. I sensed a straight line from my eye, down to my wrist, and out the barrel of the pistol.

"You snot-nosed greenhorn," Deek growled.

Deek started to turn toward me.

Without the slightest thought, I fired. The blast was strangely muffled and every movement in the room was taking place in slow motion. Deek jerked but kept moving, his gun swinging in an arc straight for me. I fired twice more and then Deek slowly crumpled on his way to the floor.

I heard a voice to my right. "Drop it or I'll kill her."

My senses were clouded and my pistol was still aimed where I had fired my last shot. I was just beginning to realize what I had done when I turned my head and saw Angelina with a shiny pistol barrel pressed against her temple. Behind her, holding a small nickel-plated hideout gun, was a grinning Anthony Ortega.

Any thoughts I might have had concerning the taking of a man's life failed to register. Instead, all I could see was the fear in Angelina's eyes.

"Drop it, kid," repeated Ortega. "None of you move a muscle or she dies."

I eased my Smith and Wesson down on the table and stepped back.

Señor Cruz, horrified and speechless, raised both hands high in the air. Ahayaca remained seated but rested both his hands on the table.

The front door of the hacienda slammed open. Fernando, rifle in hand, ran into the dining room and slid to a stop. He looked at Deek's body and then at Ortega with the gun in his hand.

"Is everything alright, Señor Ortega?"

Ortega nodded toward Deek. "Pick up those two pistols and the one on the table."

Fernando clumsily gathered the pistols, stuffing all three behind his belt.

Clutching Angelina, Ortega took a step back, making certain he was out of Monte's reach. "Go outside," he ordered Fernando, "and fire two shots in the air. Then get back in here."

Fernando ran outside. Angelina was in shock. Monte was ready to kill but Ahayaca sat calmly in his chair.

Ahayaca glanced up and saw the puzzled look on my face. To my consternation, he smiled again.

Ortega noticed the smile. "Is something amusing, Ahayaca?"

The blast of two shots roared through the open front door and into the dining room.

When the sound subsided, Ahayaca said, "My people consider gold the offal of the gods. All it is good for is making pretty things. What you do here, El Serpiente, is foolish."

Ortega tilted his head from left to right as he studied Ahayaca. "So, you recognized me?"

"I was not sure at first. You looked like him and your voice sounded like him but when you laughed at Billy, I no longer had doubts."

My head was still spinning but when Ahayaca referred to Ortega as El Serpiente, I tried my best to clear my mind. Was Ahayaca saying that Ortega was actually El Serpiente? But how was that possible? And was Fernando working for Ortega? What did the two shots signal? What would happen to Angelina? What could I do to protect her?

Fernando ran back into the dining room and then stood behind us, blocking the hallway that led to the front door.

Monte seemed to calm somewhat, but I knew that meant nothing. He was still deadly. "So why did you take the brands, Ortega?"

"Simple. For every three brands the Yaquis brought to me they got one rifle. The brand was proof they had done what I instructed. That way, I was nowhere near the rustling at any time. There was no way that anyone could trace the dead cattle back to me.

"Once I killed enough cows, I knew Señor Cruz would be in debt to me when the loan was due. Then I would, but oh so reluctantly, have to take possession of the rancho. All perfectly legal."

"Just like 'debt for service,' " I sneered. "All perfectly legal just like El Serpiente."

"Of course," boasted Ortega. "The laws I used to ensnare slaves in Mexico were the same ones I used to trap Señor Cruz. My plan was equally as simple. I would get the rancho and then take the beautiful Angelina to be my wife.

"But now, my plans have changed. I fear, the *bronco* Yaquis will have to make a murderous raid on the Rancho de la Osa . . . and its peaceful Indian village. And, tragically, the sweet and innocent Angelina as well as the fiery Rosa Bustamonte will have to disappear."

We heard the distant pounding of horses' hooves. It sounded like an approaching stampede.

Ortega shoved Angelina into my arms. "Now," Ortega announced triumphantly, "we will get the answers we want. Personally, I detest the sight of blood. However, I do not know who will be better at getting Ahayaca to talk, the Yaquis or Garcia."

The thundering of hooves grew louder and then suddenly stopped. Dust drifted through the front door and into the dining room. In seconds, Garcia and three of his rurales barged in with pistols drawn.

Ortega dropped his hideout pistol into his front pants pocket. "Are my Yaquis with you?"

"*Sí*," answered Garcia. "Nine of them."

Chuckling, Ortega said, "That should be more than enough to clean out a village of peaceful Indians, Indians that don't even own one gun."

Rosa had been uncharacteristically quiet but she finally broke her silence. "What happened to you, Antonio?"

"Rosa, Rosa," chided Ortega. "Always the same Rosa. I grew up, that is all that happened. You still believe in the revolution, that someday you will have justice. There is no justice, only power. And money buys power. It is that simple. Only fools like you waste time with causes and constitutions. I take what I want. That is how I got to where I am today. And that is how I will get where I am going.

"I gave you a chance to join me, Rosa, and look how you repaid me. For such betrayal, there can be no forgiveness. But perhaps the price I get for you in Mexico will make up for your treachery."

With a sneer on his face, Garcia sauntered up to Monte. "So we meet again, *amigo*. But this time you will not get away. Now you will see that no one makes a fool of me and lives."

"Everybody dies," said Monte. "And so will you."

Garcia smirked. "But not the way you will die. With the whip, I made Tetabiate crawl and lick my hand. Before you die, you will crawl to me and lick my boots."

"Enough of this!" demanded Ahayaca. "If you harm any one

of my friends, you will never find the treasure. You can do nothing to me, nothing to my people, nothing at all to get what we chose not to give you.

"But, as I have discovered this very day, the times have indeed changed. Our village will no longer be unseen by the world. Airplanes will change that. So, we also must change.

"My people will do as I command. I am Lord of my people. And I have the authority to change our tradition."

"What are you getting at?" asked Ortega.

"We will give you our gold if no harm comes to my friends. Especially to Montesegundo, who is my blood brother. But harm anyone here and you will never see a single piece of Montezuma's lost treasure."

"Lost treasure?" questioned Ortega. "Do you expect me to believe you have Montezuma's gold?"

Ahayaca stood up. His eyes flashed. His demeanor abruptly changed. It was as if he had become another person. "Go outside," he said with a commanding ring in his voice. "Ask the Yaquis about their silver. Do you think you could torture them and make them talk? Tetabiate was Yaqui. I know the will of the Yaqui and the will of my people is just as great. Test me and you will lose, Ortega. Our will, our tradition, our beliefs are far greater than a man like you could ever hope to imagine."

A hush fell over the room for several seconds and then Garcia swore. "He is right, Ortega. The Yaqui know how to die. They would never talk."

Ahayaca continued, but now he was defiant. "You, Antonio Ortega, are finished on this side of the border. Take the gold and vanish. Go back to Mexico and become again the snake that you are. Otherwise, you will have nothing."

Ortega was indecisive and off-balance. He had expected anything but what was happening and now Ahayaca had completely outmaneuvered him. "How much gold is there?"

"More than your men and your motorcar can carry. It was more than Cortés and his men could carry as well. Many of them drowned fleeing Tenochtitlan with pockets full of gold. You are all fools to want so much gold."

"How far is it?" asked Ortega. "How far to the gold?"

"Our village is five miles from here. It is there, hidden, that you will find what you seek."

Garcia walked around the table. He whispered something to Ortega and then they both went to the far corner of the dining room and began speaking softly.

They had been huddled in the corner for a few minutes when Fernando, brimming with newfound courage, began to strut back and forth.

"Not so important now, are you Señor Cruz? Now I am the one in charge. And your daughter, now she pays attention to me and wishes she had been friendlier to Fernando."

Holding his rifle in one hand he walked up to within a step of Monte. Fernando mockingly leaned in. "Hey, big man. You said you would shoot me if ever I swear bad things on my mother's grave."

Fernando stretched out his empty hand. "Well, gringo, I will do better than that. I will swear on *your* mother's grave. I swear that . . ."

Monte's punch came so swiftly that Fernando had no time to blink. The crushing blow landed with the muffled sound of dry twigs snapping.

Fernando's knees buckled as he spun. Then he slammed facedown on the tile.

Ortega and Garcia froze. No one in the room moved for a long count of ten.

Then, only mildly irritated, Ortega ordered, "Someone throw some water on him."

A rurale grabbed a glass of tea and spattered it onto the back of Fernando's head. He still did not move. The rurale then hooked his toe under a shoulder and rolled Fernando over.

The rurale gasped and jumped back.

Fernando's eye socket and temple were caved in. Blood was oozing out of the pulp that, seconds before, had been a taunting eyeball.

"*El es muerte!*" declared the shocked Mexican.

Ahayaca looked down at Fernando. "*Si, el es muerte,*" he said but then pointed at Monte, "*pero . . . el es* El Muerte."

The closest rurale took two steps backward. The other two rurales flinched and reached for their pistols.

Monte still had his knife but at that moment, no one, including Garcia, cared to ask for it. Staring in disbelief at Monte Segundo, the Mexicans well understood that the dining room was too small and bullets too slow to kill El Muerte. Before he died, El Muerte would surely kill some if not all of them.

Garcia glared at Monte. "So . . . are you the great El Muerte?"

Monte eyes flashed with a vicious light. "How bad do you want to know?"

"Maybe later," Garcia sneered, "I will find out. But today all I want to know is how much gold I can carry."

Ignoring the two dead men sprawled on the floor, Ortega asked, "Can I drive to your village in my motorcar?"

"Halfway only," answered Ahayaca. "The remainder must be covered on foot or horseback."

"Alright," said Ortega, as he crossed the floor and gathered the three pistols from the dead Fernando. "I will drive my motorcar. Garcia, you and your men use your horses. Our prisoners will walk in front of us."

"What about the old man?" Garcia asked. "He will be too slow."

Ortega shrugged and handed Monte's pistol to the nearest *rurale*. "He can make it. If he can't, Segundo can carry him."

CHAPTER EIGHT

With Monte and Ahayaca a few steps in the lead, and me behind them with Rosa, Angelina, and Señor Cruz, we were herded down the road under a blistering late afternoon sun. Several paces to our rear, Ortega drove his Studebaker with Garcia riding alongside. Behind them, riding in the rising dust, came the nine Yaquis and then the three rurales.

I had no illusions. Both Garcia and Ortega were barbarians and they commanded a small army of thieves and cutthroats. A few villagers might be spared but once they had the gold, I knew our lives were over. The only hope I had was that Ahayaca had a plan, perhaps a way to convince Ortega and Garcia that there was more gold to be had elsewhere. Ahayaca had mentioned the Sierra Madres and the *barrancas*. I wondered if there actually was more gold hidden there, or perhaps a silver mine? Could he, as he had done before, bargain for our lives using the location of the lost Tayopa?

Surely, I told myself, he had to have some sort of plan. Why else would he have worn such a dazzling necklace knowing full well Garcia was hiding in the hills above the ranch? But whatever his plan might be, was it worth the danger we were now in? Two men were dead already and more could have been killed or injured by stray bullets in the dining room. What could be worth taking that kind of risk? And why would Ahayaca put his own people in jeopardy?

And if there was a plan, what if it did not work? Ortega had made a fortune selling people as slaves. What would prevent him from selling an entire village? I shuddered when I thought of what might happen to Angelina and Rosa. I tried to block those images from my mind and swore that I would die, giving my last breath to defend them.

We had walked almost two miles when I noticed that Ahayaca had gotten ahead of Monte and was walking several paces in front of him. Señor Cruz was doing well on his own so I left Angelina and, in a few quick strides, caught up with Monte.

Monte glanced at me but then looked straight ahead. "Good. You're here."

"What is it?" I asked, in a near whisper.

"When we get to the village and hear a drum, be ready to run. Ahayaca says that the second we see a jaguar, all of us are to run for the buildings and duck inside the first doorway we come to. You are to take care of Angelina and help Señor Cruz. I'll take Rosa with me."

"What's going to happen?" I asked.

"I don't know. Now, go back and send Rosa up here to me. Don't tell them anything about running for the buildings *until* you hear the drum. Then, tell them about the jaguar. We don't want Ortega or Garcia getting wind of anything."

Without another word I faded back and joined the others.

I was trying to think of what to say without revealing too much, when Rosa spoke up.

"Monte will try something," she said. "He knows no other way. He will get killed."

"He would only do that to protect you, Rosa. He won't do anything if he thinks it will endanger you."

"Huh! He cares nothing for me. He left me on the train."

"You're wrong, Rosa," I said. "You were playing a game then. Monte didn't think it was a game. He thinks you betrayed him. You can imagine what he wanted to do to Ortega when he saw you with him and yet Monte couldn't so much as lay a hand on him. For a man like Monte, that was unbearable. He had no other choice but to get as far away from the two of you as he could."

Rosa sighed and then frowned. "Did he tell you this?"

"Not in so many words, Rosa, but he wants you to go up and walk with him. He said it was important."

Rosa hesitated for a moment and then quickened her stride. Gradually pulling away from us, she started to catch up with Monte.

"What's going to happen to us?" Angelina asked.

Glancing ahead, I noticed we were approaching the turn in the road where the village trail branched off.

"Nothing at all," I said. "Ahayaca doesn't care about gold. Garcia and Ortega will take all the treasure they can carry and ride across the border. They know they'll be safe there. There's no reason for them to harm anyone. So don't worry, Angelina. Everything will work out."

Angelina was unconvinced but managed a faint smile. "Thank you, Billy. Thank you for saying that."

Señor Cruz and I exchanged glances. I could see that he didn't believe me either, nor could I blame him.

When we came to the trail, Ortega stopped and got out of his motorcar. Following Ahayaca, all of us then veered onto the uneven path that led to the village.

Señor Cruz instantly began to have difficulty keeping his balance. To help him maintain the pace, I walked beside him and supported one arm while Angelina did the same on the opposite side. Neither of us spoke but we often exchanged glances. And though the worry in her eyes was obvious, I was encouraged and deeply touched to see that she embraced a grim determination not to panic.

Rosa worked her way up beside Monte. They walked for a

moment and then Monte said, "You sure got yourself into a big mess."

"Me?" snapped Rosa. "This is all your fault."

"*My* fault? How in hell is it my fault?"

"I should have gone back to Mexico," Rosa said. "None of this would have happened."

"You mean you shouldn't have gotten on the train in Columbus."

"That is right," agreed Rosa. "You did this."

"So it's my fault you took up with Ortega, is that it?"

Rosa's face flushed red. "That is not what I meant. I meant . . . that I should not have listened to you when you asked me to come with you. If I had not listened, I would not have gotten on the train."

Monte thought for a moment. "Then why did you?"

"Why did I, what?"

"Why did you get on the train?"

Rosa glared up at Monte. "Why did you ask me to get on the train?"

"You know why," Monte mumbled.

"Then say it. Say to me, why."

Monte clenched his jaws and stared out into the desert.

"You cannot say it, can you Monte Segundo?"

Monte could feel Rosa's eyes boring into him. "You understood what I meant."

Rosa groaned and shook her head. "Like I said, this is all your fault."

Monte and Rosa continued on in stubborn silence until Monte caught sight of the village fields in the distance.

"Rosa," Monte said softly, "no matter what happens, when we get to the village, you stick to me like glue. No questions. Do you understand?"

Rosa heard the gravity in Monte's voice. She realized

something was about to happen. "I will, Monte. Like glue."

As Monte and I had done the day before, we all crossed the last arroyo and then walked out onto the path that led through the fields. However, unlike before, the fields were no longer loaded with produce. In fact, every field had been harvested. Anything and everything that could be eaten was gone.

Ahayaca turned back to look at Ortega and Garcia but kept walking. He pointed at the narrow pass. "There is a break in the hills," he called out. "Our village is just beyond."

Everyone on horseback drew their rifles from their scabbards and began scanning the tree-covered hills on either side of the pass.

"If your people try anything," warned Ortega, "you will all die."

Ahayaca made no reply. He disappeared into the shadowy pass and was soon followed by Rosa and Monte. I allowed Señor Cruz and Angelina to go in first with me, only a step behind. As we began to wind our way through the narrow corridor, I was stunned to see that the walls that had been so amazingly smooth the day before were now covered with drawings, images that had been chiseled into the stone.

Everywhere, there were S-shaped spirals that first wound clockwise and then counterclockwise. There were scores of circles with dots in the center and what appeared to be insects, deer, and snakes going in all directions. The only drawings that required no imagination to identify were those depicting the sun. Dozens of them were dispersed among all the other images.

Under the circumstances, why such an idea would come to me is inexplicable, but suddenly I realized that I was looking at a type of map, a map with an urgent message included. I felt a chill run down my back. Was this a form of last will and testament, a map to a hidden treasure that only surviving members of Ahayaca's tribe could decipher? Were they expecting to be wiped out by Ortega and his men?

In minutes we were through the pass and walking on the flagstone street. But instead of seeing a bustling village, we were met with an eerie silence. Not a soul was in sight.

Ahayaca was thirty paces out in front of everyone but Monte and Rosa had slowed and were now only a few feet ahead of us.

"This is magnificent," said Señor Cruz, as he gazed at the stone buildings on his left and then his right. "I never would have imagined such a place existed."

I merely glanced at the buildings but I immediately noticed that all of the hanging flowers were gone. Gone, too, were the white awnings that had shaded the doors and windows. Now able to see past the edge of the plaza, I studied what I at first thought was a thirty-foot-high earthen dam covered with various types of cacti. As I looked closer, however, I was surprised to see a ten-foot-high wooden gate at the base of the massive berm.

Ahayaca had stopped well shy of the plaza and turned toward us. We all kept going until he put up one hand signaling for us to halt.

I looked behind us just in time to see Garcia ride out of the pass. Rifle in hand, he rode forward. His black eyes swept back and forth over the entire village as his horse's hooves clopped gingerly on the flagstone street. In the silence, the sound of hooves on stone reverberated back and forth off the steep canyon walls.

Next came Ortega on foot and then the Yaquis, all with their rifles at the ready. Now dozens of hooves clattered noisily over the street, their rumbling echoing off the walls and flooding the village.

Last to enter, riding single file, were the three rurales. The lead *rurale* was several horse lengths to the rear of the Yaquis.

When the last Mexican rode onto the street we heard the first ominous beat of what had to be an enormous drum.

Compressed by the narrow canyon, the thunderous boom startled the horses. Some reared, some spun wildly.

And then came a second boom and a third.

Monte grabbed Rosa's hand. "Get ready to run for the buildings."

I hooked my arm through Señor Cruz's. "Angelina," I whispered, "grab his arm and get ready to run for the buildings. Look for a jaguar, a jaguar of any kind is our signal to run."

Angelina grabbed hold of an arm. All of us began frantically looking in every direction for the appearance of a painting or a statue, anything that might resemble a jaguar.

I was looking back toward the pass when I saw it.

Pouncing off the precipice of one of the buildings, a huge spotted cat, paws outstretched, flew through the air and then ripped the rearmost Mexican off his saddle.

Both slammed down onto the pavement.

The horses exploded with fright.

Awestruck, I watched the cat slashing with its claws, viciously mauling the Mexican as he maniacally fought for his life.

It was Monte yelling "Run!" that brought me to my senses. I started running, only half-aware that I was pulling Señor Cruz and Angelina along with me. In fewer steps than I can recall, we lunged through an open doorway as a shot rang out over the mixed chorus of the drumbeats, human screams, and screeching horses.

Monte had run to the opposite side of the street and shoved Rosa through a doorway. He paused long enough to see the jaguar flinch from a bullet to the back. But to Monte's amazement, he saw the cat stand up on its hind legs and charge the second *rurale*.

The jaguar's mouth was wide open, where there should have

been teeth there was a human face painted black and yellow. Only then did Monte realize that the cat was, in fact, an Indian wearing the skin of a jaguar!

The wounded jaguar took another shot in the chest but still sprang onto the second *rurale*. Clutching the saddle with one hand, the Indian managed to slice open the *rurale's* thigh with a flint knife. Then, the jaguar went limp.

As the lifeless Indian slid down the side of the horse, two more jaguars simultaneously lunged from the roofs and tore the remaining rurales from their saddles. Before the Mexicans slammed onto the flagstone, wooden darts filled the sky, the ones hitting their targets popping into the flesh of man and beast as the others careened like hailstones off the walls and street.

Two Yaquis, full of darts, fell from their horses but even with the darts protruding from their bodies, they were able to run into the stone buildings. Near the fallen rurales, however, three of the Yaquis lay dead.

More drums began to beat as the remaining Yaquis, along with Ortega and Garcia, spurred their horses and ran for the plaza. Wheeling their mounts, they regrouped behind the stone platform.

The Yaquis had darts in their backs they could not reach. The ones in their bloody chests, however, they ripped out. Only Ortega and Garcia were uninjured.

Hundreds of shrill whistles and trumpets joined the drumbeats. Then warriors with bows and arrows suddenly appeared on the rooftops above us. They wore only a loincloth but their heads were adorned with long, iridescent red, green, and yellow feathers. Their faces were painted black with yellow dots.

Arrows flew toward the plaza but they were instantly answered with Springfield rifles. Immediately, an Indian fell from the roof and landed in front of Monte's doorway. Reaching out and grasping his ankle, Monte drug the Indian inside. He was dead but still had an iron grip on his bow.

Monte pried the Indian's fingers loose from the bow and then took the remaining three arrows from his quiver.

Rifle bullets began ricocheting in every direction. The noise from the drums, whistles, and trumpets was almost deafening.

Raising her voice, Rosa asked, "Do you know how to use that?"

Monte nocked an arrow and tested the draw of the bow. "I was half-raised by the Kootenais, remember. I hunted mostly with my pistol but I learned how to hunt with a bow, too."

Looking out the door and back toward the dead rurales and Yaquis, Rosa said, "There are plenty of rifles out there."

"Yeah. But that's a good fifty feet to get one and fifty feet back. And there's two Yaquis holed up on this side of these buildings just like we are."

Monte edged his way along the front wall to a window. From where he stood, he searched the buildings on the opposite side of the street but saw no one inside them. He took a quick look down toward the plaza and then ducked his head back inside.

"They're dismounting and taking cover behind the platform."

"The what?"

"It's like a wall down in the plaza. They're holding their horses but the wall is only four feet high. Ahayaca's men are filling the horses full of arrows."

Rosa glanced around the room they were in. Barely visible in the shadows near the back wall, she noticed two more openings that, at first glance, appeared to be closets. With Monte guarding the front entrance, Rosa crawled to the opening closest to her and quickly discovered the opening was not a closet. It was, instead, a small doorway and it led to the building next to them. The second portal on the opposite wall did the same. She looked again and could see that similar openings connected the entire complex of buildings. Anyone entering one building could walk along the back wall and go from one to the other.

Rosa crawled back to Monte. "There are doorways back there. You have to stoop over but we can work our way down closer to the rifles."

Taking his attention off the street, Monte strained his eyes but they were adjusted to the glare of the sun. "Where?"

"Back in the shadows. In each corner, there are doors that connect each house to the other."

"Alright," Monte said, going into a crouch. "Let's go."

They had taken only a few steps when the whistles, horns, and drums suddenly ceased. And then, so did the rifle fire.

Monte took hold of Rosa's arm. "Let me go first," he whispered. "Those Yaquis are in here somewhere."

Rosa nodded and Monte silently crept around her. She took off her sandals and then, holding them in her hand, she watched for anyone that might approach from their rear. Crouching low, Monte removed the arrow from the bow and then eased through the first doorway taking care not to bump the bow or arrows against any of the stonework. His eyes began to adjust to the dim light, and he could now see down through several of the doorways.

Nothing moved as far as he could see, so Monte rose up and nocked the arrow. With his eyes on the front entrance he waited for Rosa.

Without a sound, Rosa came up behind him. To let him know she was there, she rested her hand on the small of his back. On moccasins and bare feet, they crept along the back wall to the next portal and then paused to listen.

A faint metallic tinkling sound drifted through the portal. Another quickly followed. Monte spun around and mouthed the word "stay."

Realizing the metallic sounds were shell casings bouncing on stone, Monte knew he had to move quickly. Someone was eject-ing shells from a pistol and would, for a few seconds, be unable to shoot.

Again removing the arrow from the bow, Monte ducked through the narrow portal, ran to the next, and, without hesita-tion, lunged through it. Glimpsing the Yaqui standing near the front entrance, Monte nocked the arrow as fast as he could. The Yaqui turned and looked back, trying to see into the shadows.

Monte drew the arrow back. The Yaqui flipped the loading gate shut on his pistol and raised it. Both fired at the same instant. Monte felt the bullet whip past his ear. He crouched and nocked a second arrow, letting go as another shot smacked into the stone above his head.

Before Monte could nock his last arrow a third shot went wide and ricocheted onto the floor only to collide with another wall.

The Yaqui was staggering straight for Monte but his pistol was wavering. Monte took his time and buried the last arrow in the middle of the Indian's chest.

With a thud, the Indian fell at Monte's feet.

Monte jerked the pistol from the hand of the Yaqui. Keeping his eyes on the front entrance and the portal opposite him, Monte rolled the Yaqui over and unbuckled his gun belt. Flip-ping open the loading gate, Monte saw that the Yaqui's pistol was not a forty-five like his but a forty-four-forty.

Only two cartridges remained in Yaqui's belt loops. Monte fingered them out and then dropped the belt. After ejecting the empty casings, Monte saw that only one chamber remained loaded.

Shoving in the two remaining cartridges, Monte rotated the cylinder and then eased the hammer down.

Bending low, he waited for Rosa to glance through the portal.

When she did he motioned for her to come. In seconds she was again by his side.

Monte pointed at his pistol and then held up three fingers. Rosa nodded. Monte then took out his hunting knife and handed it to Rosa.

Pistol in hand, Monte peered through the next portal as he cautiously slid along the back wall. Again feeling Rosa's hand on his back, he stopped two steps from the opening. He knew full well that the second Yaqui could be in a hidden corner of the next room and poised to shoot the first thing that moved.

Rosa tugged on Monte's shirt. She pointed at herself and by signs indicated that she would go through first. Monte shook his head, no. Rosa frowned and then Rosa did the same. Monte took off his hat and indicated that he would stick it through the opening and use it as a decoy.

Again, Rosa shook her head but this time more adamantly. She again pointed to herself and then demonstrated how quickly she could poke her head through the portal and back again, too quickly to be in any danger.

Monte thought for a moment and then nodded.

Rosa gathered her dress, pulling it up above her knees. Kneeling, she crawled up to the portal. Leaning backward on all fours like a loaded spring, she thrust her head through the doorway and back in less than a second.

Rosa looked back at Monte as she came to her feet. She pointed to her left and whispered. "He is there, under a window, but I think he is dead."

Monte took off his hat and then ducked his head in and out of the next room. "There's lots of blood," Monte whispered. "He's full of those little arrows."

Replacing his hat, Monte bent over. He felt another tug on his shirt and glanced back at Rosa.

Her eyes were soft, almost pleading. "Antonio never touched me."

Monte stared at Rosa. Cocking his pistol, he gave a faint nod and then ducked through the portal.

Catching sight of the Indian, Monte instantly swung his pistol up. The Yaqui was lying in a pool of blood with his side braced against the front wall. He held a pistol in his right hand but he did not move. Monte took a slow step toward him. Still there was no movement.

Monte froze. He watched the Indian's chest for a full minute before he was satisfied the Yaqui was dead.

"Come on in," Monte said. "All those little arrows finally bled him to death."

As Rosa came through the portal, Monte went to a window hoping to see me.

The three of us, however, were huddling in a corner. We had been there for several minutes, our only weapon a mano used for grinding corn in a metate. Angelina had found it and given it to me. It was a cylindrical stone six inches long and quite heavy. Gripping it firmly in my hand, I was well aware that it could easily crush a skull.

Hiding in the corner, I knew I would not hesitate to use the stone on Ortega or his men. But as we crouched together, I could not help but think of the fate that awaited Angelina. I had no doubt what would be done to her. What I did not know, what I could hardly bear to envision, was whether I had the courage to do what very likely had to be done, to kill Angelina before she could be taken by Ortega or his men.

I had seen unspeakable barbarism while Monte and I were in Mexico, but Ortega and Garcia possessed a malignant cruelty that was beyond my comprehension. There was no limit to their debauchery and evil. Yet Ahayaca had said that many such men existed in Mexico, vile beasts that knowingly enslaved men, women, and children. Men that herded people like cattle onto trains and then sent them off to die slow, agonizing deaths.

My mind raced with disjointed thoughts. Visions of New York flashed before my eyes, of skyscrapers and restaurants, of theaters and museums, of Mother and Father. If I died in the village they would never know what happened to me. Ortega would take over the ranch and seal off the pass to cover up his murders. I would simply disappear and evil would reign victorious.

But would Ortega murder Angelina here in the village or would he use her first and then sell her to a brothel? If I had a choice, would I allow such a thing to happen to Angelina? Would she want me to take her life? Did I have the awful courage to smash in her skull?

Monte's voice broke into my living nightmare.

"Billy, are you alright?"

I sprang up and ran to the side of the nearest doorway.

"We're here," I called out, still holding tightly to the mano. "We're all fine."

Monte peered around the doorway and into the street. Two Yaquis and three jaguar-warriors lay among the three bloody and shredded rurales. Three more Yaquis were sprawled farther down the street along with several dead and dying horses. Beside the stone platform, there was a partially visible dead horse. Other than that, the plaza appeared empty. Not a single person was anywhere to be seen.

"Take a look, Billy," Monte shouted. "Do you see anything from your side?"

I stuck my head out and looked back at the pass and then scanned the top of the buildings. Seeing nothing, I looked down toward the plaza. I saw no one. Neither did I see anyone on the berm beyond the plaza. I did notice, however, that the massive wooden gate was still closed.

"I don't see anyone anywhere," I called out.

Monte took a good look at the pistol he held, a short-barreled Colt. He estimated that it was at least one hundred yards to the platform. There was no way to know how accurate the Yaqui's pistol might be at that distance but for anyone behind the platform with a rifle, hitting a man at one hundred yards would be an easy shot.

Rosa came up beside Monte. "What are you thinking?"

Monte looked over the pile of dead bodies less than thirty feet in front of him. "If we have to make a stand in these close quarters, I need my pistol. One of those rurales has it."

Looking into the street, Rosa pointed to the one closest to the pass. "That is the one. I remember his jacket. It was different than the others. He was given your pistol."

Facing the plaza, Monte eased halfway out of the doorway and paused. Nothing moved so he took a half step. He stood motionless and glanced at the rooftops opposite him. Seeing nothing, he took a full step out into the open.

Still, there was no movement anywhere nor was there any sound to be heard. Monte took another step and then crouched behind the back of a dead horse. Going down on his belly, he crawled toward the *rurale*. When Monte got close, he felt the warmth of the dead man's blood soaking through his shirt.

With a shove, Monte rolled the man over. His throat was torn to shreds and his chest was drenched with crimson foam.

Monte palmed his Colt and then jerked it from behind the *rurale's* belt. Rolling on his back, he opened the loading gate and checked the cylinders. All five bullets were unfired so Monte took one cartridge from his belt and then dropped it into the empty chamber.

With a Colt in each hand, Monte crawled back to the horse. Coming to his feet, he sprinted for the doorway and then bounded through it and into the shadows.

Going to Rosa, he exchanged the Yaqui's pistol for his hunting knife and then sheathed it. "That doesn't make much sense. Not even one shot."

"I saw no heads come over the wall of the platform either," Rosa said. "Maybe they are no longer there. Maybe they are getting onto the rooftops so they can shoot down on us."

Monte glanced out the window and again checked the roofline across the street. "I wonder what happened to all of Ahayaca's men. They were up there a few minutes ago."

Suddenly, the big drum began to beat again. Now, I could tell that it had to be located behind the earthen berm. I stepped out far enough to get a good view of the berm and saw the gate begin to swing open. I could make out two men pushing hard to swing the double doors open wide.

I saw Garcia appear from behind the platform. His back was to us as he faced the gate.

For a moment, I saw only the two Indians. Then, crouching and shoulder to shoulder, warriors began flowing through the opening. Some wore jaguar skins but most only wore head feathers and breechcloths. All, however, carried round shields in one hand and a weapon in the other. Some had axes, some lances or bows. Others carried sticks of some sort, but all were advancing slowly toward the plaza and Garcia.

Garcia fired a shot from his pistol. One of the Indians fell but the rest did not flinch. In mass, with the drum pounding out a slow ominous beat, they continued their guarded advance.

Garcia, facing the oncoming warriors, eased around the platform and then continued to back up. As he worked his way up the street toward us, he waved his pistol from side to side while shouting, "*Regresa! Regresa! Voy a disparar!* I will shoot you all!"

Ignoring Garcia's threats, the warriors kept coming. Splitting in two like a rushing torrent of water, the warriors swarmed around the sides of the platform and then rejoined on the far side to again form a solid wall of men.

Garcia stumbled over a dead Yaqui but regained his footing. He refused to take his eyes off the oncoming wave of Indians, now an army of at least one hundred warriors.

Angelina and Señor Cruz came up next to me and peered down the street. I glanced to my left and saw Monte standing in a doorway across from us. Rosa was beside him.

"Garcia is mine," Monte said, and then stepped out into the street.

The moment Monte came into view the warriors immediately dropped to one knee, let go of their weapons, and then placed their left palm on the ground.

Garcia spun on his heels to see Monte walking toward him with a pistol in his hand. When Monte was fifty paces from Garcia, he stopped.

"Hell is never full," Monte said and then smoothly raised his Colt to eye level.

Garcia threw his pistol up and fired. He thumbed back his hammer and fired again.

Taking his time, Monte put the front blade of his pistol in the center of Garcia's chest but then deliberately lowered it. The Colt bucked and a fraction of a second later we heard a dull *thwap*, the delayed sound of a lead slug smashing into Garcia's stomach.

Garcia folded over but then staggered upright. He raised his pistol and fired a shot that ripped through the side of Monte's shirt.

Monte stood where he was. He took careful aim before sending a second well-placed slug into Garcia's guts.

Swearing viciously and barely able to stand, Garcia attempted one more shot but his bullet blasted off the cobblestones and buzzed over Monte's head.

Garcia folded over, groaning in pain. He fell to his knees. He held there for a moment and then, with a sickening thud, fell flat on his face.

The Indians gathered their weapons and stood. In mass and with no sound but the beating drum, they marched around Monte and on up the street. We all stood motionless and watched the warriors encircle their dead. Hoisting the bloody corpses on their shoulders, the warriors solemnly carried the bodies down past Monte, back across the plaza, and then through the open gate.

The gate then slowly closed behind them but the deep base drum continued its steady beat.

Rosa was at the far end of the street nearest the pass but she was the first to walk out and into the street. I was next and then came Angelina and Señor Cruz. Monte was busy ejecting empty casings so I waited for Rosa. As she neared, a thought came to me.

"Rosa, have you seen Ortega?"

"No," answered Rosa, "but a man such as he would be the first to run in a fight."

I looked up at the canyon walls and the hills beyond them. Pointing at the thick growth along the ridgeline I said, "Even if he did get away from the village, it would be difficult if not impossible to get past all those thorns."

I was looking up when Angelina took the mano out of my hand. Surprised, I glanced down just as she handed me a Springfield rifle.

She tossed the stone off to the side and accepted a Winchester rifle from her father, who now carried a Mauser in his free hand.

For a moment, Angelina stared at Garcia's crumpled body and then she used her shirtsleeve to wipe some blood off the buttstock of her rifle. After a second glance at Garcia, she worked the action of her rifle, making certain a bullet was in the chamber.

"You know guns?" I asked.

Managing a faint smile, Angelina said simply, "I am a rancher's daughter."

I looked into Angelina's steady green eyes. "That you are," I said. "You most certainly are."

Angelina lowered her rifle and then gazed up at me. "Did you see those warriors kneel when they saw Monte come out of that building? What was that? Were they getting out of the way so he could shoot Garcia?"

I looked down at Monte, who was now coming our way. "That, Angelina, was a respectful bow. Monte is blood brother to Ahayaca and Ahayaca is their chief, their king."

With a hint of exasperation in her voice, Rosa asked, "So now El Muerte is also royalty?"

I shrugged. "To this village he is."

Holstering his Colt as he came close, Monte asked, "Any sign of Ortega?"

"No," answered Señor Cruz. "None of us has seen him since we took shelter inside the pueblos."

Monte turned. Looking past the plaza, he studied the earthen berm as we listened to the steady beat of the drum. "That means Ahayaca has him. Ortega is on the other side of that gate."

Smaller drums began to beat, keeping time with the larger drum. Beyond the berm, smoke began to rise in a billowing, dark plume. Whistles, trumpets, and conch shells blasted. Then we heard the muffled chatter of tambourines and the soft rattle of deer hooves.

The black plume of smoke rose higher into the blue sky and then dissipated into a cloud of white. The drumbeats grew louder and more rapid, and then more rapid still.

Abruptly, then, there came a deafening silence.

We looked one to another.

"What was all of that?" asked Angelina, her voice filled with trepidation.

"I would guess," Monte said flatly, "that . . . was the end of El Serpiente."

Rosa closed her eyes and made the sign of the cross over her chest. She then stared at the smoke, now beginning to thin.

"What do we do now?" I asked.

"I want to know," Angelina said, as she pointed uneasily at the smoke. "I want to know what's over there. And I have to talk to Ahayaca. None of this . . . none it seems real. I have known him all my life. It's as if he lived in two different worlds. Now, I feel like I never even knew him, never knew who he really was."

"Perhaps," cautioned Señor Cruz, "it is best not to know what lies beyond that gate."

"That gate is there for a reason," Monte said. "I agree with Señor Cruz. But, for the time being, we should stay put, at least for a while. Maybe Ahayaca will show up."

I glanced at Angelina and then surveyed the carnage strewn all around us. "I say we go down to the plaza and wait by the platform. It could be a while."

The combination of fear and excitement was starting to drain from Angelina and the horror of the ordeal she had just endured was beginning to take hold. She grew pale and wide-eyed.

I started to put my arm around her but stopped halfway and looked over at Señor Cruz. He gave me an approving nod so I lightly rested my hand on her shoulder. "Let's go down to the plaza and have a seat. We're all exhausted."

Holding her rifle, Angelina leaned into me. "Yes . . . I am tired. Very tired."

And with that, Angelina and I started off down the street with Señor Cruz not far behind.

Watching us go, Monte said, "What a way to start off."

"Start what?" asked Rosa.

Monte waved his hand in a sweeping arc. "Those two. I'd say they're on their way, wouldn't you?"

Rosa glared up at Monte. "How would you know anything about such things? You who fight everything that walks or crawls would not even fight for me. Without lifting a finger, you walked off the train and left me."

Rubbing his chin and avoiding Rosa's eyes, Monte grumbled, "I don't know how to fight like that."

Still staring at Monte, Rosa snipped, "Do you know how to kiss a woman?"

Monte looked away. "Not when it means anything."

Rosa leaned closer, "What did you say?"

Turning to Rosa, Monte looked into her beautiful brown eyes. "I said . . . I don't know how to kiss a woman when it's supposed to mean something."

Rosa was skeptical. "Never?"

Monte sighed and then said, "No, not ever."

Rosa looked deep into Monte's eyes, searching for what she desperately hoped to see.

She looked again. And then she saw it.

Reaching up with both hands, she grabbed his shirt collar. "When a kiss is shared between a man and woman who love each other, it is done like this."

Pulling Monte to her, she rose on her tiptoes. Wrapping both arms tightly around his neck, she buried her lips against his.

Several pounding heartbeats later, she loosened her grip around his neck and slid down his chest.

"That," she said without so much as a smile, "is how it is done. A kiss like *that* is meant to say something."

Monte took several deep breaths and then swallowed hard. "Damn!"

Rosa put her hands on her hips. "Is that all you have to say?"

Monte shook as if a chill had run down his back. He put his hands around Rosa's waist and gently lifted her. Pressing her to his chest he hesitated and then kissed her, kissed her as he had never kissed a woman in his life.

Still holding Rosa a foot off the ground, Monte said, "Did that say what you wanted to hear?"

Rosa again put her arms around his neck. "Yes. But I have been waiting a long time so I want you to say it again."

CHAPTER NINE

We had been sitting on the steps of the raised platform for close to an hour when one of the doors of the gate moved. Then it cracked open a few inches. A moment later it opened a few more inches. We heard a grunt and then, in a smooth arc, the door swung wide open.

Standing alone in the entrance was a young boy clothed only in a breechcloth. Around his neck was a gold collar. Silver rings hung from his ears. On his head, feathers of brilliant red, blue, and green fanned out from ear to ear in a spectacular headdress almost as long as his arms.

"It's Pedro," I said, coming to my feet. "That's Pedro!"

Everyone else stood up. Pedro remained where he was, his eyes fixed on us. When he made no effort to come to us, Monte said, "I think he wants to tell us something."

Angelina shook her head. "This is so unbelievable. It's like having a dream that never ends."

"Billy and I will go talk to him," Monte said. "I think it's best the rest of you stay here."

"That seems appropriate," agreed Señor Cruz. "You two have been their invited guests once before."

Neither Rosa or Angelina objected, so Monte and I walked over to Pedro. We halted a few feet in front of him. As soon as we did, Pedro went to one knee and placed his left palm on the flagstone.

"Lord Montesegundo," Pedro acknowledged and then stood back up.

"Pedro," Monte said, offering a respectful nod of recognition.

"I have a message from Lord Ahayaca," Pedro declared. "We have once more appeased Tezcatepuca. The Black Sun will not come. Our tribe will continue on the earth for another century. But we must move to a new home, a home where no flying machine can see."

"Lord Ahayaca bids you, his blood brother, farewell. He leaves you a gift of the Black Sun."

"I am honored," Monte said, "to be the brother of Ahayaca."

Pedro once more went to his knee and placed his hand on the flagstone. Then he sprang to his feet, spun on his toes, and broke into a run, heading back through the gate and down another flagstone walkway. In a matter of seconds he disappeared behind a growth of trees.

I was incredulous. "They're leaving? All of them?"

Monte gazed through the open gate in the direction Pedro had gone. "I'd say they already left."

Taking one step forward I peered through the opening. "Look at this!"

Monte turned back to the platform and waved. "You are seeing orchards?" he said but his comment was more of a statement than a question.

"How did you know?" I asked.

"Ahayaca told me a few things on the way over here. He said they grew their own fruit. He told me that and some other things that had to do with his tribe."

Rosa and Angelina helped support Señor Cruz to the gate and then we all stepped through. Once again we were awestruck.

Heading up the center of the narrow canyon for several hundred yards was a flagstone walkway; its entire length was lined on both sides with flowering rosebushes. Beyond the roses, groves of plum, apple, and orange trees grew in neat rows. In the tops of several of the fruit trees large, brightly colored parrots began to screech and flap their wings.

"Those birds are macaws," Monte said and then indicated the walkway we were on. "There's a stone culvert that runs under our feet. When it storms, the water comes down the canyon, goes under the street, underneath the pass we came through, and then out to the ditches for the fields."

"But where are the drums?" Angelina asked. "I don't see any drums. And where was the smoke coming from?"

Monte inhaled, testing the air. He pointed to the northwest. "Up that way somewhere beyond the orchards."

"I want to see," Angelina said.

"Are you sure?" asked Señor Cruz. "Have we not seen enough?"

"No, Father. I want to see. I have to see."

I glanced at Monte. "Do you have any idea what's up there?"

"No," Monte said, "but I have no doubts that Ortega is dead. Ever since Ahayaca escaped from the plantation down in Mexico he wanted Garcia. But coming here today, he told me he wanted El Serpiente instead. He left Garcia for me."

"I don't care if he's dead," insisted Angelina, "I want to know what happened."

"As do I," Rosa said. "Antonio and I were once friends. I also want to know."

"Alright," Monte said and then led off down the rose-lined walkway.

Rosa trotted up to Monte so I stayed with Angelina and helped her with Señor Cruz. In a matter of minutes we came to a sharp fork in the walkway. The main path went on up the canyon in the direction Pedro had gone. The fork on our left turned directly west and led through a dense grove of plum trees, the branches of which formed a thick canopy of leaves overhead.

Shortly after taking the left fork, we caught a glimpse of what had to be another plaza. As we neared it, the smell of woodsmoke grew stronger.

Monte and Rosa were first to enter the plaza. We saw them turn to their left, then stop and stare upward.

Nearing the plaza, I could see that it was almost twice as wide as the one outside the gate. In the center of the plaza I caught sight of smoking logs, all that was left of a fire that had recently blazed in a large firepit. But when the three of us stepped beyond the last trees and out into the plaza, what we saw shocked us more than anything we could have imagined.

Seventy paces in front of us, a steep hill jutted into the sky. The side facing us had been cut flat and then faced with flagstone to form one side of a towering pyramid. Extending up the middle of the pyramid, from its base to the flattened top, was a wide stairway of polished stone. Stretching from the bottom step to the top was an erratic streak of red.

"God in heaven!" exclaimed Señor Cruz as he quickly crossed himself.

None of the rest of us uttered a sound. All we could do was stare.

It was several minutes before Monte noticed a crumpled mass at the base of the stairway.

"There's Ortega," he muttered and then started for the steps.

Rosa hesitated for a moment and then, apprehensively, followed at a distance.

"What is it?" Angelina asked.

"Please stay here," I said to Angelina. "You have seen enough. Please stay."

Angelina leaned her head back, sighed heavily, and then closed her eyes. "I will, Billy. I'll stay with Father."

Easing away from her I hurried past Rosa and up to Monte. By then I could easily recognize the shirtless body sprawled at the base of the steps. Ortega's face was down and his legs and arms were horribly contorted but there was no doubt who it was.

"They sacrificed him!" I gasped. "He was a human sacrifice!"

"It looks to me like they threw him all the way down those steps," Monte said.

I pointed upward. "They must have killed him up there."

Monte knelt beside the body. There was surprisingly little blood on it.

Reaching for Ortega's shoulder, Monte rolled him over.

Ortega's eyes were wide open as was his broken lower jaw. But what killed him was the gaping incision that had been cut from his stomach to the base of his throat.

I fought down the urge to vomit.

"They cut out his heart," Monte said. "And then they rolled him down the steps."

"Aztecs," I said weakly. "Just like the Aztecs used to do."

Monte looked up the long flight of stairs. "I'm going to see what's up there. I've come this far. May as well finish it."

I swallowed the acid working its way into my mouth. "Me, too."

Rosa eased up beside Monte. She looked mournfully at Ortega. "What happened to you Antonio?" she moaned. "What happened to the boy I once knew?"

Monte stood. "Greed, I'd say. That's what got Deek, too."

"No," Rosa said, "it was more than that. Antonio wanted power. And he wanted to feel important. That is why he wanted the rancho. He wanted to be a *haciendado*, to be looked up to, not like the peon he was when we were young."

"We're going to the top," I said. "Are you coming with us?"

"I will stay down here," Rosa answered, "Antonio was not

always a bad man. I will pray that the Holy Father forgives him and then I will give him a good burial."

I saw Monte look at Rosa and smile. It was a reverent smile, a mixture of fondness and of utmost respect.

"Find a good spot, Rosa," Monte said. "Somewhere in the orchard, maybe. When I get back down, I'll help you."

I was moved as well by Rosa's compassion. "I'll help, too."

Watching Rosa walk away, Monte said, "She's a better person than I am. I'd let the maggots eat the son of a bitch."

I nodded in agreement. "I'd have never guessed Rosa had a soft side to her."

Monte started up the steps. "Lucky for me."

Being accustomed to mountain living, Monte went up the steep incline as if it were a stroll in the park. By the time I got to the top of the stairs, however, I was sweating and gasping for air.

"One hundred and twenty seven," I said, between breaths. "That's a long flight of stairs."

Careful not to stumble and fall backwards, I took a few more steps onto the flat top of the hill. Paved with sandstone bricks, it was roughly a ten-by-ten-foot-square with a rectangular block of stone in the center.

Catching my breath, I took a closer look at the block and saw that it was knee-high, less than shoulder width, and about five feet in length. The block and stone floor surrounding it was covered in pools of crimson and splattered drops of blood.

Monte was standing behind the stone block gazing down at the canyon below. He held out the pendant that Ahayaca had been wearing around his neck. "This was left on the rock there."

I glanced at the pendant and then the block of stone, which I now understood was an altar. "That's the gift Pedro was talking about."

"Yeah. It's a symbol of the Black Sun."

"Pedro mentioned Tezcatepuca," I said, "Who was he talking about?"

"That's their god of hell. He feeds on evil. Or, I should say, the hearts of the evil."

I shook my head in disbelief. "Then, Ahayaca and his people were Aztecs?"

"Ahayaca," Monte said, "is a direct descendant of Montezuma. In fact, Montezuma's father was named Axayaca."

I let that soak in a moment. "And that's why Ahayaca began calling you Montesegundo? Because it was similar to Montezuma?"

"I don't know about that part of it," Monte said. "Ahayaca didn't say. Maybe so."

"What about the gold? Montezuma's lost treasure? Was it hidden here? Did it even exist?"

"I never asked," Monte answered. "It was none of my business."

"Well, then do you know why some of the warriors were dressed in jaguar skins? That was incredibly bizarre, don't you think? At first I thought they were real jaguars."

"So did I," Monte said. "It seems the best warriors the Aztecs had used to be the Eagles and the Jaguars. And that's how they dressed, as eagles and jaguars. Skins, feathers, and all.

"The jaguars were also known as the *Ocelomeh* or ocelots."

"And the Eagles," I said, recalling the words of Ahayaca, "were called *Cuayumeh,* the tribe living down in Mexico where he was going to get his wife."

"You got it. Those two groups or tribes were the only Aztecs that Cortés fella didn't capture. They're the ones that took off with what was left of Montezuma's treasure so Cortés wouldn't get it.

"Some Eagles went south with some of it and the Jaguars came north with some. This is as far as the *Ocelomeh* got.

"But their ways of doing things changed some in all that time. Like when the Jesuit priests came and set up where the ranch is now. Ahayaca told us that the priests never converted the *Ocelomeh* but he said the padres did have some effect. Those old *Ocelomeh* toned down quite a bit."

"Like how?"

"Well, take this Tezcatepuca, their god of hell. He used to have a big appetite for human hearts, just like all their other gods. But the Jesuits taught them about turning the other cheek, not stealing or murdering, that sort of thing. So, they eventually decided to only sacrifice one man, a really bad man, to Tezcatepuca once every fifty-two years. And that was only to prevent the Black Sun from coming and wiping them all out."

I looked down over the walkway and the orchards below. I could see Angelina and Señor Cruz sitting in the shade of a tree. Gray clouds were starting to roll in from the northwest and a wind was stirring the air.

From where I stood, none of the village was in sight. The façade of the pyramid was completely hidden from the village and the village hidden from anyone on the desert side of the pass. Only an airplane flying over would ever glimpse any of trace of the *Ocelomeh* people.

"A storm's coming," Monte said. "We better get down. I hear when the wet season hits in this country, the wind howls and the rain comes down in buckets."

Avoiding the slippery blood, we started down the steps and, to my surprise, I soon discovered that going down was harder than climbing up. By the time we reached the body of Ortega, my legs were quivering and close to buckling.

Rosa came over to us as I was rubbing my thighs and trying to ease the pain. She avoided looking at Ortega.

"I found a shovel and have dug a shallow grave," Rosa said. "There are flat rocks nearby. We can cover the grave with those.

It is enough. The rains will come soon. We must hurry."

Monte glanced at the mutilated corpse and grimaced. At that moment, I was certain that he was thinking of his father and how he had endured a similar death at the hands of the Apaches. However, if that gruesome memory did indeed cross his mind, Monte hid it well.

The corpse was lying face-up and Rosa kept her back turned.

"You take his hands," Monte said, "I'll take his feet. If he gets heavy let me know and we'll set him down."

I went around to Ortega's head and grabbed his wrists. They were still warm. I lifted. The head dropped backward and dangled loosely as if the neck were broken. I kept my eyes level, concentrating only on lifting my share of the heavy load.

Following Rosa, we made it to the edge of one of the orchards before I had to rest. Then we started again, this time getting him alongside a three-foot-deep trench before setting him down.

Monte waited for half a minute and then asked. "Rosa, do you want to say any words?"

At that point, Rosa took a long, sad look at the remains of Antonio Ortega. She then reached down and ripped off the bottom portion of her dress. Stooping low, she carefully folded the cloth over Ortega's face.

"No words," she said. "He would understand."

Knowing what to do next, Monte and I picked up the body and then eased it into the shallow grave. Monte then picked up the shovel Rosa had used. Starting at the feet, he slowly began filling the hole. When he got to the cloth covering Ortega's face, Monte hesitated.

Rosa looked away and did not look back until Monte was finished shoveling. By then the wind was gusting and the sky had turned into a churning sea of black clouds.

Working together, it took only minutes to cover the mound of loose sand with several layers of heavy flagstones. We then grabbed our rifles and hurried to the walkway.

With Angelina and me aiding Señor Cruz, we walked as fast as we could back through the gate and across the plaza. Before we got to the street, the wind was roaring down the canyon and picking up bits of sand.

Sidestepping the dead men and horses we rushed up the street. The rain started to fall before we were through the pass. By the time we reached the fields it was pouring rain, a warm hard rain. It fell in watery sheets, many of which were driven sideways by whipping gusts of wind. We were soaked in seconds but, oddly, I was not at all uncomfortable.

I took off my hat, reached across Señor Cruz, and placed it on Angelina's head. She wiped her beautiful green eyes and managed a smile. "For a salesman," she said over the wind and pounding rain, "you come in kind of handy."

Squinting as raindrops pelted my face, I said, "I hoped you would notice."

We trudged across the harvested fields. When we reached the wash Monte came back and took over for Angelina. Then, together, we carefully waded with Señor Cruz across a knee-deep torrent of red sandy water.

An hour later we reached Ortega's Studebaker and immediately helped Señor Cruz get behind the wheel. Monte gave the engine crank a spin and we were greatly relieved when the engine fired up on the first attempt.

Utilizing the miracle of modern machinery, we were back at the hacienda and out of the rain in a matter of minutes. When we slopped through the front door, Kim Lee, with a bandage around his head, came running to meet us.

"You alive!" he shouted. "You alive! All you alive!"

Being occupied with our own survival, none of us had so much as thought about Kim Lee, much less what had happened to him.

All of us paused. Dripping wet, we stared at Kim Lee as if he were some sort of a phantom.

"Where have you been, Kim Lee?" asked Señor Cruz. "What happened to you?"

Kim Lee adjusted the bandage around his head. "When bad men come, I hide in kitchen cabinet. I hit my head and bleed but I no move until everybody go. Then I hide in hay for horses but nobody come looking. So, I drag those men out of house and bury in garden. I get hungry, so I get out and come to kitchen.

"I in kitchen to get food and then I see you come. You not dead. None of you dead. Why you not dead?"

"Please build a fire in the living room, Kim Lee," said Señor Cruz. "It will be dark soon and the air will chill. The storm is just getting started."

I looked down at the puddle of water at my feet. "I have a change of clothes in the bunkhouse. I'll go there and then come back."

Angelina handed me my hat and then gently took Rosa by the hand. "Come with me Rosa. We'll change in my room. I have plenty of things that will fit you."

Señor Cruz gave Monte a measured glance. "Sorry, Señor Segundo. I have nothing big enough for you to wear. All I can offer is a blanket."

Monte took off his hat. "If I could just get out of this shirt, I can dry off by the fire."

"Good," said Señor Cruz, "Let me show you to the living room. The fireplace is there. I will bring you a towel and a blanket."

Monte followed Señor Cruz as I ducked out into the storm and growing darkness and ran across the plaza to the bunkhouse. I hurriedly changed into a white shirt and a new pair of denim pants. My city shoes were dry but wearing them was out of the question. Quickly changing my socks, I shoved my feet back into the wet boots and laced them up.

My hat, however, was too wet and floppy to do any good so I grabbed a saddle blanket. Holding the blanket over my head, I raced through the downpour and back to the front door of the hacienda.

I leaned the dripping blanket against the outside wall. Stepping through the front door, I heard Angelina's voice coming from a room that was off to my left.

"In here, Billy."

Following her voice, I made my way down a short hallway. Wanting to remember the moment, I paused at the edge of the living room. It was small and cozy.

A blazing fire filled a massive stone fireplace. Monte was standing with his back to the flames holding a blanket around his shoulders. Two leather sofas lined the walls. Rosa was sitting on the sofa closest to Monte. She was barefooted, her wet hair was in braids, and she was wearing a beautiful white lace dress.

Angelina was sitting in the middle of the other sofa. She was also barefooted, her hair was combed straight, and she wore a green print dress that matched the color of her eyes.

The only light in the room came from the fireplace.

With the firelight glistening off of her hair, Angelina patted the space to her right. "Sit here, Billy. I don't bite."

A stinging jolt of surprise and excitement suddenly shot down my arms and legs. I felt myself flinch. I smiled, trying to suppress a wave of what is best described as skittishness.

"Where is Señor Cruz?" I asked.

"He is making coffee with Kim Lee."

My attention was focused on Angelina but out of the corner of my eye I could see Monte and Rosa watching me. Feeling stiff, I awkwardly crossed over to the sofa. Leaving a foot of space between us, I sat down but did not lean back.

Rosa looked up at Monte. "Are the two of you related?" she asked sarcastically.

Monte adjusted his blanket to expose more of his pants to the flames. "We're just cautious."

Falling back on a tried and true tactic, I asked about the weather. "How long does a storm like this last?"

Angelina ran her fingers through her hair. "Hours. The rain will fill all the arroyos. They will flow throughout the night but by morning, except in a few holes, the water will all be gone. It comes quickly and leaves quickly."

Señor Cruz came into the room carrying a platter with six steaming cups of coffee on it. He served everyone and then took the last cup for himself and sat down on the other side of Angelina.

"I have been thinking," he said. "I do not want to return to the village. Not ever. I do not want anyone to return. I will leave it for the buzzards. And to the ghosts of the dead. It is a place that has always been hidden and I wish it to stay hidden."

"People will be looking for Ortega," Monte said. "He was a big man in Tucson."

"Yes," agreed Señor Cruz. "But if we report what happened the authorities will come to investigate. We cannot allow that. Then they would pursue Ahayaca and his people. Ortega must simply disappear."

"But what about the Studebaker?" asked Angelina.

"I have thought of that also. Tonight, I will drive it to the big arroyo near Sasabe and roll it down into the water. People will assume he went off the road and was lost in the flash flood.

"Someone must follow me in my automobile and bring me back. All of the tracks will be gone by morning."

"I can drive," I offered. "And I believe what you have planned is the right thing to do. Ahayaca has suffered enough."

"So, Señor Cruz," asked Monte, "after all of this, do Billy

and I still have jobs here at the ranch?"

"Certainly," answered Señor Cruz, "but with all the cattle that have been stolen, I will have difficulty paying you for quite some time."

"There's the rustling that's been done already," Monte said, "but this close to the border, rustling will still be a problem unless we work to put a stop to it. With the war in Mexico going the way it is, bandits are running free all along the border. And the Yaquis are looking for any way they can to get enough money to buy guns. And then, too, you've got a jaguar out there that likes the taste of beef. I'll stay and work as long as you need me. Pay me when you can."

Angelina glanced expectantly at me. "And you, Billy Cabott, what about you?"

Feeling my face flush with heat, I said, "I'll stay as long as you want me to."

Señor Cruz sipped his coffee but, at the same time, looked knowingly over the rim of his cup at Rosa and then at Monte. Taking a moment to swallow, he asked, "And Señorita Bustamonte, will you also stay with us? There is much to be done and we have plenty of room."

Rosa looked down into her coffee cup. "I would like to stay but if I am to do that I would require two things."

"And what would those two things be?" asked Señor Cruz.

"First," Rosa said, raising her eyes and turning toward Angelina, "I would want to borrow this dress from Angelina."

"And the second thing?" asked Angelina.

Setting her coffee cup on the floor, Rosa stood up and tiptoed over to Monte. Reaching up, she grasped the blanket on both sides of his neck, pulled him to her, and gave him a light kiss.

"The second thing that I will need . . . is a priest."

Monte's eyes narrowed with genuine concern. "Rosa, I don't have anything to offer a woman. Nothing at all."

Sliding her hands down Monte's arms, Rosa said, "You have all I want, Monte Segundo. I ask for nothing more."

Monte looked deep into Rosa's eyes. "Are you sure?"

"I have known from the very beginning. We both knew."

Looking at Monte and Rosa that night I knew I was witnessing a rare triumph of good over evil. No two people could have endured more suffering and hardship and yet there they stood undefeated, undeterred, and joyously happy simply to be together.

What, I wondered, had endowed them with such indomitable courage and strength? Was it the harshness of the land itself? Did nature teach them that cruelty was something to be expected, that it was as much a part of life as the wind and rain? Was hardship for the two of them merely a consequence of living, just another desert to cross or mountain to climb?

However it had come about, I knew Monte Segundo and Rosa Bustamonte possessed an abundance of what I severely lacked. I also knew, for me, that missing ingredient was only to be acquired on the leading edge of civilization. And I was well aware the only remnant of our country's frontier resided in the untamed borderland of the Southwest.

It would take men and women like Monte and Rosa to inhabit that land and to hold it. It would take women like Angelina as well. And it would even take men like me, men willing to learn, to adapt and ultimately to draw a hard line in the sand.

With Mexico awash in corruption and chaos, and a world war on the horizon, I realized the border would be a region of conflict for years to come. And that night I could think of no place I'd rather be than the Rancho de la Osa, no friends I would rather be with than Monte and Rosa, and no person I wanted to know more intimately than the green-eyed and saucy Angelina Cruz.

ABOUT THE AUTHOR

Paul Cox was born in rural Arkansas. When he was ten years old, his family moved to California. There, he had a successful athletic career, culminating as an NCAA Division II All American in track and field at Cal State Fullerton. After graduating, Paul attended dental school in San Francisco and graduated in 1976. In 1994, he moved with his family to North Idaho. He is an avid outdoorsman and artist. Paul has ridden horses for thirty years and raises cattle on a small ranch outside of Sandpoint.

The employees of Five Star Publishing hope you have enjoyed this book.

Our Five Star novels explore little-known chapters from America's history, stories told from unique perspectives that will entertain a broad range of readers.

Other Five Star books are available at your local library, bookstore, all major book distributors, and directly from Five Star/Gale.

Connect with Five Star Publishing

Visit us on Facebook:
  https://www.facebook.com/FiveStarCengage

Email:
  FiveStar@cengage.com

For information about titles and placing orders:
  (800) 223-1244
  gale.orders@cengage.com

To share your comments, write to us:
  Five Star Publishing
  Attn: Publisher
  10 Water St., Suite 310
  Waterville, ME 04901